**I had one chance, and if I blew it, I was a dead man…**

Jerry crushed his cigarette brutally into the ashtray with the look of someone about to do something important. He strutted over to me and hovered with hunched shoulders and a pointed gun. It was easy for me to feel like the helpless prey of some deadly animal.

"I'm going to ask you a question. And if I don't like the answer, I'll offer you a prompt. In the foot, then in the belly, so you can roll around a long time, thinking it over. I'm sure you know how it works. A Socratic dialogue."

"Socratic?"

"I encourage you to reflect, and together—" He wagged the gun back and forth. "—we search for the truth to an important question. No philosophical training is needed, but if I think you're not trying to help us reach a consensus. Well, you remember what happened to Socrates? His fellow Athenians forced him to put a gun to his head and blow his own brains out. So, who told you?"

I frowned to buy time. Even went so far as to say, "Huh?"

Jerry pressed the gun barrel against my foot. "You'd better clean out your think pipes."

"Geesh, this is hard. You know how it is, you're talking to somebody and he says something and the next fellow says something, and before you know it, you've heard something."

Jerry cocked the gun. "Last chance."

I was imagining my life hopping along on one foot when the answer popped into my mind. "Ah, now I remember. Chief Parker told me."

Jerry's coal-like eyes darkened. "Is that so?" He backhanded his gun barrel across my face. My cheekbone caught fire. Blood splattered on Trixie, and she yelped.

"Very convenient since Parker's dead. I don't believe you."

My face hurt like a fucker. I yanked out a handkerchief. Time was running out. I had to do something. Now.

A soft thump sounded outside the front door. Jerry froze like a lethal animal with a scent. He dashed to the window.

Shit! He'll see the shotgun.

A chilling locked room mystery! Impossible for the murderer to escape…yet, he did.

Powerful officials conspire against Chief Bucky's attempt to solve the case, including the KKK, whose members particularly resent Bucky's friend, Charlotte, a Harvard-educated "Negro" lawyer. When they drag her off to a hanging—her hanging—Bucky reaches the end of his rope.

KUDOS for *The Killer Who Wasn't There*

"Newly appointed Police Chief Bucky Ontario wields the power to hunt and arrest criminals, or does he? Still learning the ropes of his job, he's up against the KKK knotting ropes into nooses. A wonderfully mysterious and thrilling Killer Who novel, with the unique '50s charm we loved in the series debut, *The Killer Who Hated Soup*."~ Edith Parzefall, author of the *Hangman of Nuremberg historical mystery series*

"We've come to expect a lot from author Bill A. Brier, and he didn't disappoint in this newest mystery. On a par with Sherlock Holmes, Brier has us—and new Police Chief Bucky Ontario—scratching our heads and trying to figure out how the killer got out of a locked room ... locked from the inside. A chilling and thoroughly intriguing mystery, one you won't be able to put down." ~ Pepper O'Neal, author of the award-winning *Black Ops Chronicles* series

"As usual, Brier tells a chilling, intriguing, and fast-paced story, combing mystery, humor, and suspense. If you like a good mystery, you're going to love this one." ~ Taylor Jones, The Review Team of Taylor Jones & Regan Murphy

"Written in Brier's unique voice, filled with wonderful characters, an intriguing mystery, and lots of heart-stopping action, you'll be biting your nails all the way through—and loving it." ~ Regan Murphy, The Review Team of Taylor Jones & Regan Murphy

# THE KILLER WHO WASN'T THERE

## THE KILLER WHO SERIES
## BOOK 2

# BILL A. BRIER

*A Black Opal Books Publication*

GENRE: PSYCHOLOGICAL SUSPENSE/MYSTERY/THRILLER

This is a work of fiction. Names, places, characters and incidents are either the product of the author's imagination or are used fictitiously, and any resemblance to any actual persons, living or dead, businesses, organizations, events or locales is entirely coincidental. All trademarks, service marks, registered trademarks, and registered service marks are the property of their respective owners and are used herein for identification purposes only. The publisher does not have any control over or assume any responsibility for author or third-party websites or their contents.

THE KILLER WHO WASN'T THERE
Copyright © 2017 by Bill A. Brier
Cover Design by Tammy Seidick
All cover art copyright © 2017
All Rights Reserved
Print ISBN: 978-1-626947-57-3

First Publication: FEBRUARY 2018

All rights reserved under the International and Pan-American Copyright Conventions. No part of this book may be reproduced or transmitted in any form or by any means, electronic or mechanical, including photocopying, recording, or by any information storage and retrieval system, without permission in writing from the publisher.

**WARNING: The unauthorized reproduction or distribution of this copyrighted work is illegal. Criminal copyright infringement, including infringement without monetary gain, is investigated by the FBI and is punishable by up to 5 years in federal prison and a fine of $250,000. Anyone pirating our ebooks will be prosecuted to the fullest extent of the law and may be liable for each individual download resulting therefrom.**

ABOUT THE PRINT VERSION: If you purchased a print version of this book without a cover, you should be aware that the book is stolen property. It was reported as "unsold and destroyed" to the publisher, and neither the author nor the publisher has received any payment for this "stripped book."

IF YOU FIND AN EBOOK OR PRINT VERSION OF THIS BOOK BEING SOLD OR SHARED ILLEGALLY, PLEASE REPORT IT TO: lpn@blackopalbooks.com

Published by Black Opal Books **http://www.blackopalbooks.com**

# THE
# KILLER
# WHO WASN'T
# THERE

### THE KILLER WHO SERIES
### BOOK 2

# CHAPTER 1



*Defiance, Oklahoma, February 1957:*

A Negro in a phone company vest ran onto the road, arms waving. I slammed on the brakes. He rushed over to my window, panting, "A girl—a young'un—in the ditch! Ya gotta come!"

I flew out the door of my Ford Roadster and raced after the man scrambling through knee-high grass and into a ravine.

"I was on a pole, workin'," he hollered over his shoulder, "spotted an animal circlin' around somethin' in the brush. Looked like a kid all rolled into a ball. I ran over, and a coyote ran off, jus' as I heard your car."

I gasped. A Negro girl lay on her side, whimpering, welts on her arms and legs. Her blood-splattered gingham dress in shreds. I needed to get her to a doctor as fast—

"Leave her alone!" a harsh voice hollered.

Startled, I glanced up the ridge. Two state troopers. One was small and muscular, the other large and muscular. The small one started toward the girl.

"We'll take care of it, fella," the other said, shooting his hand up like a traffic cop.

"Anything I can do to help?" I offered. "I'm the new Defiance Police Chief."

"That's nice, but this is a family matter. You run along, she'll be fine."

Fine? What was he thinking? "She doesn't look fine to me."

"Listen, Chief, this isn't your jurisdiction. Now take off!"

The small trooper lifted the little girl and started back up the ravine.

The Negro whispered to me, "Ain't no family matter. Was the Klan."

Stunned, I stared at the man. The Klan, here?

# CHAPTER 2

Ten minutes later, I pulled into the Texaco station, still shaken. The image of the little girl and her bloody dress was stamped on my mind, and my stomach knotted at the thought of the Klan being around. Geesh! Thought I'd left them back in Louisiana two years ago.

"Be with you in a jiffy, Bucky," Marge, the attendant, yelled over from the next pump. She was cleaning the windshield of an old Dodge pickup while the driver read a newspaper behind the wheel.

"Fill 'er up with regular," I told her after she finished ringing up the other customer.

"Congratulations on your new job, Bucky. Twenty-one years old and chief of police." She plucked a piece of sage from my sleeve. "Don't you look handsome in your pressed blue shirt? And I like the blond curl coming out from under your hat."

I couldn't help smiling. "Try to always look my best. Say, what's with the Klan being around?"

She blew air between her lips. "A rotten bunch if I ever saw one. Every few years they sprout like weeds. If they were any dumber, they'd have to be watered twice a day. Just yesterday, one of them tried to sneak past me into the women's restroom with an armload of recruiting posters. I told him to hightail it. He'd already stunk up the place by plastering a poster above the men's urinal."

"Recruiting posters, huh? Something's got their feathers ruffled."

"You watch yourself. They don't take too kindly to the law, sometimes. They killed one of your predecessors—stabbed him straight through the heart."

⌇⌇⌇

When I opened the door to my new office, I saw a small white box sitting on my desk, next to the name-plate, *Chief "Bucky" Ontario*. It was the object beside the box that stopped me.

A Colt revolver.

I swallowed, my heart kicking in a little rhythm. I'd gone from a carefree car salesman to police chief, and already I had the Klan to worry about. And the little girl. Something told me that gun was calling my name, though I didn't know why.

I padded to the window beside the desk. A night rain had left the parking lot glistening with puddles of gasoline rainbows. Sitting down, I opened the box, took out a silver badge, polished it on my sleeve, and pinned it to my shirt. Not bad.

A face with touches of humor near the mouth and eyes appeared from around the doorframe. "Mornin', Chief, I see you've found your gun and badge."

"Hello, Sergeant."

Hazelwood hobbled inside holding a cane. He stood like a bent nail, hunched over and chuckling. "There's a dusty old picture down by the evidence locker you oughta see. It's of Chief Wade 'Cowboy' Wallis. He's sitting where you are, except he's got a knife in his heart."

"Kind of you to point that out." I could only hope Cowboy Wallis was the police chief Marge had told me about. I didn't care to follow a long tradition of stabbed chiefs. Well, with Parker getting killed by a dog and Harman shot by a killer, there was at least some variety in violent retirements of police chiefs.

"A little humor for your first day, Chief. You'll need it when I tell you who's back in town, getting juiced up over at Uncle Lewy's."

I tossed my hat over the revolver. "If it's the ghost of Cowboy Wallis, he can have his gun back."

"It's your former cellmate, Tyburn."

That was a name to rattle people's bones. "Jail mate, not cellmate. And unfortunately, he was let go."

Hazelwood rested on his cane and crossed his shiny black boots inlaid with silver. "But I heard you said he did it."

"He robbed the bank, all right. He told me."

Mrs. Rheingold chirped over the intercom, "Chief, a Mr. Oswald is here to see you."

It took a moment to find the correct button. "Who?"

The door burst open, and a short, thick man with bushy white muttonchops and an owlish face strode in and thrust out a business card. "Otto Oswald, National Insurance."

I stood and took his card as Sergeant Hazelwood excused himself and shuffled off.

"I'm here to inform you," Oswald said, tugging his blue-and-white plaid vest, "that I'm on the hook for a substantial sum of money."

"Gee, sorry to hear that. Because of the bank robbery, huh? Have a seat."

We sat. He took off his big curly cowboy hat, put it in his lap, and brushed back his hair, so white and fluffy it looked like a snowdrift. "Goddamn right. You should know, sir, that the man responsible is in your town." He jabbed a finger toward the window. "Right this moment."

"You don't say." I tried to sound surprised.

"Tyburn Newgate's a thieving scoundrel!"

"Lots of folks would agree with you, and if I had my way, he'd still be in jail, but a jury found him innocent."

He smacked the desk with his palm then sniffed and rubbed his nose. "Only because those nincompoops were bamboozled by his hotshot lawyer. A shyster trained to do things a rat won't do."

"It's a darn shame, all right." I got the feeling Oswald wasn't finished, so I leaned back and folded my hands in my lap. "Anything else?"

Retrieving a gold tin from his vest pocket, he opened it and snorted a pinch of snuff into each nostril. He rubbed his nose again, this time with a lace-fringed blue handkerchief. "Damn right there's something else. I expect you to see that justice is served."

I raised my palms. "The jury rendered its verdict. In the eyes of the court, justice has—"

Oswald's owlish pupils got small, and he gave the desk another wallop. "Don't give me that horseshit. I've read the reports. If you had testified about how he'd confessed to you while you two chummed it up in jail, he'd have plea-bargained. The bank would have their silver back, and I wouldn't be out ten thousand goddamn dollars!"

Heat rushed into my face. "Wait just a minute! First of all, we weren't in jail *chumming it up*. I was there under trumped-up charges. And besides that, I didn't testify because I was in Louisiana helping my sick daddy. The fact is, Mr. Oswald, Tyburn is now a free man, and that's that."

"That's not that. I want the silver back and expect you to get it."

I clenched and unclenched my hands under the desk. "You can expect all you want, but I have no idea where it is. Tyburn had two accomplices, who slipped across the border into Mexico. For all we know, they have it."

"They don't. For two days I watched Tyburn in the courtroom, all smug as a fox savoring *my* company's money. He has it." Oswald lifted his pointed chin. "Twenty-eight years."

A trickle of sweat itched my right ear, but I ignored it. "What, twenty-eight years?"

"More than a quarter century in this business, that's what." Oswald leaned across the desk, smelling like a stale cigar. "And I've never been wrong."

I'd heard enough. I swiped the trickle from my ear, gripped the chair's armrest, and stood. "Tyburn didn't tell me where the silver was, so I can't help you."

Oswald shot to his feet. His hat slid from his lap onto the floor, and he planted his thick knuckles on the desk. His eyes looked about to jump out and do something dangerous. "What I say next has an *or else* after it. You can, and you will."

I didn't say anything. I was trying to think of what he meant.

Oswald's eyes got back to normal. "Now look, Chief. I'm aware you got this job because of your fine work uncovering city corruption. God knows, it came at the town's most crucial time. Nevertheless—" His eyes turned scary again. "—you've got until six p.m., day after tomorrow to come up with the silver."

Two days! He was off his rocker. "And what's this *or else* supposed to mean?"

"Or else you'll be back hawking cars." He collected his hat from the floor and strutted out.

That was a fine how-de-do. I'd never even heard of the guy, and he's one to get me fired? I doubted that. On the other hand, if I were to get the boot, I'd have hell to pay from Uncle Rupert. I came from a proud family of shrimpers and public servants. If I was to fulfill my dream of following my uncle's example by becoming mayor, losing this job was not an option.

I needed a drink.

"Mrs. Rheingold," I said into the intercom. "Call Sally's and have them deliver a chocolate malt."

"Right away, Chief," she said crisply.

I rocked in my chair. If I got fired, I couldn't even get my old job back selling cars. My former boss would've already replaced me.

I pressed the intercom again. "Make sure they don't forget the extra malt from the mixer."

"As you wish, sir. Incidentally, in your drawer are life insurance papers to fill out. The town foots the bill. Your relatives might welcome your having coverage. God knows, those of the last chief—well, those of the last several chiefs appreciated the benefits."

I paced across the room, hardly listening. Who'd that guy think he was? I stopped and inspected his card. *Otto Oswald*. Pretty damn cocksure of himself. Better check him out. But first, it wouldn't hurt to mosey over to Uncle Lewy's and pay Tyburn a visit. See how far he'd go to keep his secret hidden.

I grabbed my hat. Mrs. Rheingold fluttered in, patting a giant wave of silver hair above her forehead. "Sally's doesn't deliver before lunch. Want me to run over?"

I shook my head. "No time. I have to see a man about some silver."

Mrs. Rheingold tossed a glance at the gun. "Aren't you forgetting something?"

I didn't like what those notches in the grip meant. "No need to lug that thing around."

She picked up the pistol and slid it into a holster from the hat rack. "You'll get used to it."

I waved my hand. "Some other time."

She studied me over her pink-rimmed glasses. "You never shot jackrabbits as a boy?"

"Huh?"

"Growing up. You nev—"

"Boars."

"What?"

"I shot wild boars, not jackrabbits."

"Then what's the problem?"

"No problem, just don't need it, that's all." Damn, I hated sounding whiny, but I didn't feel like explaining that, as a boy, I had mistakenly shot and killed my three-legged pet raccoon, Tripod. Finding him cornered by a wild boar, I had run and grabbed Daddy's pistol. I'd been good at shooting bottles and cans, but the trauma of shooting Tripod had made me vow to never again fire a pistol. Of course, back then, I never imagined being a policeman.

She took my hat and settled it on my head. "I know just what you need," she said, her eyes sparkling with an idea. "But later. You run along."

# CHAPTER 3

**D**efiance was a small town located north of Kingfisher between Tulsa and Oklahoma City. I liked living here. Folks were friendly.

Even bank robbers.

As entertaining a jail mate as he was, Tyburn lacked any moral or ethical sense. Like someone with no sense of humor. There was nothing to say about it, except that it wasn't there. He had bragged to me about how he and his two associates—that's what he called his outlaw partners, associates—had outsmarted, outshot, and outrun the cops after robbing the bank and slipping into South Texas. According to Tyburn, his associates had crossed the border into Mexico to visit the senoritas, leaving him passed out in a Laredo bar, where the police nabbed him.

I trudged through the cold and turned onto lower Fifth Street, hands jammed in my pockets. A car honked, and a Dodge Coupe splashed to the curb. It was Lamar Fromm, City Councilman and undertaker.

"Bucky!" he called, whirling an arm.

I ambled over, put a foot on the running board, and bent down to the window.

"Listen here," Fromm snapped. "What the hell is that thieving Tyburn up to? I've seen him twice this morning.

First leaving Gustafson's then going into a beer joint. For someone just out of jail, he gets around like a stray dog."

"Already on top of it, Lamar." Since he was going to continue calling me Bucky, he'd hear no more Mr. Councilman from me.

"That's good. We don't want him around anymore. He's been a criminal since he was knee-high to a louse."

I waved and started off. "You have a pleasant day, Lamar."

Tyburn was a toddler when his parents brought him over from England. He was their only child, and, for that, they should be thankful. His daddy had been taken on as a butler for the Overstreets, one of the richest families in Defiance, and Tyburn had taken on crime. He'd roll around the mansion on his tricycle and snatch anything from cookies to loose change. Folks called him a bad seed.

Gustafson's Grocery sat up ahead with a new sign in the window. *Big Bargains on Dry Goods*. I'd stop off and ask Abby, the new proprietress, a few questions. Before becoming a car salesman, I had worked as a clerk for the previous owner, Gus Gustafson.

I got there just as a Cheyenne boy in a coonskin cap raced out. Looked about the same age as the little colored girl.

Abby, broom in hand, was at his heels. "Scat!" she snarled, whacking his bottom. "Another stunt like that, and I'll be talking to your mother."

I held the door and followed Abby inside. She wasn't bad on looks. Not a knockout, nothing like that, but pretty enough to turn heads.

"It's mighty early," I said. "Your grandfather didn't open up until ten." Gustafson had recently been thrown in the clink for crimes, which I'd helped uncover. Abby Gunness, the old man's eldest granddaughter, had been given the store in return for caring for her invalid grandmother. The younger granddaughter, Kindra, was a good friend of mine but away at college, and I sure missed her.

She put down the broom, pushed out her lower lip, and blew. Her black bangs fluttered in the breeze. "I'll leave it for the banks to work half days," she said. "We're open six days a week now, eight to six. Business is up seven percent, even with sales items."

"You're a savvy businesswoman, and dangerous with a broom."

"The little snot tried to shoplift. He told me there was something gooey on the floor by the tar soap. I went to check and heard a clink, ran back, and caught him with his hand in the jawbreaker jar."

"Your grandfather moved it behind the counter because kids used to steal them. One of those thieves was Tyburn Newgate, who I heard was in here this morning."

Abby turned quickly and straightened the gum display. "There were no children in here this morning."

"He's not a child anymore. He's a bank robber. Scrawny. Maybe your age. Late twenties. Remember seeing him?"

"We were kind of busy."

"Hair's yellow, like straw."

She turned back to me, her forehead wrinkled. "Oh, yes, I remember him now. He bought a pack of Camels."

She had that phony surprised voice people get when trying to pull a fast one.

"Camels, huh? You sure about that?"

"Real sure. I even gave him a box of matches."

"He say anything?"

"Uh-uh. Guess that's why I forgot about him."

"He didn't pay in silver dollars, did he? That's what he stole from the bank."

She shook her head. "Just regular dollars."

"Okay, then. I don't mean to scare you, but he's a criminal. An acquitted criminal, but a criminal."

She let out a trill of laughter. "Gee, you make him sound dangerous."

"No one's accused him of being harmless."

She brushed scraps of lettuce from the counter onto her apron. "Why was he acquitted?"

"It's a long story. Let's just say, he's put me in a tough spot."

Tough wasn't even the right word. Because of him, my plan to become mayor might get shot down the tubes. Sure, Uncle Rupert wouldn't throw his nephew out in the rain. Folks didn't do that to relatives. He'd give me a job—maybe as an errand boy—and provide a roof over my head. Even if it was a covered pigsty.

She shook her apron over a wastebasket. "Sounds serious. Is he suing for false arrest or something?"

"It's kind of complicated."

⁊⊃⁊⊃

My stomach felt queasy. Wished I'd had that malt. Uncle Lewy's was up ahead, and I had no idea how to get Tyburn to hand over the silver. He probably believed he owned it legitimately since he got off the hook for stealing it.

The write-up in the local *Prairie Duster* said he was captured alone while driving into Laredo with a shovel. But Tyburn had told me he was arrested *in* Laredo while passed out in a bar. Something didn't jive, and I could think of only one something: he had double-crossed his partners.

The three robbers likely buried the silver in the desert before bouncing into Laredo—that explained the shovel. When Tyburn's associates danced across the border into Mexico, Tyburn could've taken the car, dug up the silver, moved it somewhere else, and then got arrested returning to town. It was only a theory, but if it was true, I might scare Tyburn into giving up the silver.

Uncle Lewy's was a dance club and one of three beer joints in town. The sign in front read *Conway Twitty, This Saturday Night.* I stepped inside and waited for my eyes to adjust. It smelled of stale cigarette smoke and sour beer. A stage took up the back portion of the room, and two covered pool tables filled a dark alcove. The bar ran along a side wall, and behind it hung pictures of all-time conference football champions, the Oklahoma Sooners.

The beer joint wasn't the kind of place I frequented at nine-thirty on a Monday morning. Or any morning. No clinking glasses, cheerful voices, laughter, good times. The few customers there slouched glum-faced at the bar while pounding down drinks. For them, alcohol served as a kind of oxygen. The workingmen—the blue collars with scraggly faces and grease on their hands—had already cleared out. They worked the farms and fields and factories near town that manufactured everything from typewriters to pinball machines to crystal sets. One plant printed baseball cards packaged with bubblegum. They also cranked out girlie playing cards.

Tyburn sat propped up at one end of the bar, talking to a hog farmer with wading boots and a weathered face. A cigarette bobbled in the corner of Tyburn's mouth while he lectured. He'd sing out to anyone willing to listen.

He had on the same clothes as ever: black vest, white T-shirt, jeans stiff and beltless. His yellow hair was thick enough to finger comb, and he had a thief's darting eyes that squinted against his cigarette smoke.

With creepy awareness, he turned his bony body to me and twisted his mouth into a grin. He pulled away his cigarette and let loose with a Texas-style whoop. "Yahhhh hooooo!"

He wasn't even from Texas. Just shows he'd steal anything.

"Well, goose me with a bullfrog. If it ain't my old jail-pal, Bucky-boy." He flicked his sputtering cigarette to the floor, slipped off his stool, and signaled me over. "Gimme five."

I automatically shook his hand, but wished I hadn't. After all, why would a police chief shake hands with a bank robber? Then again, he did have something I wanted-ed. Maybe shaking hands was a good thing.

"Hey, Tag," Tyburn called to the beer puller. He wagged his finger between the two of us. "Pour a couple."

Tag had a big head with a patch of growth beneath his lower lip. He'd been to prison for killing his first two wives. He was now single. I spun a quarter on the counter. "Make mine a Nehi." I'd have preferred milk, but didn't want to hear wisecracks from Tyburn.

I tossed a thumb toward the back.

Tyburn grinned. "A little privacy, huh?" He had a small bandage stuck over the right side of his upper lip that made the grin lopsided.

I tried a smile, but couldn't manage it. We walked to a corner table, Tyburn in a slow, swaying, knocked-about gait. I rubbed a circle of smooth skin on my face. A swamp mosquito had bitten me there, and I'd never had to shave it ever since. Occasionally, I found myself rubbing it when someone made me feel uneasy.

"You look mighty serious, Buck." We screeched back chairs and sat. "So before you say somethin' I won't like, I wanna congratulate you on your rise to stardom." He pointed to my seven-point badge.

My stomach clenched. Maybe I should've ordered

milk. "What brings you back to…uh…you know, these parts?" Damn, I didn't like the way that came out.

"These are my parts, remember?"

"Right, okay. Then why now?"

Tyburn's voice hardened. "Why not now?"

"You robbed the bank. Even told me so. Whole town knows."

Tyburn clawed open a fresh pack of Camels. "Whole town knows shit. I was just yakkin' jailbird talk to impress ya. Admired the way ya risked your life tryin' to save those Injuns at the town's birthday bash. Even made Sparks all giddy."

Officer Larry Sparks had been our jailer and witnessed me trying to protect two Indians from getting brutally gunned down by my predecessor, Chief Harman. I failed and was arrested. In lockup, Officer Sparks and Tyburn had exchanged some pretty tough words. The conversation had ended with Tyburn burning Sparks with a cigarette and Sparks threatening to kill him. Clearly, there was no love lost between the two of them.

Tyburn put a cigarette between his lips and tugged it from the pack. Lit it with a wooden match he struck with his thumbnail. Sucked in a lungful of smoke and let it char his lungs a moment. "The way I see it," he went on, his words on a stream of smoke," we both got thrown in jail under false charges."

I bent forward. "And the way I see it, you may soon be—"

Tag plunked down drinks and a glass with ice. He popped the cap off my Nehi and poured. He shifted his slow-moving eyes to Tyburn, then to my hip, as if expecting to see a gun stuck to it. "Everything okay?"

I nodded. Tyburn wouldn't try anything here. Tag laid down a straw from behind his ear and ambled back. I tore off the wrapper. "As I was about to say, you'll be taking a hit soon enough for that number you pulled."

Tyburn blew a smoke ring at me. "What number?"

I swatted the circle away. "Two. As in the number of associates you double-crossed. They know you're out of jail, so visiting hours could be anytime." I jabbed the straw into my drink. "And another thing, I wasn't at your trial to testify, but I'll be at your next one. Right after the judge gets word of our jailhouse chat."

"And what judge would that be?"

"That's not the point to be focusing on."

Tyburn raised his beer and tilted his head back. His Adam's apple slid up and down like a piston. He burped. "Uh-uh, Chief. The US Constitution don't allow double jeopardy."

Damn. Tyburn knew too much to fool with that one. I took a long draw of pop through my straw. Years back, a mayor got busted for installing a secret recording device in the council chambers. Maybe Tyburn would go for a bluff.

I glanced over both shoulders and leaned in. "Double jeopardy doesn't count in your case. Your hotshot lawyer planted a listening device in the jury room. The prosecution has the evidence. That means you can be retried."

Tyburn's lips tugged at his cigarette, and he reached for his beer. "Is that so? Well, I ain't got nothin' to worry about."

"Let's suppose you did rob the bank and—"

Tyburn banged the bottle on the table. "I ain't supposin' shit."

I sat back, stared into my drink, and stirred it with the straw. I bent forward again. "Let's say, hypothetically, Joe Blow and his associates robbed the bank."

After taking a near-lethal drag, Tyburn rolled his cigarette between his thumb and finger and studied it while smoke oozed from his nose. "Okay. Hypothetically."

"Let's say Joe Blow tells Lawman where the silver's hidden, and then Lawman gets it and returns it to the bank."

"Joe Blow's pretty fuckin' stupid."

I raised a finger. "But Lawman never mentions Joe Blow's name."

Tyburn flashed a sly grin. "So Lawman's in cahoots with Joe Blow."

"Let's just say Lawman's following orders to recover the silver."

"But how's Lawman gonna say he found it?"

I thought a moment. "Maybe Joe Blow and his associates don't know it, but a Cheyenne boy happened to see them bury the silver in the desert, and he took it. Later on, the boy got caught trying to buy out Gustafson's jawbreaker supply with pockets full of silver dollars."

Tyburn stretched his back and tilted his head from one shoulder to the other.

He was thinking. Maybe, just maybe…

"Sorry, but I don't see Joe Blow givin' up his silver."

"But that way, no new trial, no time in jail, and Joe Blow's associates would have every reason to believe that the Indian boy dug up the silver from where it was originally buried. That's better than them thinking Joe Blow stole the silver for himself."

Tyburn took a swig from the bottle, swished it around in his mouth, and swallowed hard. "You've got a wild imagination, Chief."

I took a long draw of pop, then stood. "What happened to your lip? Roughhousing with cellmates?"

"Rough razorblades. Thanks for asking."

"Six p.m., day after tomorrow. If I don't have the silver by then, Judge Thompson will issue a warrant for your arrest." I snatched the cigarette from between his lips, dropped it, and crushed it with my foot. "Smoking stunts your growth."

Someone whistled, and I turned to the bar. Tag held up a phone.

I took it. "Chief Bucky here."

# CHAPTER 4

The phone call from Mrs. Rheingold was still on my mind, along with the little colored girl, when I returned to police headquarters. I told Officer Sparks to keep Tyburn under surveillance and to call the station if he left town. It was a long shot that he would exchange silver for freedom, but six o'clock was coming fast, and I had no better ideas. He might have had enough confidence in his attorney not to sweat out another trial, but if my theory was right about him double-crossing his partners, he'd have plenty to mop his brow about.

With a groan, I strapped on my revolver. Mrs. Rheingold had arranged shooting lessons for me with former deputy chief Ham Wentworth. I'd never met the man, but heard he now raised llamas. I'd also heard he was impossible to predict.

I turned off the main highway onto Old Griffin Road South and took a deep breath, hoping to calm my nerves.

Two miles up, a red barn-shaped mailbox that said *Wentworth* sat on a post. I steered the cruiser over a cattle guard and onto a muddy dirt road with tall weeds in the center that battered the car's underbelly like they wanted in.

A single-story wood frame house stood on a small

rise among a grove of willow trees waving in the breeze. A black Ford pickup, stacked with hay, was parked near a corral in back. Beside the barn sat a rusty tractor.

I parked beside a well with a bucket and hand pump. I barely got one foot on the ground when a llama trotted up. I yanked my foot back and slammed the door. A dozen more wandered over. A light yellow one with horizontal pupils pressed its wet nose to the window.

I grew up around wild animals in Louisiana. Most were harmless if unprovoked and not hungry, even the alligators I'd wrestled. So I opened the door and stuck out my hand. The llama's smell reminded me of my goats back home. Nice.

A screen door closed with a bang, and the animal jolted back. A beefy man about fifty, wearing a tan sheepskin coat, labored down off the porch.

"If it's not the new chief," the man said with a tight smile or grimace, I couldn't tell. He squinted in the late morning sun and pointed to the yellow llama. "She's the one to worry about. Piss her off, and she'll spit and scream. If she's sex-starved, she'll rub against you and moan." He shooed the animal away with his hat and offered his hand. "I'm Ham."

A familiar sense of dread washed over me. I had sensitive hands, and Ham's were thick and heavy, like his shoulders and arms. I used a maneuver I'd perfected when greeting professional gator wrestlers. I shoved my hand in deep, keeping my fingers safe from wreckage. "Nice meeting you."

Ham peered inside my squad car. "Nice shotgun setup. Upright. Easy and quick."

I wanted to hurry up, get out of there, and check on that little girl. "I guess Mrs. Rheingold talked to you about maybe giving me some pointers on how—"

"Lessons."

"Huh?"

"She said you needed shooting lessons."

I put an unsteady hand on my gun. "Yeah, well, I've never—"

"Never what, killed a man?"

I jerked my hand away. "Jesus, that's not it."

"Not what?"

"I don't plan to kill anyone."

"Who said you did?"

"You asked if I did."

"Police work is more than killing people."

I frowned. "I don't want to kill people."

"You may have to."

"Maybe as a last resort."

"Or maybe not, if you're prepared." He scraped a line along the pea gravel with the toe of his boot. "You start out using the Golden Rule with people. But if they cross the line, you do this—" Ham pivoted and plunged his elbow hard into my stomach.

I grunted and crumpled to the ground, gasping for air.

Ham bent over and peered into my face. "You don't feel like getting up and doing anything right now, do you?"

I shook my head. Now that I could breathe again, pain seared through my body.

Ham reached under my arm and heaved me to my feet. "Sorry, but I had to do that. I could've explained all day and you still wouldn't get it."

"Don't worry, I got it." I wanted to strangle the man but doubted I'd reach his throat before suffering more pain.

"The longer you're on the job, the more likely you are to be attacked, injured, or shot on your day off. You need to learn more than just how to shoot. Let's say you stop a fellow for speeding. You don't know hell's first whisper about him. He might be an Injun with a trunk full of white lightning or a bank robber with guns. Be prepared. And if you have to hit a man, do it hard enough so you only have to do it once. Now, you still want those shooting lessons?"

I grabbed a box of rounds from the car and followed Ham behind the barn and away from the llamas. A row of tin cans had been arranged against a berm about twenty yards downrange.

"What you've got here is a .38 Special Colt Official Police revolver," Ham said, loading my gun. "Now I'll show you how to use it."

"Not by shooting me, I hope." Ham didn't seem to get the humor, so I added, "You know, like the punch."

"Like this?" Ham jabbed the barrel into my stomach and cocked the hammer with a terrifying click.

I hurtled back and onto my butt.

"I make the jokes around here. Now get up."

They weren't kidding about him being unpredictable. I got to my feet, considering whether I should pour salt in Mrs. Rheingold's sugar bowl.

Ham handed me the gun. "Hold it firmly and extend your arm. Now take aim and align the front and rear sights."

"I got it."

"Maintain focus on the front sight and—what the—" He stared at my hand which shook like a shivering Chihuahua. "You're all limp-wristed."

I dropped my arm and wiped sweat from my eyes. "It's kinda heavy."

"If you can't hold steady for three fucking second—"

"Maybe if I use two hands."

Ham snorted. "Are you a pussy or a man?"

I glared at him. All at once, a calm resolve took over

my body as my old feelings of guilt and shame were replaced by determination. I raised my gun and squeezed off the first shot. A can flew in the air and the recoil jerked my arm up. Aiming again, I sent five more cans flying. My ears were still ringing when I turned to my drill instructor.

Ham started for the house. "I'll meet you on the front porch."

I didn't understand what had happened. Couldn't explain it even to myself. I reloaded the gun and swaggered back around front, mighty pleased with myself. I waited for Ham on the porch in a chair constructed entirely of tree branches with a wagon-wheel-shaped back.

"Hope you like your coffee strong and black," Ham said, backing out the screen door and holding two mugs.

I tasted it and about gagged. "Wow!" It practically needed a knife and fork. I set the sludge down on a tree stump I assumed served as a table.

"A piece of advice," Ham said. "Defiance police chiefs live short lives." He took a long slurp of coffee. "One way to lengthen yours is to keep that shotgun in your car close at hand. It'll give you a leg up in the respect department."

That insurance man, he knew how to get respect. "I had a visitor this morning. Otto Oswald. Ever hear of him?"

"Owns National Insurance Company. A powerful man."

Exactly what I didn't want to hear. "What do you mean?"

"There's not a politician in the state that wouldn't take his call in the middle of dinner. As for Defiance, he's got dirt on more than one city councilman and wouldn't be afraid to spread it around. At least one of them's a Klansman."

"He said if I don't recover the bank's silver in two days, he'd have me back selling cars."

"Knowing Oswald, you'll have more than your job to worry about."

If I had looked at my breast pocket, I would've seen it thumping. I told Ham about the deal I offered Tyburn.

"That deal's not worth a Chinese nickel. Tyburn's a punk, but he's not stupid. He knows the DA can't afford to lose to that slick lawyer again. Not if he wants to get reelected."

"Tyburn's still got his partners to worry about if he double-crossed them."

"Your theory that he moved the silver may be right. Proving it is another thing. Detective work is simple, but not easy. Trust your instincts. Inexperienced investigators think only of clues and evidence. Without it, they sit on their butts. Instead, it's best to form theories based on what you know, and sometimes things fall into place."

"How did Tyburn manage to hire that hotshot snake-charming lawyer who leaves jurors thinking he can see around corners? A man like Jefferson Davis can't come cheap. Tyburn's daddy's only a butler."

"A butler to a rich and powerful man."

"But that powerful man's in prison."

"For someone who put him there, you outta know."

"Are you saying that Overstreet paid Tyburn's legal fees?"

"Wouldn't be the first time he's pinch-hit for that punk kid."

"But Tyburn's not a punk kid stealing jawbreakers from Gustafson's anymore. He's stealing silver from banks. Why should Overstreet care about him now?"

"That's what you need to find out. But whatever the reason, you'd better find out before it jumps up and bites you in the ass."

A block of ice formed in my stomach. "Do you think Tyburn's two accomplices will come after him?"

"If so, I'm sure Tyburn's figured out how to handle them."

"Like how?"

Ham shrugged. "Maybe make a deal or—" He ran a finger across his throat. "Sometimes the worst has to happen before you can hope for the best. Right now you're holding more loose ends than a blind carpet-weaver."

I chuckled uneasily. "What else can Oswald do besides get me fired?"

Ham gulped his coffee and smacked his lips. "I wouldn't stick around to find out."

The block of ice hardened.

# CHAPTER 5

Headquarters to car one. Headquarters to car one, over," Sergeant Hazelwood droned over the radio.

"Hi, Tom, it's me."

"Chief, where are you?"

"Just left Ham Wentworth's place." I put a hand on my bruised stomach. "What's cooking?"

"We've got a big one. A stabbing at the Mayfair Hotel. Sparks is there now."

My mind raced. "How bad?"

"Real bad. Like dead bad. I sent Murphy for back-up."

"Do we have the guy? The one with the knife?"

"The victim's the one with the knife."

"What? Never mind. Have Mrs. Rheingold bring my camera."

I was a professional photographer, of sorts, and always kept my camera handy.

"You might not know this, Chief, but the Mayfair's not under our jurisdiction. Sparks just happened to track Tyburn there."

"I'll be there in ten minutes." My foot slammed the accelerator like a brick, and the Fury lurched forward in an eight-cylinder roar. Looked like another one-for-the-books Mayfair killing.

The hotel sat isolated right at the city limit, screened from the highway by a grove of bayberry trees. It had sheltered important guests for more than three decades.

After swearing me in, Judge Thompson had said I'd have enemies and should get acquainted with the files in the police station's basement. Files about people and events never intended to reach the light of day. Those files included the Mayfair.

I had wasted no time that same afternoon pouring through documents. A folder labeled *Mayfair Hotel* told of several mind-blowing events. One was of a Mayor Potter and his wife. Suspicious of her husband's many visits to the hotel, she'd barged into his suite and found him in the arms of a "floozy." She shot the woman between the eyes and dragged the mayor down the back steps by his ear. No easy feat—the mayor weighed three hundred fifty pounds. He eventually died of a heart attack and was buried in a square coffin. The police never officially recorded the murder. The files showed lots of Mayfair cover-ups.

I screeched to a smoke-swirling stop at the hotel entrance. The exterior looked like a rundown Atlanta mansion. Nothing General Sherman would've wasted a match on: busted shutters, cracked windows, nettles shooting up through the porch. A crooked *No Vacancy* sign was nailed to the door.

The lobby was deserted. I gave a bell on the counter three sharp raps. Man, what a dump. Faded stuffed chairs and couches, old-fashioned oil paintings of scenes like men on horses, and salivating dogs chasing foxes. On a stand in the corner sat a Motorola TV with tinfoil on its rabbit ears to improve reception.

A short, spindly man with narrow uplifted shoulders

appeared from the back regions of the lobby. He was clenching a cigar between stained teeth and had a bushy mustache that might've crawled off at any moment. "Come with me," he snapped. "You shouldn't be here, so be quick about your business."

He lifted the hinged section of the countertop and came out. His thumb appeared deformed, and his cigar-stained fingers looked dipped in gravy. He led me up a timeworn staircase and down a hallway a few coats of paint above gloomy. I was very interested to know who this dead person was. I heard voices coming through an open door at an end room. The door had a jagged fist-sized hole near the doorknob. The clerk stopped at the doorway and motioned me inside. None of the three people in the room paid attention to me, although only one of them was dead, the one on the floor staring at the ceiling and clutching a knife in his heart. I didn't recognize him.

"I'm telling you," Officer Sparks was saying, "there's no way he could've done that to himself."

"And I'm telling you," Officer Murphy blasted back, "he committed suicide. You don't see anybody else in here, and the room was locked from the inside." Murphy, only a few years younger than Sparks and the force's first academy graduate, had the stiff-backed appearance of a recruit who had just jumped to attention.

"What are you saying?" I asked, while examining the door and noting a key in the inside lock.

"There's—um," Murphy stammered, "—uncertainty about how he died."

Sparks blew air, lips fluttering. "Not died, nitwit, how he got stabbed."

The clerk leaned against the doorframe, cleaning his fingernails with a match. "Y'all gotta clear out by one o'clock." He nodded at the corpse. "Especially him. Big shots are coming and won't like dead bodies around. Or, for that matter, local cops." He pointed his cigar stub at Sparks's feet. "Don't appreciate it, fella, you tracking blood around."

Sparks moved his foot and found a blood spot.

The clerk removed the door key from the lock and started to leave.

"Hold it!" I said. "Give me that." I took the key, and he left. Damn, Sparks screwing up was bad enough. Now I might've lost the killer's fingerprint from the key.

"Like I say," Murphy went on, "suicide, pure and simple. Look at him. He's gripping a knife big as a drum-stick."

The man seemed surprisingly serene—maybe a slight wince. The wound wasn't as gruesome as the late Chief Parker's. In the chief's case, a dog had torn out his throat. I almost tossed my cookies with that one.

The victim probably got up from the crumpled bed to answer the door. I examined his left hand, the one not holding the knife. It had a rag around it, still damp with blood. I removed the rag. There was a half-inch cut be-tween the first and second knuckle. I felt the man's bare arm. It wasn't cold, but not very warm either.

Sparks's head had disappeared up the chimney. I tapped his back. "Roll it out for me, Larry. From the be-ginning."

His head came back out. His hair was cut military style and brushed up stiffly. He put on his hat. "I was sit-ting over at Smiley's. Not getting a haircut, just waiting for Tyburn to leave Uncle Lewy's across the street."

I peered out one of the two corner windows at a shabby brown barn. Handkerchief in hand, I carefully un-latched the window, but it was sealed closed with a cen-tury of paint. "Go on, I'm listening."

Sparks smacked his lips. "So after about an hour-and-a-half of watching Smiley whittle a piece of wood and listening to him yak about fishing, I got pretty bored. You know how he talks your brain numb."

The second window was also locked. I unlatched it, and it rose easily. "You say you were bored?" I stuck my head out. There was an oak tree about ten feet away, and the ground about twenty feet below.

"Well, yeah. I'd been there a long time, so I sent Smiley over to check on Tyburn. I'd have done it myself, but knew you didn't want him to get wise that he was being watched. Anyway, Smiley hotfoots it back saying the beer puller told him that after you left, Tyburn tore out the back like a boar for a mud hole."

Maybe our little chat had spooked him. I brought my head in, speculating whether someone could've jumped onto the oak tree or made it to the roof. "This was Tag, you say?"

"What? Oh, the beer puller. Yeah, him."

I checked my watch. "That was almost two hours ago."

"I guess," Sparks said. "So I ran over there to see if Tag knew where Tyburn had gone. He didn't, but a hog farmer said Tyburn had mentioned the Mayfair. I went to the car and radioed in, but Mrs. Rheingold said you were out at Ham Wentworth's getting shooting less—"

"Right, right, so then what?" Mrs. Rheingold probably blabber-mouthed to the whole town.

"So Larry came here and saw Tyburn's rusty old Chevy Coupe parked in back," Murphy chimed in. "But it's gone now."

"Did you come inside and talk to him?" I asked Sparks.

"Came in, but didn't talk to him. Didn't even see him."

I stepped over the body and knelt at the open door. "Who'd you talk to?"

Sparks tossed a glance toward the hallway. "That little shit, Dusty, the clerk. He didn't want to say anything at first. I told him no problem, I'd start making phone calls. He right quick changed his tune. Said Tyburn came in and asked what room some fella named Gregory was in."

"Gregory, huh?" I'd never heard of him. "First or last name?"

Sparks shook his head. "Didn't say. Just Gregory, room two-thirteen."

"It's his last name," Murphy said. "Driver's license says Willard Gregory of Santa Fe, New Mexico."

"So, anyway," Sparks continued, "I went back to my car to radio you again. See what you wanted me to do."

"Back up a second. Did this guy, Dusty, did he say Tyburn had gone up to room two-thirteen?"

"Yeah."

My mind filled with questions, but I wanted to go slow and cover everything. "Okay, so you tried to call me again from your car."

"That's what I said. But Mrs. Rheingold told me you were still…preoccupied, so I decided to pay a personal visit to Tyburn and this Gregory guy. Maybe they had the silver up there with them. But when I knocked on the door, no one answered. I tried the knob, but it was locked."

"Did you hear anything inside? Noises, talking?"

Sparks shook his head. "Nothing. Even stuck my ear to the door."

"When you came inside the hotel, did you go through the lobby or up the back way, through the emergency exit?"

"The lobby."

I bent over and glanced inside the chimney. "So you what, kicked the hole in the door?"

"Yeah, but first I called for Dusty to get his ass up here with a passkey."

"But it didn't do no good," Murphy chimed in.

Sparks shot him a hard look. "Do you mind?" He turned to me. "While I was waiting for Dusty, I looked through the keyhole and saw a key in the lock from the other side. When Dusty got up here, I told him his passkey wouldn't work because of that other key, and that I'd tried to push it out with my pocketknife, but it wouldn't budge. That's when I booted the hole in the door, reached through, and unlocked it."

"This must be the place," a voice sang brightly. A middle-aged white-coated man swished his narrow hips into the room. A familiar set of moves I had seen before. Doc Carrington modeled himself after the romantic swashbuckler, Errol Flynn. A cape and sword would've completed the image.

The doc dropped his bag, gazed down at the body, and stroked his pencil-thin mustache. "Tsk, tsk, tsk. Poor devil."

Mrs. Rheingold and two colored orderlies with a white stretcher trailed the doc into the room. Mrs. Rheingold handed me my camera bag. "I was told you wanted this. Oh, and Mr. Oswald called from the insurance company." She slipped me a folded *While You Were Out* note that I jammed in my pocket.

"Doc, I need to take pictures before you start touching anything." I shooed everyone out the door and photographed the entire room. Afterward, the doc directed his orderlies to deliver the body to Fromm Mortuary. I grasped an orderly's arm. "Hold on. Doc, aren't you going to do an autopsy? We need an autopsy."

The doc's eyebrows took off skyward in fake surprise. "You suppose he died from something other than heart failure?" Murphy snickered. The doc paced around the body, studying it. "I'd put him at about thirty, so we can rule out old age." He stopped and raised a finger. "Perhaps poison."

"I'm just saying," I said. "We don't know if it was murder or suicide."

The doc gripped my shoulders and gave them a little shake. "Fear not. I shall examine the body carefully."

"Be sure to check the entry wound. The angle may be important in ruling out suicide. Murphy, dust the room for fingerprints. But first, you and Sparks come with me."

On the way out, I read Oswald's message. *The day after tomorrow is a bank holiday. Must have the silver by 6:00 p.m. tomorrow.*

I crumpled the note and groaned. *Or else.*

# CHAPTER 6

Sparks led Officer Murphy and me to where he had seen Tyburn's car parked. Tire tracks in the gravel showed the car had exited the lot and headed toward 81 South. I sent Sparks back to the station to write up his report. "Murphy," I said, "come with me."

Maybe after escaping from the room, Tyburn had left the hotel by way of the stairs outside the rear emergency exit.

The soil was still damp from rain. Some footprints led to the barn, others toward the parking lot. "Before dusting the room, make impressions of these prints," I told Murphy.

I got back to my office, still thinking. Tyburn must've killed Gregory and took off toward Laredo to dig up the silver. Why else would he head south out of town?

I grabbed a book from my bookshelf: *Oklahoma Law Enforcement Procedures and Protocols Manual*. "If a murder suspect flees a town or municipality," the volume said, "the county sheriff and state patrol must be notified."

That made sense. The police chief's jurisdiction was confined to a city or town, and the sheriff's included an entire county. The state patrol, of course, covered the whole state. I reached for the phone and dialed.

While waiting for the sheriff to come on the line, I thought about Oklahoma's strict rules on jurisdiction. Those state troopers had practically ordered me away from the little Negro girl in the ditch.

Jeb Rakoff, Garfield County sheriff, came on the line, and I told him about the murder. "The victim's name is Gregory from Santa Fe."

"Gregory, huh? That the first or last name?"

"Last," I said. "And Tyburn Newgate is our prime suspect. We think he fled south."

Rakoff didn't say anything for so long, I thought we'd got cut off. The only sound was Mrs. Rheingold's typewriter. Finally, he said, "I suppose I can issue a bulletin for Tyburn's arrest and notify the state patrol."

"Thanks for your help," I said, wondering why the long silence. "Um, one more thing, Sheriff. A little Negro girl was found hurt in a ditch this morning, and I want to follow up and be sure she's okay. The thing is, I don't know where she lives. Two state troopers took her and told me to pretty much mind my own business. I'm hoping you could tell me how to find her."

"A little Negro girl, you say. Yes, that's, um—Was this ditch in town?"

"Actually, just north of town."

"Well, there you have it."

"What do you mean?"

"That's out of your jurisdiction, so it's not your concern."

"Maybe not as a police chief, but as a citizen, it sure as hell is. So I'll ask you again, how might I find this little girl?"

Another silence, then a long audible exhale. Finally, "Chief, I know this is only your first day on the job, but don't you think there are more important things for you to do than worry about some colored girl? You said the state troopers were handling it. Now I suggest you not insult them by sticking your nose where it doesn't belong. I hope I've made myself clear. Goodbye."

જ્જ

What a bastard. You'd think I was trying to start a turf war. Screw him. He was right on one count, though. I did have important things to do—such as solving a murder, finding Oswald's stolen silver, and keeping my damn job.

I called Sergeant Hazelwood and told him to get hold of the Santa Fe police and learn what he could about Gregory, then I went to the window, opened it, and took in a lungful of fresh air. Gazed out at the miles of Indian prairie grass and cornfields. Fresh air made my mind work better, and my mind told me to track Tyburn's movements since he arrived in town this morning and screwed up my life. Just thinking about him rolled my stomach.

Lamar Fromm said he got around more than a stray dog. He was in the beer joint and, before that, Gustafson's. What about even before that? His daddy's? I reached for my hat. Time to go question a butler.

જ્જ

I sped up the spiral road under a canopy of arching oaks, through midday shafts of yellow sunlight, past neighborhoods of rich people in big houses behind walls and hedges, all the way to the top of the crest—to the Overstreet mansion.

I had less than thirty hours to get Oswald's silver— *or else*. He really screwed me with that bank holiday. He could just as easily have granted me an extra day. But, no, the slime ball had to take a day away.

I reached the road's end. Ahead loomed the Overstreet estate. The house was a massive construction of stone and mortar, looking every bit like a medieval castle, minus the gun turrets, but with spires and lots of little windows. It was designed and built by Overstreet himself. I steered through the open gate and toward a herd of fancy new cars. I parked between a Cadillac and a Rolls Royce, extra careful not to bang anything with my door when I got out.

The castle-sized front door had swirling moldings, and the doorbell sounded like something from a clock tower. The door opened, and a gorgeous, glassy-eyed blonde in an oversized yellow dress grinned and waved a champagne glass like it was New Year's Eve.

"Well, who have we here?" She squinted at my badge and swayed as if the ground was shaking. "Wait!" Up shot her free hand. "Don't tell me. You're a policeman." She grinned again, but bigger, as if she'd won the sixty-four-thousand-dollar question. Her teeth sparkled like those of Ham's llamas.

"I'm here to see…um…" I forgot Tyburn's daddy's name. "Is the butler around?"

Mrs. Overstreet's long head appeared at the door, and her mouth opened like a pink clownfish. "Bucky Ontario!" She spat my name like a curse. "What the devil are you doing here?"

I tipped my hat. "Hello, Mrs. Overstreet."

The shorter and younger woman, now standing behind Mrs. Overstreet, tapped her shoulder. "He wants to see Martin."

Mrs. Overstreet shot her a wide-eyed look then turned back to me, her eyes now like Oswald's—set to kill.

I cleared my throat. "That's right, ma'am. Is he in?"

Her lips pulled down like bent steel. "What's this about?"

I coughed into my hand. "Police business."

"Well!" She raised her chin. "You've come at a bad time."

The other woman threw a hand to her mouth and giggled.

Mrs. Overstreet wheeled around to her. "Trixie! Go back inside." She turned again to me. "If I wasn't a Christian woman, I'd spit in your face for what you did to my husband."

"Mrs. Overstreet, your husband's in prison because he broke the law."

"Poppycock. Toying with ballots goes on all the time, and *you* know it."

Toying? That's what she called election rigging? "You could be right, but I insist on talking to Martin."

"I don't know what games you're playing, but—"

I raised a hand. "I'm a police chief, ma'am. I work at it, I don't play at it."

Her blood seemed to drop a few degrees, because her glare became colder than her husband's cell bars. "I hope you rot in hell," she spat, spun around, and marched inside, adding, "You'll find Martin in the dining room."

I entered the vestibule and glanced around. Mrs. Overstreet had joined several women in the living room, standing in streaks of sunlight from the windows, drinking champagne, and clucking like hens.

I padded down the hallway, recalling that Martin wasn't the butler's real name. Martin was Mrs. Overstreet's previous butler's name, and she liked it so much, it stayed with the job.

I found the scrawny butler bent over in a corner, ironing a polka dot dress. "Excuse me, Martin, I'm—"

"I know who you are, Chief Bucky." He had Tyburn's same yellow hair. He also had a flat voice and pointed chin he didn't bother raising. "What can I do for you?"

"I need to talk to you about your son. Happen to know where he is?"

"I've not the slightest idea."

"When did you talk to him last?"

He placed the iron down with the hot bottom facing me. "I would say…maybe two, three hours ago."

Things were looking up "What'd he say?"

Martin shrugged and turned the dress around. "Not much."

*Yeah, I'd bet. He's trying to protect his thieving, killing son.* "Where'd he call from?"

"Call?" Martin's forehead creased like a washboard. "He didn't call, he was here."

"Here!" My mind jolted and spun at the same time. He must've fled south from the Mayfair and doubled back. "Why'd he come here?"

Martin dipped his hand into the pocket of his black trousers, and out came a pipe. "A Dunhill."

"I'm impressed. What about it?"

"My birthday present."

"Your son came here, didn't say much, but gave you a pipe. Then what?"

"He left." Martin pocketed his pipe with a smirk, picked up a sprinkle bottle, and dribbled water on the dress.

"I saw him earlier at Uncle Lewy's with blood on his shirt. You must've noticed it yourself."

"His shirt looked fine to me."

"Your house in the back, where he grew up, did he go there, change shirts maybe?"

Martin scoffed. "My son moved out quite some time ago—along with his shirts."

Disappointed that my blood trick didn't work, I moved on. "Does he own a hunting knife?"

Martin shrugged and started in on the hem. "I know he did as a youngster. All the boys did."

"Where is it now?"

"It probably disappeared over the years."

"Your son was pretty good at making things disappear around here. Loose change and such."

Martin closed his eyes and breathed in deeply through his nose. "Tyburn was a lonely child. The missus and I, she's passed now, we worked long hours."

"What do you know about Willard Gregory?"

Martin blinked suspiciously. "Who?"

"You heard me. Who is he?"

"I'm afraid I don't know."

I heard women gathering in the hallway and tried again. "Never heard the name?"

He put the iron down and scooped up the dress. "I've told you, no. Now what's your point here?"

"Two points. Your son's not only a bank robber, but also a suspect. A prime suspect, a very prime suspect, in the murder of Willard Gregory. Now I'll ask again, where's your son?"

Trixie trotted into the room, her blonde hair pulled behind one ear. "Martin, you are such a dear." She took the dress from him and buried her nose in it. "Fresh and clean. My husband—" She rolled her eyes. "Why, if I came home reeking of champagne, he'd think I'd been with another man. No telling what he'd do." She giggled and flitted to the door then turned with a cuddly smile. "Martin, your son's a dream," she cooed then twirled and left.

Martin reached down to unplug the iron.

I yanked it from the socket. "You haven't answered me."

Martin straightened and gave his coat a sharp tug. "Look, Chief Bucky, he was here only a minute. That's it. And you're wrong." He jerked the cord from my hand. "He's made some mistakes, but he is *not* a murderer."

Mrs. Overstreet whisked into the room. "Chief Bucky, you're keeping Martin from his duties. In the future, I suggest—"

"I'm just leaving. Thank you both for your time."

I got into my cruiser and took off. Butlers! They were all the same. Lonely creatures, silent as shadows, lurking in corners like cockroaches, antennae taking in everything and transmitting nothing. Almost nothing. Martin blinked suspiciously when he heard Willard Gregory's name. Ham said that Overstreet was protecting Tyburn, and it was obvious his daddy did so too. Ham also said something was going to jump up and bite me in the ass. I tried to remember if I'd reloaded my gun.

# CHAPTER 7

Leaving the Overstreet residence, I decided to take the old frontage road, winding through a broad landscape covered with shadows of clouds shaped like cotton balls. As I crested a hill, I came to a herd of goats in the road.

An old man wearing a World War I army uniform used a stick to prod the animals to the side.

I got out of the car and helped get them onto the shoulder, where they nibbled pigweed along a fence.

The man eyed me suspiciously. "Who the hell are you?"

From the smell of his breath, I guessed he was a stranger to a toothbrush. He had a sun-beaten face and smelled goaty enough to be buried. A ragged and stained buckskin hat hung cocked over one eye.

"Bucky Ontario, Defiance Chief of Police." I threw out a hand. "How do you do?"

The man frowned, mumbled something about not doing well, and gave my hand a quick up-and-down pump. Surprised by the old man's strength, I flexed my fingers to make sure they still worked.

"Not to be rude, sir, but why do you wear the uniform?"

"Why shouldn't I wear it? I served our country and am damn proud of it."

I started to tell him that was three wars back, but decided against it.

"Speaking of uniforms," the old man grumbled, "why are you wearing Chief Parker's?"

"Chief Parker died some time back."

The old man squinted his visible eye. "That kind of rings a bell. Killed by dogs, maybe? You be careful."

One dog had killed Chief Parker, and I was the chief's second successor. But rather than explain, I pointed to the goats. "Nothing better than goat's milk cheese. Back home they separate the bucks from the does."

"What the hell for?"

"Otherwise, they say the goaty smell of the boys is absorbed into the milk."

The old man grimaced. "Hogwash. Where'd you say you're from?"

"Louisiana." Not wanting to rile the old man further, I said, "I'm sure there's a variation between breeds from place to place. You say you're not doing well?"

"Doing fine. The other day I—uh, no, that wasn't me. What are you talking about?"

"Earlier you said you're not doing well."

"Oh, yeah. Those damn cars. Scared the dickens out of my goats."

"What cars would those be?"

"Three of them, all black. Barreled by like hell on wheels."

I checked my watch. Almost one-thirty. That hotel clerk wanted everyone out by one because big shots were coming. "Were the cars long, like limousines?"

"Yeah, like them."

❧❦❧

My radio crackled. "Calling car one. Over."

I picked up the mic. "What is it, Murphy?"

"Chief, it's me, Murphy."

"I know that. Why'd you call?"

"I'm back at the station with the prints. Just a couple sets. The room was pretty clean."

"Clean! It's a hotel room. There should be prints all over the place. How about water faucets, you check those?"

"Everything, Chief. Gregory was only there a short time before stabbing himself—that is, maybe stabbing himself. The maids must be pretty good about—"

"I understand. But you got some good ones, huh?"

"One on the toilet lever, and another on the outside doorknob."

"How about the mortuary? Did you go there and check the knife?"

"It only showed Gregory's prints."

"Figures."

"Another thing, Chief. Gregory had eight silver dollars in his pocket. That pretty much cinches it, don't ya think?"

"Cinches what?"

"That he was the second of the three robbers."

"How do you know Tyburn didn't plant the dollars?"

"You mean, maybe he wasn't the second robber?"

"I think he was, but not because of the dollars. Compare those prints you've got to Tyburn's. They're on file."

"One more thing, Chief. Sparks and me, we were talking about Gregory and everything."

"Yeah?"

"Well, you sure we outta be messin' with this?"

"Messing with what?"

"You know, the stabbing. The Mayfair's outside our jurisdiction."

"So I've heard. Who says?"

"Just is, that's all. State troopers always handle Mayfair cases."

"Well, in this case, so do we. Sheriff Rakoff's got them searching for Tyburn, and I want you to get busy identifying those prints."

"Whatever you say, Chief."

I hung up the radio and drummed a little beat on the steering wheel. First day on the job, and I was on my way to solving a murder. Not bad for a brand-new chief with no law enforcement experience. I might be out of my depth, but I'd always been a good swimmer.

# CHAPTER 8

I turned onto an unmarked dirt road and nosed into a thicket of ironweed that offered a hidden view of the Mayfair, about two hundred yards away. Slapping a telephoto lens on my camera, I peered through to the corner room, top floor.

How the hell did Tyburn get out of there? Both windows had been locked, and one was even stuck closed with paint. But even if he got out the unstuck window and managed to lock it from the outside, the oak tree was too far away, and without a rope and grappling hook, he'd never gotten to the roof.

The upstairs emergency door was now propped open. The stairs led to the back parking lot where Sparks had seen Tyburn's car. On the other side stood the brown barn I'd seen from the window.

I put down my camera and watched a hawk soar on a sweeping updraft. Like me, it hunted vermin, except its prey wouldn't escape from locked rooms. About to tuck away my camera, I glimpsed a figure emerge from the barn. I put the lens back to my eye. A man in a chauffeur's uniform carried luggage toward the stairs. He probably drove one of the limousines the goat herder saw on the road.

I drove back to the main road and pulled into the hotel's front lot behind the bayberry trees. Why would bigwigs with limos stay in such a dump? The Encore Hotel or even the Holiday Inn would be a million times better.

The hotel entrance was locked, and I couldn't see anything through the peephole. I gave the door four hard raps.

Seconds later, thumping footsteps approached. I imagined Dusty opening the door in a huff. But when it swung open, a tall, hard-faced state trooper filled the doorway. He ducked his head and came out like a frigate pulling alongside a shrimp boat. The trooper had a dimpled chin, captain's bars on his collar, and a shotgun in his hand. "Where's the fire, Chief?"

I swallowed. "No fire. I'm here to see Dusty."

"If it's about the murder, and I'm sure it is, it's been taken care of. So get lost." He backed inside and swung the door.

It stopped at my foot. *Here we go with that jurisdiction thing I'd been hearing so much of.* "It's about a robbery, and I'll wait here for Dusty." I withdrew my foot.

The captain glared. I glared back.

Finally, he turned and closed the door. I had power tripped him. Stare at a man's ear and he'll think you're looking him in the eye. In this case, I stared at the captain's dented chin.

I waited on the porch, watching quail scratching in the brown grass beneath the bayberry trees. As a kid, I used to shoot them out of the sky with my BB gun, and Zeke, my dog, fetched them. When Zeke died, I lost interest in shooting birds. Live and let live became my philosophy.

I went to the peephole again and squinted. That trooper with shiny captain's bars must be one of the hot shots in there. Suddenly the caustic breath of Dusty blew like a hair-drier on the back of my neck. I swung around. "Jeez. You might consider coughing or something."

"What the hell do you want now?"

"I have questions for you, if you don't mind."

"And if I do?"

The front door opened and a trooper appeared. A different one. A sergeant with ears like club steaks and stripes up and down his arms. His nametag said Hale. Maybe troopers were having a convention. He stood arms folded—biceps bursting out of his shirt like a bare-fist fighter's. He'd probably been a middleweight boxer. Not a man I wanted to see rolling up his sleeves in search of answers.

I ignored him and gripped Dusty's reedy arm, lifted him to his tiptoes, and dragged him away.

"Go ahead and mind," I said. "You'll answer my questions anyway. I'm after Tyburn and the silver he robbed."

Dusty shook his arm free. "I ain't got it, so piss off."

"Don't fuck with me, Dusty." I glanced at the trooper and lowered my voice. "Tell me how Tyburn got out of Gregory's room."

Dusty twitched his thin shoulders. "Maybe a window."

"And locked it from the outside? Try again."

"I don't know. The chimney."

"Okay, forget about Tyburn. What do you know about Gregory?"

"Gregory?"

"Yeah, the dead guy."

"I know his motorcycle's still in the back."

I had wondered how Gregory got to the hotel. "Keep going."

Dusty flicked a glance over my shoulder. "Someone had called in a room reservation for him."

I leaned close. "Who?"

A vise-like hand gripped my shoulder. "Conference is over, Chief."

Trooper Hale's rough voice sounded like he gargled with battery acid. His lips turned down and his ears flattened like a rabid dog's. "I'll walk you to your car."

Dusty scurried inside. I considered my options, but couldn't think of one that didn't risk losing blood. As we walked, the trooper pulled out a pack of Luckies from his shirt pocket and tapped it hard against his forefinger. An uneven cluster of cigarettes popped up like a cityscape. He offered me one. I shook my head.

We reached my cruiser, and the trooper leaned against the door and lit his cigarette. "I'll tell you something." He spit a piece of tobacco off his tongue. "I knew Chief Parker. He was a good chief. Folks respected him. I respected him. Even went bear hunting with him once. Came home with a three-hundred-pounder." His chest swelled with a lungful of smoke.

"Why would you respect him?" The troopers certainly didn't respect me when I found the little girl just hours earlier.

Jets of smoke streamed from Hale's nostrils. "Chief Parker respected protocol. So did the chief before him and the chief before him. It's like this. Yesterday I saw a chicken crossing the road. I asked it why. It said it was none of my business."

"I see. Protocol."

The trooper gave me a friendly shoulder punch and chuckled. It sounded like a drain emptying. "Now you've got it. The captain knew you'd understand. And to show his appreciation, he wants you to know you can count on him to cover your back anytime." He clucked his tongue twice. "Anytime."

"Well, that's—you tell the captain I appreciate that."

"I'll tell you something between you, me, and this car of yours with the fancy shotgun rack. The lieutenant governor is arriving here for some R and R in about—" He pulled back a cuff and checked his watch. "—thirty minutes." He winked and opened my door. "Any little thing you're not clear on?"

I shook my head. "Nope. Things are pretty clear." Bullshit clear. My neck felt hot. The troopers were hiding something.

The trooper dropped his cigarette, gave it a good grinding with his foot, and drove his fist hard into my solar plexus. My stomach took a whirl, and I crumbled to the ground, the air knocked out of me. The trooper swung his leg back and kicked me in the side as if going for a field goal.

I found my breath and howled like a coyote.

"Wrong answer, Chief. Not pretty clear. One hundred percent crystal clear." Another kick, and the trooper started for the hotel, his face twisted to one side. "You're swimming with sharks, Chief. You'd best find another pond."

# CHAPTER 9

Once I finally caught my breath, I peeled myself off the ground and clawed into the front of my car with the kind of reaction I normally reserved for cold toilet seats. *A-a-a-a-hahhhhh!!*

I sat for a minute, recuperating, before reaching for the ignition. Fuck! The slightest movement caused a jabbing pain in my side and a hefty dose of wooziness. I closed my eyes and sat still, hoping the pain would stop. I gave up waiting and, sloth-like, reached again for the starter. I had to get my ribs looked at.

The engine growled to life.

Which way? Would Doc Carrington be at the hospital or his office? His office might have fewer people around to ask questions. I turned east, then south. Slow and easy. These weren't the smoothest streets in the world.

After a few miles, the pain in my side lessened and I began thinking clearly. Find another pond, Hale said. Screw him. *A-a-a-hahhh.* Damn potholes.

Doc Carrington's house lay just ahead, with his office tucked into a section in the rear. The ranch-style plank house sat isolated among acres of willows, elms, pines, cedars, and beside a lazy creek. Excellent for hunting game, fishing, and swimming. Doc always swam in the nude. That's what he told everybody.

The doc's Chrysler New Yorker was parked in the driveway. Hard to believe I had sold it to him less than a month ago. Boy, had my life changed. Ouch!

Above his front door was a gigantic pair of ivory tusks. I managed to get out of the car, inch my way to the back door, and knock.

"Damn, Bucky, what'd you do to yourself?" the doctor asked as soon as he opened the door and saw me leaning weakly against the wall.

"I didn't do anything," I said, grimacing as I followed him inside. I explained what happened as we walked to his office, where the doc helped me onto the examination table. The room looked like a regular doctor's office, except for a floor-to-ceiling photograph of the doc in khakis and a pith helmet, holding a humongous gun and resting his foot on a dead elephant.

He removed my shirt. "Can you lift your arm?"

I raised it a little. "My side really hurts."

He poked around.

"Ouch! Jesus, easy."

He grabbed a stethoscope from the cabinet and pressed the cold disk to my back. "Breathe in and hold it. You say you were kicked? Exhale."

"Twice, after being punched in the gut."

The stethoscope moved to a new spot. "Again." A new spot. "And again." Doc put down the instrument. "Looks like you're going to live. Go ahead and jump down."

"Very funny. Do I have broken ribs?"

"Maybe a crack or two." He helped me off the table. "Raise your arm again. See these two red marks?" He wagged his finger at my tortured side.

"Like I said, I was kicked twice."

He handed me my shirt. "By someone quite charitable."

I buttoned my shirt. "That's a laugh."

"Where I'm from in South Texas, they call kick marks like yours love taps. Made by the top of the foot. They're not intended to break ribs. For real damage, the toe is used."

"Love taps, huh?"

"Sends a message." He helped me with my coat. "Those who ignored it usually returned on stretchers. Often with collapsed lungs. Or dead. Who is this person?"

"Someone who doesn't like outsiders swimming in his pond." I put on my hat. "Speaking of dead, do you think Gregory's stab wound was suicide?"

"As I informed Officer Murphy, the person thrusting the knife was either lucky or had knowledge of anatomy. An upward angle will do more damage where there are fewer bones and more soft things that bleed than someone thrusting downward."

"So the angle was upward?"

The doc raised his right hand. "That is my testimony. I should also mention the knife appeared to be new."

"I'll note that. Could Gregory have done it to himself?"

"The wound supports that possibility. It also supports that he did not." He handed me a bottle of aspirin. "Careful where you swim. You may not be so lucky next time."

☙❧

I popped some aspirins on the way to my office and lay down on the floor as soon as I arrived, hoping that my head would stop spinning. About when the pills started kicking in, the phone rang. I slowly reached up for it.

"Chief, it's Ham. I've got information that should interest you. But not on the phone."

I felt a hard thud in my stomach. Maybe it had to do with Tyburn and the silver. It was past lunchtime, and I was hungry. "How about Sally's?"

"Already got my coat on."

☙❧

I took two more aspirin and my time getting to the car.

I ate at Sally's a lot. At home, I had cereal for breakfast, sometimes with a banana, if it hadn't turned black. Supper was usually Campbell's soup heated on a hotplate and eaten from the can. My old girlfriend back home taught me that trick. It's simple and meant fewer dirty dishes.

I arrived before Ham and slid into my favorite booth by the window. Jolene, a long-faced waitress with blue hair and loose-fitting skin, dropped by and swiped the table with a rag and emptied the ashtray into it. She wasn't the type for chitchat but did congratulate me on my new job.

"Thanks," I said, glancing toward the door. "I'm waiting for someone."

She left two ice waters, and I left for the restroom. Above the urinal a poster showed a rearing horse and hooded rider. It said *KKK of America. For membership, write P.O. Box 62-126, Oklahoma City.*

I wondered how to find out about the little colored girl without ruffling anyone's feathers. Had one idea, but no time for it right now. I tore off the poster and crammed it in my pocket.

Back at the booth, my stomach sprang backflips as I worried about what Ham wanted. I flicked glances at the door. Wished I'd ordered a malt. Doc Carrington wasn't much help in the Gregory-suicide department. Not that it mattered much. It seemed clear that Gregory had been in bed when Tyburn came to the door. Gregory let him in, Tyburn stabbed him, and then he put Gregory's hand around the knife.

I ran a finger along the edge of my frosted water glass. In my pocket was the room key that Dusty had removed from the lock. Maybe he only wanted to put it away. But in a murder case, it was probably not good to assume anything.

Ham slid in across from me. He had strands of hay on his coat. I straightened and took a sip of water.

Jolene appeared. "Give me a custard pie and coffee, black," Ham said.

I ordered a hamburger, fries, and chocolate malt. "Wait," I called after her. "Bring the malt right away." My stomach needed it.

Ham eyeballed me hard. "I got a call from Sheriff Rakoff."

Uh-oh. Didn't like Ham's look. Maybe Rakoff's deputies found Tyburn. And without the silver. "Is there a problem?"

"Rakoff talked to some trooper captain, and he thinks you're swirling down the drain by chasing after this stabbing case and what's-his-name."

Jolene dropped off Ham's pie and coffee.

"Gregory," I said. "The dead guy's name was Gregory." The mention of the trooper captain got me jittery. I took a straw from the container.

"First or last?"

"Last. What the hell's Rakoff talking about?"

Ham picked up his coffee. "You tell me."

I ripped off the wrapper and jammed the straw into my water glass. "Gregory was Tyburn's accomplice in the bank robbery, and Tyburn stabbed him. That is, I'm pretty sure it was Tyburn. Anyway, I called Rakoff because I suspected Tyburn had skipped town."

Ham blew on his coffee. "You're *pretty* sure Tyburn stabbed Gregory, and you *suspected* Tyburn had skipped town."

"Well, I—yeah, I guess." I looked around for Jolene and my malt.

Ham slurped his coffee and put down the cup. "That's not what's important."

I knew where this was going, since Rakoff had talked to the trooper captain. "I know, protocol's what's important. A trooper delivered that message personally."

"Love taps?"

"Jesus! How the hell did you know?"

Ham shook his head. "You've got more to worry about than losing your job. Fucking with State Troopers can get you—"

"What was I supposed to do, not call Rakoff?"

"Mind if I finish?" Ham slurped more coffee.

I leaned back. "Sorry."

"It's as simple as this, if you don't play ball, you're off the team."

A tiny bee buzzed around in my stomach. "So I fouled by calling Rakoff. Is that what you're saying?"

"Call it a swing and a miss. No Rakoff. No anybody. Got it?"

"Does the Mayfair provide stay-out-of-jail cards? Because I didn't see them on the counter."

"To its guests it does. Has for almost forty years."

Jolene appeared from nowhere, splashed coffee in Ham's cup, and was gone before I had a chance to remind her of my malt.

Ham poured spilled coffee from his saucer into his cup. "Back in the twenties, when Oklahoma was the big cheese of the oil world, local oilmen got word that President Harding would pass through town with his poker cronies. The president had planned to veto an oil rights bill, so they formed a syndicate to purchase land and build a retreat near the outskirts of Defiance. Close enough to Oklahoma City for quick and easy access. They furnished it with poker tables, whiskey, and women."

"Let me guess. The president showed up, had a wonderful time, and then signed the oil bill."

Ham nodded. "The place was boarded up afterward. Years later, one of those young oilmen became a state senator and crafted a deal with the county. He would re-open the retreat as a sham hotel and operate it with the autonomy of a foreign embassy."

"Meaning hands off to local law enforcement. But why?"

"To protect its distinguished guests. It was, and still is, a devil-may-care playhouse where anything goes."

"But it's dumpy. I've seen it."

"Overstreet likes it dumpy."

"Overstreet! What's he got to do with it?"

"He was the senator who put the deal together, and he's run the place ever since."

"But he's in prison."

"So was Al Capone, and he still ran The Outfit. Remember, the hotel's a front. Overstreet has deliberately allowed its appearance to deteriorate to discourage would-be lodgers. People of importance enter through the rear. Behind the front desk is nothing short of a New Orleans cathouse."

"I didn't see any girls." I tried to catch Jolene's eye. Could never get a waitress to see me until she was ready to see me.

"The ladies are brought in for parties. Chauffeurs and

aids stay where it's not so classy, in the west wing near the front."

"Wait a minute. Gregory had a room. How'd he rate?"

"Considering how things ended for him, not highly." Ham slid his pie away and picked up his coffee. "Shouldn't you be out prospecting for silver?"

"If Tyburn left town, he won't get far with the whole state after him."

Ham's eyes turned cold. "Haven't you been listening?"

I gulped. "You mean troopers and deputies aren't out looking for him?"

"Three things you need to get through your head. First, state troopers protect the governor, and by extension, the Mayfair. If Overstreet tells them to shit, they ask how big a pile. Secondly, they operate by their own rules."

Jolene laid down my hamburger and fries. "Oops, I forgot. I'll make your malt now."

I glared at her as she walked away. Holding my stare, I said to Ham, "What's the third thing?"

"Your conversation with Rakoff never happened. You're flying solo."

That little bee just stung.

# CHAPTER 10

I grabbed my car's mic. "Murphy, anything on those prints?"

"I was just gonna call you. I've got a match. Well, two out of three anyway."

"I'm listening."

"Gregory's was in the bathroom. Sparks's was on the outside doorknob, along with an unidentified one."

"What about Tyburn's?"

"His weren't anywhere. Not even on Gregory's silver dollars. I checked them, just in case. I was right, right?"

"What right?"

"Suicide, right?"

"Don't bet your pension on it. What about the unidentified print? That any good?"

"Real good, but it doesn't belong to anyone on file. Maybe one of the maid's. I could check."

"Not yet." Talk about suicide, I wasn't about to send my officers to the Mayfair with state troopers there. *That* could be suicide. "Send it to the FBI. They've got some new national fingerprint collection. Tell Hoover's boys to rush it through. We've got a killer on the loose. Let me know the minute you hear back."

"Roger that."

"I'm on my way to question Abby over at Gustafson's and see what else she knows. Thinking about it, there's another woman I need to question, too."

"Who's that, Chief?"

"Someone who thinks Tyburn's a dream."

c∽e∽

When I pulled up to Gustafson's, I tossed down a few more aspirin to wrestle the pain still hanging on.

"Hey, Dexter, how's it going?" I called.

Dexter, a good-natured high school dropout with ears that stood out like the handles on a sugar bowl, was sweeping the sidewalk under a dim, late afternoon sun. A country boy so weedy I found it hard to look at him. His red hair sat straight as the bristles of an inverted broom, and his shoes were always high-top sneakers with red shoelaces.

I had recommended him as my replacement when I quit to sell cars. At age twelve, he'd lost a leg trying to hop a train. Gustafson wouldn't hire him because he didn't think Dexter could climb the shelves. But using his wooden leg and foot, he clumped up the ladder just to show him. After that, Gustafson pretty much had to hire him.

"I'm doin' *real* good, Bucky," Dexter said, like he'd just gotten a raise. "I mean, Chief Bucky. That's a real swell gun. Say, isn't that somethin', Tyburn bein' back, and all?"

"Did you talk to him?"

"Nah, but I saw him here this mornin'."

"He's on my list of most wanted, so if you see him again, give me a shout."

"Abby told me he didn't rob no bank. She said that's what the jury said."

"I've got news for you. Abby's wrong. Wait a minute. When did she say that?"

"This mornin'. Right after he left."

That was before I told her about Tyburn. No wonder she acted cagey. She was in for it now.

I opened the door and saw her working the checkout stand. I whistled to Dexter, waved for him to come inside, and then paced over to Abby, who was checking out a familiar customer.

"Good afternoon, Mrs. McCoy." I patted the little dog sitting in her cart.

"Why, hello, Bucky." She hugged me and kissed me like a long lost friend. I pointed to her purchase of prune juice. "Still working surefire?" I winked.

She winked back. "Oh, yes. Surefire."

I'd told her my grandmother swore by the stuff. Six ounces every morning made her regular as the summer breeze.

I gently but firmly took Abby's arm. "Abby has to come with me, Mrs. McCoy, and check the prune juice inventory. Dexter will take over."

I ushered Abby to her back office.

"What are you doing?" she yelped. "Let *go* of me."

"Get inside and sit down." The space was small. A desk crammed with paperwork, a phone, a safe, sacks of onions, and a tortoiseshell cat bathing itself on the chair. Abby dropped the cat onto the floor and sat stiffly in the chair, arms crossed. I snagged an empty apple box and planted a foot on it. "Let's talk about Tyburn Newgate."

"I—"

I raised a finger. "He's wanted for murder, so no lies."

She opened her mouth then closed it then opened and closed it again. Like a fish trying to suck air.

"Even a white lie, and I'll charge you with aiding and abetting." I wasn't exactly sure what the abetting part meant, but it sounded good.

"Who's he supposed to have murdered? Because I don't believe it."

"Why wouldn't you believe it?"

"Just wouldn't, that's all."

"You might save a life if you did."

"I don't understand."

"Understanding comes after telling me where he is."

"I don't know where he is. Why do you say he murdered someone?"

"That'll come with understanding. How do you know him?"

She leaned back, giving her chair a squeaky little rock. "We met in school."

"His school was right here in Defiance."

"Not here, New Mexico."

"New—What the hell was he doing there?"

"Reform school. All right?"

Knowing Tyburn, I wasn't surprised. I wondered what her ticket was to get in, but didn't want to get sidetracked or push her into being defensive. "So he's a friend from the old days."

She blew air up into her bangs. "I have lots of friends."

"We all do. He your boyfriend?"

"No," she snapped quickly. Too quickly.

"Earlier, when we talked, why'd you pretend not to know him?"

"I knew you didn't like him."

"Who said?"

"He did."

"When?"

"When he came in the store. Said you had it in for him."

"He say why?"

"Because you think he robbed the bank."

"That's what he told me. I'm sure he told you, too."

She raised her chin. "Well, he *didn't*."

I heaved a deep breath. "Willard Gregory. Ever hear of him?"

Something in her face shifted.

"I don't, no, never—Who is he?"

"Not *is*, was. He suffered heart failure that I believe your boyfriend had a hand in." I eyed her closely.

"I—I…" Her voice trailed off and came back with a rush. "What are you talking about?"

"So Tyburn is your boyfriend."

"No!" She jumped up, her chair shot back, and the cat squealed. Her nostrils fluttered like wings. "What do you mean heart failure?"

"Gregory was stabbed through the heart. Probably by Tyburn."

She stared at me, eyes sharp. "Probably? Or he had a hand in it?"

"More than probably. Now look, there was a third person involved in the bank robbery, and his life could be in danger. You might save him by telling me anything else Tyburn said or did."

She picked up the cat, sat back down, and petted it. "Nothing else."

"You're sure?"

"Yes. Unless…" She ran a finger across a tear under each eye.

I held my breath. "Unless what?"

"Unless you count the pipe."

"Pipe?"

"He bought one along with the cigarettes."

The phone rang, and I stood. "We're done here. I may need to talk to you again." I opened the door, and she picked up the phone.

"Chief, it's for you."

I took the phone.

"Hazelwood here, Chief. Murphy said I might catch you there. I just heard from the Santa Fe PD."

I turned my back to Abby. "Go ahead."

"Gregory has a teen arrest record from the time he was eligible for one. Set fire to his house. His parents fried, but his sister got out. Now he's wanted up in Wichita."

"What for?"

"Bank robbery, for one."

"Figures. His stock and trade."

"He also killed a teller. Wanna guess how?"

"Surprise me."

"Stabbed her in the chest. And here's the good part. I told Murphy about it, and he thought to go check the mortuary."

"For what?"

"Check Gregory for a knife scabbard."

"And?"

"An empty one was strapped to his calf."

# CHAPTER 11

I left Gustafson's and climbed into my car. I should question Dusty again. He may know more about Gregory than he'd let on. But first, the troopers would have to leave the hotel. In the meantime, I had someone else to question about Tyburn.

I picked up my radio mic and asked the station to patch me through to the Overstreet residence.

"Martin," I said. "This is Chief Bucky. That woman with the polka dot dress, Trixie. She still there?"

"Mrs. Hale is preparing to leave."

"Put her on the line."

I heard the phone being set down. A minute later, a voice purred in a southern accent, "This is Trixie."

"Mrs. Hale, this is Chief Bucky. I need to meet with you right away."

"Meet?" She giggled. "Whatever for?"

"I'll explain later."

I heard a little breathy sound. "I'm afraid that's out of the question. I have to grocery shop and prepare supper for my husband. He won't tolerate my—"

Someone said something in the background that I couldn't make out.

"Please hold on, Chief Bucky."

The voices sounded muffled, as if Trixie had covered the mouthpiece. It took a while before she came back on the line. "I'm sorry, I had to say goodbye to some friends. You were saying?"

"It won't take long, Mrs. Hale. I'll meet you in the Speedy Mart parking lot just down the hill. It's important."

"Well, if I have to."

"See you in twenty minutes."

I wheeled off from the curb and waved to Dexter, who'd returned to his sweeping.

I drove west through town. Much of the light had drained from the sky, leaving blurred streaks of red, orange, and gold. Folks were knocking off work, and most of the shops had closed. I stopped at a light across from the Ellis movie theater. The matinee had just let out, and young people poured onto the sidewalk, some with cigarettes glowing. Girls laughed and jumped like they had crickets in their pants. The marquee said *Invasion of the Body Snatchers*. Must be creepy good. I'd remember to check it out.

But first, I had to find Tyburn. The fact that Gregory carried a knife didn't mean he stabbed himself. Maybe Tyburn knew about it, but had him at gunpoint and took it from him. Or maybe Gregory pulled the knife on Tyburn, and Tyburn somehow turned the tables. If the knife belonged to Gregory, and the empty scabbard meant it probably did, it made sense for Tyburn to use it rather than a gun. That way, nothing like serial numbers could be traced to him. Plus, a knife was quieter.

Only a few cars dotted the Speedy Mart lot when I pulled in. One was an empty powder blue Caddy I'd seen at Mrs. Overstreet's house. Maybe Mrs. Hale had gone into the store to grab something for her husband's supper. Probably all the women at Mrs. Overstreet's house cooked fancy meals for their rich husbands. French dishes like Cordon Bleu, whatever that was.

Mrs. Hale came out of the store opening a pack of cigarettes, spotted me, dropped the cigarettes into her purse, and started over while adjusting her hair. I hopped from the car, raced around, and opened the passenger door.

"Oh, dear," she said brightly, gliding onto the seat in her freshly ironed dress, "a policeman and a gentleman."

I climbed back in. The car now smelled of perfume. Nice, not the pukey floral stuff old ladies use.

Her eyes flitted like a sparrow's. A dark mole under one eye contrasted with her milky complexion. "My," she said, "I've never been in a police car. So many gadgets." She fiddled with the radio knob and left it on a different channel.

I reached over and changed the setting back. "I need to ask you about Martin's son, Tyburn."

"How come?"

"He's suspected of murder."

She raised a hand to her mouth and yelped between red fingertips, "Oh, my goodness!" Reaching down, she stroked the shotgun barrel braced between us and gazed at me with a lazy smile. "I'll bet you're pretty handy with this."

"No touching. It's loaded."

"Why, I would hope so. It feels cold."

I removed her hand. "Please, Mrs. Hale."

"You may call me Trixie. You have gentle hands, Chief Bucky. Why do people call you Chief Bucky? Why not chief whatever your last name is? Or are you Bucky Bucky?" She reached into her purse and pulled out a pack of Encores and a cigarette lighter in a pink crystal case.

"I know you're pressed for time. I have a few questions."

"You haven't answered mine." She took out a thin, filtered cigarette, stuck it between her full red lips, and handed me the lighter. "Do you mind?"

I struck a flame. "The judge swore me in as Chief Bucky. He liked the sound and hoped to give me something my predecessors lacked."

"What was that?" She held my hand and sucked in a deep drag.

"Longevity. Encores must be a new brand."

She blew smoke out the side of her mouth. "Can't taste a damn thing."

"Then why smoke them?"

"Appearances. Now, what did you want to know about Martin's son?"

"Right, Tyburn. Did you talk to him?"

She took a hefty puff and held the long cigarette ash upward like a hypodermic needle. "What makes you ask?"

I opened the ashtray and gave it a little tap. "Well, you said Tyburn was a dream." I kept my eyes on that growing ash.

"I did, didn't I?"

The ash fell to the floor, and it looked like she'd flicked it there on purpose. "I also told you," she went on, "that you have gentle hands. Did that make you nervous, Chief Bucky Bucky?"

"Of course not. Why would it make me nervous?"

"So it did make you nervous." She drew on her cigarette.

"Look, Mrs. Hale."

She blew out a soft stream of smoke. "Do you find me attractive? You can be honest."

I coughed and cranked down my window. "We're talking about Tyburn. Did you talk to him?"

She withdrew a compact from her purse, opened it,

and peered closely into the mirror. "See my eyes?" She turned and put her face close to mine. Her eyes were blue as mountain lakes. "Do you see wrinkles? There are no wrinkles. Only a couple little ones that everyone has."

"You look great. That is, I mean normal, you know for a—"

"For a what? An old hag?"

"Jesus, no. Listen, I know you need to go cook for your husband and all. Tyburn, you saw him, where, inside the house?"

She threw a hand to her face and wept with the suddenness of a five-year-old. "My husband doesn't love me anymore."

"That's not true. Like you said at Mrs. Overstreet's, he's jealous. That proves he loves you. Besides, you're—you're beautiful." And that was the truth, especially with those big boobies. Except, her ears stuck out. Though handy for holding her hair back.

She took out a pink hanky from her purse and found a tear to wipe before gazing back into her mirror. "Today was a complete waste of makeup." She giggled. "I'm acting silly." She dragged on her cigarette and exhaled a blast of smoke into my face. "Okay, so about Martin's son. I was in the kitchen, opening a bottle of champagne when a car pulled into the back. A young man jumped out in a big hurry and—I saw him through the window in case you're wondering—and then he opened the garage door. By the way, you should know, his car's a real junker. Anyway, then he got back in, the car that is, and drove it into the garage." She drew a hard pull on her cigarette. "That's everything I can tell you."

"How did you know he was Martin's son?"

"Oh, we said *hi* to each other in the hallway, and he told me. He has yellow hair like his daddy."

"Did he say anything else?"

"Um, no. Not really. But he does have a playful swagger that some women might find sexy."

Sexy until his playfulness turned lethal. A Lincoln pulled into the parking spot on her side. "Where was this hallway?"

The ember of her cigarette had crawled almost to her fingers. "Outside the kitchen. I was leaving with the champagne just as he came in through the back door."

"Did you see him leave? Hear his car or anything?"

She raised and lowered a shoulder. "I don't know. Maybe he did, maybe he didn't."

"Okay, then. That should do it. I appreciate your talking to me."

She leaned across the shotgun and threw her cigarette out my window. Her big boobies squished against my chest, and my toes tingled. She put her arms around my neck. "Do you really think I'm beautiful?"

I leaned my head back. "Definitely. You've got nothing to worry about."

Her face beamed all over. She pulled my head to her and planted a long kiss on my lips. "Thank you, Chief Bucky Bucky." She reached for the door. "Oh, my God!" She scrunched down in the seat. "Did that man in the car see me?"

Someone had gotten out of the Lincoln and was walking toward the store.

"I—I couldn't see."

She raised her head and took a peek out the windshield. "I've got to get home." She opened her door and scampered off.

I watched her go, still a little dazed. My lips continued to tingle from her unexpected kiss. Considering how well some of my official interactions had gone lately, this was a pleasant surprise. I preferred a kiss over cracked ribs any day.

# CHAPTER 12

The low, orange sun shone through the trees as my cruiser tore around the curves on the road back to Overstreet's mansion. If Tyburn had planned to give his daddy a pipe and then leave the house, he wouldn't have parked in the garage. Pretty sly of him to hide under everyone's noses.

I was still dizzy from Trixie's kiss. It had moved through me like a warm light, one I would keep on for a long time.

Up ahead, a yellow-striped telephone van sat on the side of the road, red cones beside the front and rear wheels. I screeched to a stop, hoping to learn what happened to the little Negro girl.

"Hi there," I said to a colored fella, about forty, in a yellow vest. He had just opened the van's rear door and was unbuckling his tool belt. He was heavy-jawed, with thick eyebrows and a neatly trimmed mustache.

The man pointed to a cone in the street. "I'm parked legal and proper, officer."

I shook my head. "That's not why I stopped."

"Then whatcha want?" he asked, scowling, as he tossed his tools into the truck.

He'd probably had his share of police harassment. "I

want to ask you about one of your co-workers who was out on Campler Road this morning. A young Negro, maybe twenty-five. Do you know who I'm talking about?"

The man picked up a cable on the ground and began looping it between his thumb and elbow. "I just know to do my job."

"The man flagged me down. Took me to a little girl in a ditch. A Negro girl. She looked like she'd been beaten, and I want to find out why."

The man shook his head. "It wadn't done by him."

"So you do know him."

"I also know where he is, thanks to your kind."

"My kind?"

"If you wanna whoop me for mouthing off and put me in the hospital with Ernie, go ahead. I don't care anymore." He threw the cable in the van and slammed the door, then started to walk away.

"Wait a minute. What do you mean?"

"State troopers. That's what I mean. And I ain't sayin' no more." He climbed into his truck and drove off.

What the hell was with these troopers around here? I considered going straight to the hospital and talking to Ernie. Maybe the girl would also be there. She sure looked like she'd need serious treatment. I glanced at my watch. Time was short. First, I had to apprehend that murdering Tyburn.

Twenty minutes later, I pulled up to the Overstreet residence and found the mansion gate closed. Most of the guests must've left. I didn't dare use the intercom to announce my presence. That's all I'd need. Tyburn would either kill me or takeoff into the back woods. Radioing for backup would be just as dumb. I needed stealth, not the cavalry.

I parked my cruiser out of sight from the house and

climbed the iron gate, a tricky task with those sharp spikes to maneuver over. I crept through a thicket of trees along the lot's perimeter, keeping away from the open grass. Somewhere nearby, a peacock called for a mate. I stopped at the rear of the house and peeked around the corner.

Mrs. Overstreet's twenty-year-old son, Vester, known as VO, strolled toward the swimming pool, carrying a towel and fancy transistor radio. He had the lanky build of a swimmer.

VO liked me even less than his mother did. Probably because I had dealt his daddy a Go-to-Jail card, so Daddy was no longer around to sponge money from.

It wasn't yet dark enough to reach the back without VO spotting me. I had an idea. "Psst."

VO stopped and turned.

I put a finger to my lips and motioned him over.

He glared at me, pulling his lips back like a guard dog.

"Come here," I said in a loud whisper.

He padded over on feet suited for an albatross—large and flat. No wonder he lettered in swimming. "What the hell are you doing here? And what's with the cloak and dagger?"

I gripped his arm and pulled him out of sight. "Is Tyburn back there in his daddy's house?"

"I thought he was in jail."

"He's come home to roost."

"No shit. He bust out?"

"No, but with your help, I'm going to arrest him."

VO blew out a blast of air. "Like hell!"

I yanked out my gun. Didn't point it at him, just yanked it out.

He jerked back. "Jesus!"

"Listen, numb nuts. Maybe you haven't noticed." I

pointed to my badge. "I'm chief around here now."

"Maybe you haven't noticed." VO pointed to his trunks. "This is a swimsuit, not a flak jacket. This chief thing's gone to your fucking head."

I waved the gun. "Let's go."

"I don't feel good about this. And why are you arresting him, anyway?"

"He murdered someone. Feel better?"

"*No.* Really?"

"Stabbed a guy."

VO stared at the gun. "You gonna shoot him?"

"Only if I have to." My stomach tightened at the thought.

We skirted past the pool and headed toward the red-brick house. Cutting through the flower garden, we tiptoed onto the front porch and took opposite positions at the door.

I whispered, "I'll knock. If he doesn't answer, call to him. Say you have an important message from his daddy. Insist he open up. When he does, I'll take over."

"Wait a minute. What's in it for me?"

"You can play with my handcuffs later." I tapped my gun barrel on the door three times.

No answer.

I tapped twice more and thumbed the hammer back with a loud click. I winced. Damn! A sound, inside. I pressed my ear to the door. Running feet. "Son of a bitch—the back!"

I jumped over the porch railing and ran along the side of the house. At the corner, a denim blur came at my head. I raised my left arm and deflected the blow from crushing my skull. Dropping my gun, I fell to the ground.

Tyburn hovered over me, a two-by-four raised above his head, eyes wild.

"Drop it!" I shouted. His eyes flicked to the gun.

I dove for it.

Tyburn dropped the two-by-four and sprinted for the thick woods, twenty yards away.

"Stop or I'll shoot!" Sweat dribbled into my eyes. I fired once in the air.

Tyburn flinched, glanced over his shoulder, and tripped.

"Don't move!" I clutched my arm and ran to him.

Tyburn stayed on his belly while I cuffed his hands behind him.

"You're under arrest for the murder of Willard Gregory."

# CHAPTER 13

T he next morning I sat hunched over my desk, my left forearm sore and swollen. I moved it around a little. It didn't seem broken. I leaned back and sighed. Only eight hours left to meet Oswald's deadline, and I was fresh out of ideas.

On the off chance Tyburn had brought the silver to town with him, I obtained a warrant from Judge Thompson authorizing officers Murphy and Sparks to search both Tyburn's car and his daddy's house. In the house they turned up a brand new hunting knife the same make and model as the one used on Gregory, and a book of matches from a Santa Fe beer joint were found in Tyburn's car.

Very interesting since Gregory lived in Santa Fe.

I racked my brain trying to think of where Tyburn might have hidden the silver. He must've buried it somewhere between Defiance and Laredo.

Mrs. Rheingold strolled in, swinging a pair of handcuffs. "Don't be so glum. Only twenty-four hours on the job and you've already nabbed a murderer." She tossed me the cuffs. "You may need these again." The phone rang, and Mrs. Rheingold picked up. "Chief Bucky's office…Not so fast, sir." She glanced at me. "Did you say goats?"

I knew who it was and took the phone. "This is Chief Bucky."

"What's the matter with her? Another foreigner who doesn't understand English?"

Mrs. Rheingold overheard and stuck her tongue out at the phone.

"Good help's hard to find, sir." I winked and waved Mrs. Rheingold out.

"That's why I don't believe in it. Help, that is. But I'm not calling to lollygag about the incompetence of the American worker. I got a complaint."

I realized I had never learned the man's name, so I asked him.

"Name's Boots. Remember those maniacs who damn near ran over my goats yesterday?"

"I sure do, Mr. Boots."

"Not Mr. Boots, just Boots. Now listen, I want you to arrest those lunatics. They've got no call racing around on public roads."

"I don't think I can do that."

"You're a police chief, aren't you?"

"Yes, and if I'd witnessed them speeding yesterday they'd have been ticketed."

"I'm not talking about yesterday, dang it. Same thing happened this morning."

I slouched in my chair. More R and R arrivals at the Mayfair. No telling when I'd get to question Dusty again about Gregory. "I'll put a patrol in the area."

"No patrol, just a cop behind a billboard. And make sure he checks both ways."

"Both ways?"

"Certainly. Ones this morning were heading the other way."

I said I appreciated the suggestion and hung up. Hot diggity. The lieutenant governor and his troopers had left the Mayfair. The coast was clear.

Mrs. Rheingold's scolding voice came from the other room. "Mr. Davis! You cannot just walk in there."

The door swung open and in waltzed Tyburn's lawyer, Jefferson Davis the fourth. A hefty man of about sixty, he had a big round jaw and a belly that fought the buttons of his dress shirt. He had gotten Tyburn acquitted for bank robbery, and earlier that morning he met with the murderer in his cell. Before leaving the station to see the judge, Davis told me the murder charge against his client was laughable and then proved it by laughing in my face.

"Pardon the intrusion, Chief." Davis held up a tan folder, strode to the desk, and dropped it from about a foot high. "We have an important matter at hand."

I stayed seated, relaxed. Even slouched a bit to show I wasn't intimidated. I gestured to a chair in front of my desk. Davis shivered his butt into it and opened a tin of breath mints. His thick fingers snatched one like a trout taking a fly, and he popped the mint into his mouth.

I asked him, "What can I do for you, Mr. Davis?"

Davis tugged a trouser knee and crossed his legs. "Your name has a nice ring to it. Chief Bucky. Country sounding. Puts a man at ease."

I straightened in my chair. "Now that you're at ease, what's on your mind?"

Davis grinned and showed his well-kept teeth. "Straight talk also puts a man at ease." He leaned forward, placed a finger on the folder and slid it over to me slowly. "A little something from Judge Thompson." He leaned back and chuckled. "And I thought I'd seen everything."

A rap came at the door, it opened, and an arm appeared waving an envelope.

"Come in," I said.

Murphy scurried to the desk. "This just arrived." He handed me the envelope and left.

I glanced at it. *FBI*. My heart did a little flutter. The fingerprint identification from Gregory's doorknob. I set the envelope aside and opened Davis's folder. "You say you thought you'd seen everything?"

He shook his head and clicked his tongue as if unhappy. "Stupid, stupid, stupid. First, you tried bullying Mr. Newgate into giving you silver he doesn't have, nor ever had. Then you accused him of murder. A baseless charge without evidence or witnesses." His gaze dropped to my bandaged arm. "Not to mention the way you apprehended him without proper warning. Don't even think about charging him with assault of a police officer, or you might find yourself deemed unfit to wear a badge."

He was right. I didn't have a bit of proof. Not yet, anyhow. "If my stupidity leaves you with a bitter taste, go right ahead and pop another mint." I pressed the intercom. "Mrs. Rheingold, instruct Officer Murphy to make impressions of Tyburn's shoes. After that, he's to be released to Mr. Davis."

Davis's eyebrows bunched together. Stiff like the little vegetable brushes the Fuller Brush man gave away. "You're kidding."

"Evidence, Mr. Davis. Your client remains a suspect. If his shoes match footprints behind the Mayfair, that would show how he left the building." I stood. "Y'all come back and visit."

Davis laughed. Not mean this time, but friendly. "Like I said, you make a man feel right at ease. Makes me want to forget that ridiculous rumor I heard about me planting a listening device in the jury room. You certainly wouldn't spread such a cock and bull story about me, now would you, Chief? As for your jailhouse chat with

Mr. Tyburn, we both know he likes to make up fairy tales and boast about crimes he'd never dare commit." Davis got up and chuckled out the door.

I tore open the FBI envelope.

*Wanted for murder. Bobby Joe Jenkins. Born 11-11-02, age 14, height 5'2", weight 87 lbs.*

I stared off and did some quick arithmetic. This kid—this man—was now fifty-five years old. The picture showed a boy in prison stripes wearing a sad face and a sign. *Georgia 0917347.* Below, it read *Escaped from Georgia chain gang January 15, 1916. Distinct features: appendix scar and partial right thumb.*

The meaning hit me like a trooper's boot.

Hard to believe, but this Jenkins guy's fingerprints could prove I'd been wrong about Tyburn. Maybe Jenkins murdered Gregory. If so, he was no beginner. I buzzed Mrs. Rheingold. "Send in Murphy and Sparks."

"Right away, Chief."

They arrived, and Murphy flopped down in a chair by the desk. Sparks drifted to the window and lit a cigarette.

I said, "You guys ever hear of a fugitive named Bobby Joe Jenkins?"

They exchanged glances and shrugged.

"I went to school with Mary Joe Jenkins," Murphy said. "Maybe Bobby Joe's her brother."

"Holy shit!" Sparks burst.

I stiffened. "What?"

Sparks had picked up the wanted poster from the desk and waved it like a flag. "Look what it says." He slapped the poster. "A partial thumb. We know this guy."

I got up and snatched the poster from him. I looked closely. "I don't—" Then recognition struck, and *I* slapped the poster. "I got it. Dusty's deformed thumb." I handed Murphy the poster.

"I saw it when he tried Gregory's door just before I kicked it," Sparks said.

"Do you think Dusty killed Gregory?" Murphy asked, wide-eyed.

I shook my head. "Dusty just had the bad luck of leaving his fingerprints on the doorknob. I'm afraid it looks like Tyburn's back to being our number one suspect."

"So it could've been suicide," Murphy mumbled.

I ignored him and grabbed my hat. "I'm going to bring Dusty in and turn him over to the Georgia authorities. Meanwhile, let's keep this to ourselves." I didn't want word getting out that I'd locked up Dusty for murder. To troopers, that would mean swimming in the wrong pond.

# CHAPTER 14

I left the station at noon to arrest Dusty. I had only six hours to come up with the silver. My brilliant scheme to scare it out of Tyburn flopped, and Gregory was in no condition to help. Maybe Dusty'd provide the answer. Wring more information out of him before springing the bad news. Once in custody, he'd be like a clam at high tide: impossible to pry open.

The lobby looked the same as ever—seedy and run-down, but surprisingly clear of cigar smoke clogging the air like soot.

I gave the bell a light tap and sang, as if this were a friendly visit, "Dusty, Dusty come out wherever you are." It was awfully damn quiet. All at once I felt a jolt of panic and smacked the bell again and again. "Dusty! Where the hell are you?"

I ducked under the counter and dashed behind the wall of empty mailboxes. Maybe the troopers or someone wanted to shut him up. I grabbed the office doorknob. Locked. I shook it.

*"Dusty!"*

Maybe he was somewhere rolling on the floor suffering love taps. The barn! Suppose they'd hanged him? Made it look like suicide. I ran down the hallway, out the rear exit, and across the parking lot. I reached the barn door and—

"What the hell you doin'?"

I whirled.

Dusty was standing on the upper staircase by the emergency exit and holding something.

After a long sigh, I said, "I've been looking for you." I started toward him and stopped. He held a rattrap, and in it, a large rat. "Put away your friend and meet me up front."

Back in the lobby, I was admiring the artwork when Dusty emerged from behind the mailboxes. He patted his shirt pocket. "Got me a phone number, right here. Direct line to your favorite trooper."

"Hold on now, Dusty. I'm not here about the murder. That's outside my jurisdiction." Dusty stuffed his right hand into his pocket. Couldn't blame him for not flashing that stub around. I went on, "I'm cool with that, so let's be nice. What I'm not cool with is Tyburn taking personal charge of the bank's silver. And I'm particularly uncool with not knowing why Gregory had a room here."

"Read the sign on the door. It says hotel."

"We both know he didn't stroll in off the street. You even told me someone booked him a reservation. A friend, maybe, who did him a favor?"

"No friend."

"Who, then?" I whipped out my notepad and pen.

"I got a call."

"What call?"

"Someone. Ain't sayin' who. Said a fella's coming in named Gregory. Been boozin' all night, and I was to let him sleep it off in a room."

"You said a fella. Are we talking one or two fellas?"

"A fella means one."

"What time did Gregory come in?"

"Let's see, the call was around eight. I'd say he arrived about eight-twenty, eight-thirty, maybe."

I scribbled all this down. "Could you tell he'd been drinking?"

"He wasn't sober, I can tell you that."

"Did he have a rag around his hand?" He had a cut between two knuckles.

"No, but I gave him one after I saw the blood. Didn't want it dripping in the room."

"Did he say what happened?"

"Said he fell getting off his motorcycle."

"What else did he say?"

"His name and that he had a reservation."

"That's it?"

"He asked what time the bank opens."

"And?"

"I told him. He mumbled something about making a deposit and went upstairs."

"A deposit, huh? When did Tyburn show up?"

Dusty hiked up his shoulders. "I don't know. Maybe ten, a little after, little before. I don't memorize those things."

"Then what?"

"He asked for Gregory's room number. I gave it to him, and he went up."

"Did this caller mention Tyburn? Say that he'd be coming too?"

"You tryin' to trick me? I already told you—"

"Just wanting to get it written down right. So, Tyburn came in looking for Gregory. He say anything else? 'Nice day. How ya doin?'"

"Nope. Just that his friend Gregory was here, and he wanted to know the room number."

"What then?"

"He went upstairs."

"That was around ten, you say. When did Officer Sparks come in?"

"The bright one who stepped in the blood? Probably an hour later."

"Elevenish. What'd he say?"

"That he saw Tyburn's car out back, and asked where he was."

"And?"

"I said he was visiting a guest. Then the smartass asked if the guest had a name, and I told him."

I nodded, knowing Sparks went to his squad car and called the station. "Go on."

"About…I don't know, twenty, thirty minutes later, your man comes back, asks for the room number, and goes on up. Then he hollers down for the passkey. You know the rest."

"The door was locked from the inside, and Officer Sparks booted a hole in it."

"That reminds me, who's payin' to replace it?"

"Maybe the person who ordered you to give Gregory the room. Who was it?"

"I told you, I ain't sayin', and you can't make me."

"Let's say you give me the name, and I give you a little information I learned about someone from Georgia."

He squinted at me. Hard to say what was swirling around upstairs.

"Why should I care about someone from Georgia? Besides, I said all I'm gonna say."

He wasn't going to give me that name no matter what. Too bad, since the mystery person might have been a link between Tyburn and Gregory. "In that case, you'd better come out from behind the counter."

Dusty scowled. "What the hell for?"

I lifted the hinged countertop. "Now!"

Dusty's eyes narrowed with confusion. Finally, hesitantly, he came out and found himself being handcuffed.

"You're under arrest."

Dusty laughed, a nervous, this-can't-be-true laugh. "I ain't done nothin' wrong."

"That's not what the folks back home in Georgia say."

A horror-stricken expression replaced Dusty's cockiness. In a matter of seconds his lips trembled, and he transformed into an old man undergoing a new form of shock treatment.

Rather than let him collapse onto the floor, I held his arm. "Easy." I got him to a chair and let him crumple into it.

I wasn't feeling so hot myself. What had I done to this pathetic man? But then, he was a murderer.

☙❧☙

I parked behind the station and led the prisoner in through the basement and straight into a cell. I would call the Georgia authorities and then get back to saving my job, with what few hours I had left.

"You said we were gonna be nice to one another." That came from Dusty when the cell door slammed in his face.

I scoffed. "Being nice stops with murder."

Dusty stared at the floor. "How'd you find out?"

"I saw an old photo of you in a striped shirt." I turned to leave.

"Ain't what you think," he mumbled.

"Sure. You were on a chain gang because you believed in highway beautification."

"Can we talk?"

"Sure, if it's about where the silver is, because I have until six o'clock to turn it over to the bank."

Dusty continued staring at the floor. I tramped up-stairs to my office, looked up the number of the Georgia FBI, and dialed.

"FBI, how may I direct your call?"

"Hello, this is—"

Mrs. Rheingold's voice came on the intercom, "Chief, there's a very upset woman named Trixie on the line for you."

I pressed a button. "In a minute."

Back into the phone, I said, "This is Chief Bucky with the Defiance Police Department. I'm holding a fugitive and—"

"Chief! She's hysterical."

"You're with who? The Defiant Police?"

"No, I'm with—" I stared at the intercom. "I'll call you right back." I pressed the flashing line. "Trixie, what is it?"

"Chief Bucky, my husband," she sobbed. "He knows about us. And—"

My jaw tightened. "What do you mean, knows about us?"

"About the kiss. In the parking lot, that man saw us. Oh, Chief Bucky, I'm scared."

She must have meant the man who parked next to us at the Speedy Mart. "Your husband, has he done something? Hurt you, threatened you?"

"Oh, no. Well, a slap or two, but you—he wants to kill you."

My blood suddenly chilled. "Is he there now?"

"Wait a minute. Let me peek out the door."

I heard clicking footsteps and then a door latch. She must have been in the bathroom. A minute later, she trot-ted back. "It's okay. Thank goodness, he's passed out."

"Passed out! Has he been drinking? It's the middle of the day."

"Uh-huh, for several hours. He works graveyard."

"I'll be right over. What's your address?"

"That's okay. Jerry will be fine when he wakes up."

"Great, then he'll want to kill me."

"Heavens no. He won't even remember."

"Yeah, until he reminds himself about that kiss."

She gave me the address. And to think, until then I had only worried about losing my job.

# CHAPTER 15

I lit the fire to my Fury, jammed it into gear, and peeled away in a churning haze of smoldering rubber. Hopefully, I'd catch Trixie's husband while he was still asleep and unarmed. But what should I do with the guy? Arrest him for threatening murder? That was no good. He'd deny it, and Trixie couldn't testify against her husband. I was pretty sure about that. Maybe charge him with battery. Trixie said he slapped her—maybe twice.

I pulled into the driveway at 1448 Cliff Road. A modern ranch-style home with a two-car garage, spacious yard, and a front window big enough to drive a truck through. I got out with my shotgun. It might help in the respect department Ham talked about.

Trixie appeared at the front door, smoothing her skirt, touching her hair. No slap marks, but her mascara was pretty messy. She rolled her eyes at my shotgun. "You certainly don't need that."

I entered the foyer. "Where is he?"

"I told you." She adjusted the hem of her tight pink sweater that molded around her breasts. "He's okay now."

I peered over her shoulder into a living room. "Is he in there?"

"On the couch, but—"

I swallowed the lump in my throat and sidestepped around her.

"Shh! Don't wake him."

The room had a high ceiling with turquoise drapes and charcoal carpet. A seven-foot upright mounted bear with huge jaws and claws took up an entire corner by the fireplace. A matching pair of gold wing chairs sat just inside the doorway.

And there on the green sofa, snoring like a—

I stopped mid-stride and gulped. For one dizzy moment, my leg muscles threatened to collapse. Lying there, open-mouthed, was my protocol instructor, Trooper Hale.

I turned to Trixie standing just outside the room, a hand on her cocked hip, and chewing gum. I pointed to the man and mouthed, "This is your husband?"

She beckoned with rapid arm motions. I tiptoed to her. She clutched my arm and dragged me back to the front door.

"Just a minute," I said, maybe too loudly, and pulled free. "You didn't say he was a damn trooper."

She flapped her hands. "Shh! What difference does it make? Besides, as you can see, everything's fine."

"It makes a big difference, and everything's not fine." I glanced back toward the living room while my pulse settled down into the high hundreds. "What does he think he knows about us?"

Her eyes closed, and she inhaled like she was going to count to ten. Then she exhaled air that smelled like spearmint. "He believes we were making out."

"*What?*"

She pressed a red-tipped finger to my lips. "Not so loud."

Her pink fuzzy breasts were close enough to produce heat. My heat.

"That's what blabber-mouth across the street told him. He saw us in the parking lot, and he's jealous."

"Jealous?"

"He once made a pass at me. He was here playing pool with Jerry, and while Jerry was in the bathroom, he tried to kiss me. I told the creep to get lost. I should've told Jerry. He would have—"

"Wait! Let's stick to us. Didn't you tell him the truth?"

"Are you kidding?" She glanced nervously in Jerry's direction. "Heavens, no."

"Well, I think you sure as hell should. What *did* you tell him?"

"At first I denied it, of course."

"Oh, of course," I said, really pissed.

Her face wrinkled up like my kid sister's before starting to bawl.

"Okay, I'm sorry," I said, trying to sooth her. "You denied it. What then?"

She snapped back to only looking nervous. "I told him you wanted to meet me in the parking lot. You know, to talk about Martin's son."

"That's good. What else?"

"Just that…um." Her eyes darted to the next room. "That in appreciation, you kissed me."

I held a sharp finger to her face. "That's a goddamn lie, and you know it."

Her eyes turned hard. "What'd you expect me to say? I told you what he's like. And if you remember, I didn't even want to meet with you. So don't blame me." She opened the door. "You need to go. Or if you prefer, I'll wake him and you two can shoot it out."

Those lake-blue eyes flashed like she really meant it. But even so, if her husband were a civilian, I would've gone in there and shaken him awake, stood over him, and explained the facts. Except Jerry Hale wasn't a civilian. He was a goddamn trooper.

She was right. No point spoiling his nap.

# CHAPTER 16

I left Trixie at her door, glanced around, and got in my car. I hoped that neighbor guy didn't see me to report back to Trixie's trooper husband. Then he'd really think I had something going with Trixie. The next time I saw him, he'd probably be awake and bloodthirsty as the Mayfair's salivating dog picture. Ham had said that troopers operated by their own rules, and Jerry didn't seem like one to buck tradition.

I headed to the hospital to talk with Ernie, the man who found the little girl in the ditch.

I approached the receptionist, an older woman chewing gum like a teenager and trying to appear like one. She had bleached-blonde hair, a tight-fitting sweater, and silver beer mug earrings hanging from each slug-shaped ear.

"I'm here to see a man named Ernie," I said. "I don't know his last name, but he works for the phone company. A colored fella. Probably admitted yesterday morning."

She peered at me over her blue-framed glasses and winked like she was fighting off an eye infection. "My heavens," she said in a husky voice. She took off her glasses and put the tip between her front teeth. "I know you. You used to work at Gustafson's."

She gave me an up-and-down scan that said I could put my shoes under her bed anytime. "Aren't you the limit?" The corners of her lips rose almost enough to be called a smile. "You must be pretty special."

"My business is special. It's urgent you do whatever it takes for me to see this man."

Her smile dropped like a loose eyelash. I had just been demoted to something on the bottom of her shoe.

"Okay then," she said, pushed herself out of her chair and strutted off. "I'll be back."

She returned a minute later. "Room one-forty. It's in the back. Way back."

"Thank you."

"You're welcome. And by the way, his name's Ernest, not Ernie. Ernest Crawford."

I found the room and went inside. The door closed with a click. The room was musty, windowless, and stank like it hadn't been cleaned since the last bloodletting. Negro men occupied six beds along two walls. One man's leg was in a cast, hoisted high off the bed. All but one patient turned away when I entered the room.

Cops had probably meant trouble for them their whole lives. Ernest Crawford gaped at me. He had the first bed, and bandages covered his midsection.

I took off my hat and went over to him. "Hi, Ernie. I'm Chief Bucky from yesterday morning. What happened to you?"

Ernie glanced nervously at the other men.

I said softly, "Come on, Ernie. I'm on your side."

"How'd you know my name and where to find me?"

"I bumped into one of your co-workers. Now tell me what happened."

Ernie looked at his thumbs, twirled them a minute, then shook his head. "I can't."

Not wanting to tower over him, I sat on the foot of the bed. "What do you mean, can't?"

"I could get hurt real bad talkin' to you."

"This'll just be between us." I pulled up my shirt. "Love taps. You can guess how they got there—might've been from a mutual acquaintance."

Ernie's eyes got big. With a grunt, he wiggled himself upright. "When you left, one of them troopers took the little girl to their car. The other one questioned me about what you was doing there. I told him I flagged you down, and he pulled out his nightstick and gave it to me good." Ernie touched his side. "He said I better get fitted for crutches if I ever think of talking to cops again."

"Sweet Jesus! You only tried to help the little girl."

"Don't matter. Remember, I told you it was the Klan that done it."

"Yeah, but why?" The troopers must be protecting them.

Ernie flipped a glance at the man across from him with his leg in a cast. "I can't tell ya."

"I'll tell you," the man said.

"That's Jim," Ernie said. "He's the little girl's poppa."

A compact guy with thick lips and sad eyes said, "Jenny got beat up because she heard something she oughta not heard. Yesterday was a school holiday, and the wife brought Jenny along with her to her cleaning job at a rich man's house. Jenny sat in the man's office twirling in his big chair like kids do. She heard two fellas at the door and hid behind a couch. The men walked in, talked awhile, and then left the office. Jenny ran to her mamma and hollered about a party where they planned to vote for a new grand dragon, and she wanted to go. The men overheard, and then whooped the child. My wife ran to the phone and called me at work. When I finally got to the house, Jenny had already run off, and the men broke my leg with a baseball bat. Fortunately, they left my wife alone."

"How's Jenny now, do you know?"

"She's got some pretty ugly marks on her, but she'll be all right."

"What do you think it means, voting for a new grand dragon?"

He shook his head. "Don't know Klan talk."

I turned back to Ernie. "When you found Jenny, how did you know it was the Klan that beat her up?"

"I didn't, till those troopers came and told you to leave. Everyone knows they protect the Klan."

# CHAPTER 17

I dialed Sergeant Hazelwood. "Tom, the prisoner I brought in earlier, has he eaten?"

"No. Is he hungry?"

"Probably. He's been locked up awhile. I could use a bite myself. Call Sally's and tell them we have a prisoner. Get me whatever they make for him. I'll pay for mine separate."

"I just talked to Murphy. He's got a match on a footprint from the Mayfair."

I held my breath. "And?"

"It's Tyburn's."

"Finally! Solid evidence. Now we know how he left the motel—if not the room. He was lucky since, I guess, no one saw him go down the back stairs."

"What's happening with Oswald, the insurance guy Mrs. Rheingold told me about?"

"Nothing yet. But the ticking clock's about to explode my head off."

"When are you supposed to hand over the silver?"

I peered at my watch. "In just a few hours. Six o'clock. Maybe Oswald will give me an extension."

"I wouldn't count on it. Betty, my wife, works at the bank and said he has an appointment with the president at six-fifteen to hand over either the silver or a check. She also said Oswald's meeting with the city council at six-thirty."

"I guess he was serious about the 'or else.'"

"Or else?"

"I recover the silver, or I'm history."

"Sorry about that, Chief. Of course, considering the fate of your predecessors, there's worse ways to go."

"Thanks for the pep talk. Say, why was Chief Cowboy Wallis stabbed to death?"

"He got on the outs with the Klan."

I swallowed and shifted the phone to the other ear. "How come?"

"He'd hired a Negro deputy, who was hanged on his first day. The chief, well, you know about the chief."

"Tell me about the Klan around here."

"Years go by and you never know they're around. Then something ruffles their feathers, and someone wakes up to a burning cross in their yard. Or gets dragged out of bed and beaten. It only takes one or two to crawl from under a rock and the whole town stinks."

"I think they beat up a little Negro girl, and a couple of state troopers may be covering it up."

"Where'd this happen?"

"North of town, yesterday morning."

It sounded like Hazelwood sucked in air. "That could mean more trouble."

"How come?"

"Once an incident like this occurs, more follow."

We hung up, and I checked my watch. Almost four o'clock. Two more hours. Even though Alsop had hired a new salesman, maybe he'd give me my old job back. I had set a record for most cars sold in one day—five—but would anyone in Defiance buy a car from the shortest-serving police chief in history? Getting the boot at the end of my second day wouldn't earn me community re-spect—or a seat in the mayor's chair.

I took Dusty's poster downstairs to the jail.

Dusty lay on his cot with his hands clasped behind his head. The other three holding tanks were empty. A slow day.

I dragged a steel chair along the cement floor over to Dusty's cell. "I thought you might be hungry, so I ordered you something."

Dusty's eyes stayed fixed on the ceiling. "Ain't hungry."

"Food's pretty good around here. Comes from across the street. Prisoners get hotcakes for breakfast. Hamburgers, soup, or chili other times. Like I say, food's pretty good."

"Don't imagine I'll be around long enough to appreciate it."

"That's right. You've got unfinished business back home." I showed him the poster. "Here's your picture."

He only glanced at it. "How'd you know it was me?"

"Let's see." My eyes flicked back and forth between the two gloomy faces. "Hmm…hair's thinner, face fuller. Ah, of course. Right here it says partial right thumb."

Dusty raised his hand and showed me his middle finger.

"That may've been the finger that fingered you. You had the bad luck of leaving a print on Gregory's doorknob. What did you mean earlier when you said the murder you were convicted of wasn't what I thought?"

A door clanged down the hall. Sergeant Hazelwood limped in holding two paper bags. He had injured his leg back in '42 when he met head-on with an armadillo during a Baja motorcycle race. "You want yours in the office, Chief?"

"Here's fine. I'll keep our prisoner company."

Hazelwood left, and I jammed a bag through the bars to Dusty. "Let's hear your story."

"Won't do me no good now."

I unwrapped my hamburger. "I'd like to hear anyway. According to the poster you were fourteen."

"My birthday was the day before it happened. Mamma made me a chocolate cake. Best cake I ever had." Dusty tossed the bag onto the cot and padded to the window. After a long time of staring out, he said, "Pa had it comin'."

I bit into my hamburger.

"I knew if he hit Mamma again, I'd do it."

I chewed and wondered what *it* was. "So he hit her again, and you what, shot him? Clubbed him?"

Dusty snapped his head around. "Clubbed him? Is that what you said?"

"I just…" I shrugged, having no idea why I said that.

"I had my own twenty-two but never shot him." He went back to looking out the window. "It was four-oh-five in the mornin'. I know because I saw the clock." Dusty spoke evenly, as if watching images pass before his mind's eye. "I wanted to cover my head, block out her screams. But when I heard him leave Mamma and stomp into the bathroom, that's when I knew." He stared intently out the window.

I grew impatient. "Knew what?"

"He was goin' for his razor strap." Dusty turned, his face hard. "Oh, how he loved his razor strap. He'd rear back and put everything he had into the lash. Crack! Like a gunshot."

My Jesus Christ, I thought, or maybe said aloud.

"It was the sound—that sound in my head that made me crazy. Had to stop it. Stop it before it started. I ran through the hallway to the back porch, grabbed my rifle, and loaded a single shot. I had to get him before he started in again on Mamma. I ran back. It was dark, and I tripped over the dog in the hallway. Their room was at the far end. Hardly lit at all. But I saw him. Saw him raise that strap back like a slave master about to bring down the wrath of hell. I shouldered my rifle, as Mamma turned and looked at me. I took a wobbly aim at Pa and—and killed her."

"*What*?"

"She flung herself in front of Pa just as I fired."

"Fuck, man. Then what? I mean, what happened next?"

Dusty swallowed hard, and his eyes looked as sad as I'd ever seen in a man.

"Mamma fell to the floor. Pa stared at her for a long time, like he was trying to figure out what happened. Then he turned her over. She had blood coming out of her eye. I was scared and dropped the rifle. Pa looked up at me all big-eyed and said real soft-like, 'You killed your mamma.' Then his eyes grew even bigger, and he yelled over and over, 'You killed your mamma! You killed your mamma!' He charged at me, and I ran outta the house. He hollered from the door, 'You'll pay for this, you rotten kid.'"

"Where'd you run to?"

"The depot to hop a train. I had to get out of town because I knew Pa would call the cops."

"That's how you got away?"

"Not before losin' this." He raised his stubby thumb.

"Dexter, over at Gustafson's, lost his leg jumping a train. Must be a tricky jump."

Dusty snorted. "Wasn't a train that done it. Was a gator."

"A *what*?"

"The quickest way to the depot was through the swamp. By the time I reached the water, the sun was comin' up and dogs were chasin' me. Someone yelled fire, and I dove in the water. Almost landed on a gator." Dusty shook his head as if shaking off the memory and shuffled to his cot.

"Lucky the gator only nipped your thumb."

"Everything happened so fast, I didn't even know it was gone." He gave a little wiggle of what was left of it. "When I finally realized, I figured it had been shot off. But then I read in the papers that the cops thought the gator had eaten me, so they cut him open and found my thumb." He reached for his hamburger. "There you have it."

I sat wondering if Dusty ever allowed himself to shoot a rifle again after killing his mamma by mistake. It took me over ten years to pick up a pistol after mistakenly killing Tripod, my raccoon.

Dusty tottered to his sink and turned on the tap. Leaning his head sideways, he guzzled. He wiped his mouth with a sleeve and sat back down. "When are they comin' for me?"

The Georgia authorities would likely have no more sympathy for him now than they had forty-one years ago. His pa probably told them he shot his mother in cold blood. Bastard.

Dusty couldn't have made up such a story. It would be easy to let him go free and forget the whole thing. Then again, I wanted to know who made Gregory's room reservation. My daddy always said there's nothing immoral about horse-trading.

"I haven't notified them yet." My daddy also said, never make the first offer. It weakens your position.

Dusty turned to me and didn't say anything, just nodded slowly. Like he was *really* thinking. I took a last bite of my hamburger, stuffed the wrapper in the bag, and stood up. "I'll be seeing you." I walked down the hall and reached the door—

"Wait a minute."

I smiled to myself and opened the door. "Don't worry, I'll let you know when your escorts arrive."

"Hold on, goddammit!" he yelled, as if his life were at stake. "You want that silver, don't ya?"

My heart gave a sharp thump. "Silver?"

"Thought that would wiggle your ears. Didn't you say you had to get it for the insurance company?"

I strolled back to the cell wearing my best poker face. "You mean you have it?"

"I ain't got it. O' course not."

"Then what are you talking about?"

"I'm talkin' about somethin' else that ain't what you think."

"Like what?"

"Like maybe Tyburn and them got away with more than just sacks of silver."

I threw him a suspicious eye. "I never heard of anything else besides two or three safe-deposit boxes getting busted into."

"There's a lot you ain't heard."

"I guess I'd like to hear what I ain't heard."

"And I'd like to tell ya, but you have to promise to unlock this cell and make that poster go away."

I laughed. "For that to happen, I'll need more than stories about gold watches lifted from bank customers. I want ten thousand dollars' worth of silver. You tell me where it is, and we'll talk about unlocking this cell."

"I can't tell you where it is, 'cause I don't know." Dusty stood and gripped the bars, his face, a weaselly smile. "But I can tell ya how to get somethin' better."

Something better? "That might be a story I'd be interested in. What is it?"

"Do we have a deal?"

Doubtful, but curious, I said, "Okay, but your better had better be better than silver."

Dusty's bushy upper lip curled into a grin. "Tyburn wasn't the brains behind the bank robbery. Overstreet was."

Excitement raced up and down my spine. "That's—that's one hell of a surprise."

"He set it up and got Tyburn and two others to carry it out. Those three got the silver, but Overstreet got the gold. State Senator, Oliver Stempson's gold. And I ain't talkin' bout his watch."

I dropped back down on my steel chair. "This senator, Senator Stempson you mention, didn't he die?"

"Collapsed dead on the senate floor from heart failure two days before the robbery. He and Overstreet had been cronies goin' back to their senate years together. Overstreet knew Stempson had a secret safe-deposit box in the bank. Stempson had been stashing kickbacks from state contractors since the Harding days. Overstreet wanted to get his hands on them before Stempson's wife—and ex-wives—beat him to it. Along with grabbing the silver, Tyburn broke into Stempson's box, and a few others to make it look random. Stempson's heirs couldn't raise a stink because the box contained the senator's ill-gotten wealth."

"But how much gold can one safety-deposit box hold?"

"When I said gold, I meant good as gold. The cash was converted into Mexican bearer bonds worth—I don't know the exact figure—but in excess of a hundred thousand dollars. Overstreet got the bonds, and Tyburn and his pals kept the silver."

So that's why Overstreet hired Davis to keep Tyburn out of jail. "All very nice, but what about the silver?"

"Don't you get it? You don't need the silver."

I cocked my head. "You're not making sense."

"The insurance company doesn't care about silver."

My heart started slamming around. I got it. Oswald was indebted to the bank for ten grand. It didn't matter if it was paid in silver dollars, gold ingots, or wampum. "I see," I said with a smile in my voice.

"For a bird-dog, maybe you're not so dumb after all. What you do is, you call Overstreet's butler and tell him you want ten K in cash by, when do you need it?"

"Hold on. What do you mean, call the butler?"

"Martin is Overstreet's right-hand man while he's away. His eyes and ears. He's also authorized to act on Overstreet's behalf. Now, when do you need it?"

*I'll be goddamn. Butlers! Shoulda guessed.* I checked my watch. "In two hours."

"Fine. Tell Martin he's got an hour. If he balks, give him a choice. Hand over the ten thou—and you forget the whole thing—or you'll notify the FBI, and they'll call in those Mexican bearer bonds."

I nodded. "But first, I want to know something. The person who called you about giving Gregory a room. Was that him, the butler?"

"You catch on quick."

# CHAPTER 18

I left Dusty and hurried up to my office to call Martin. I liked Dusty's plan. I'd tell the stinking butler that the cash was for the insurance company, not myself. I didn't like letting Overstreet off the hook for bank robbery, even though he was already in prison. I consoled myself with the knowledge that one crook stole from another crook and the bank would get their money back. Plus, of course, I'd keep my job.

Martin was Mr. Cool on the phone. Not a hint of emotion. He made none of the usual butler remarks, "Very good, sir," or "As you wish, sir." He said only, "I'll call you back in ten minutes," and hung up.

Ten minutes later, I watched the phone ring—three, four, five times. Let Martin sweat a little. I picked up and listened.

"Potter Park. One hour." *Click.*

I scrubbed my damp hands up and down my pant legs, got up, and moved to the window. The late afternoon sky was charcoal, the color of tombstone. Where would Martin get all that money so fast? The bank? Maybe from a secret safe stuffed with cash and—and perhaps those Mexican bearer bonds.

Overstreet must be America's biggest crook. Horse

racing scams, election rigging, and now bank robbery. What next, the Klan? All with the help of corrupt state troopers, at least one shady sheriff, and a shifty butler.

I sank into my chair, thinking that me, an officer of the law, was protecting that scoundrel. Overstreet should be prosecuted for bank robbery. This wasn't what I thought police chiefs were supposed to do, and I didn't like it. Not for one cotton-pickin' minute.

∽∾∽

I got to Potter Park ten minutes early and parked among the willows by the north end of the library. It was here that I once found a dead rattlesnake that had been run over. It seemed fresh, so I cooked it, ate it—and puked for two days.

The sun had dropped from the sky and settled behind the park. The sickle of the moon would give enough light for Martin to find me. I tramped across the dead grass to the empty picnic area and sat on a table with my feet on the bench, gun at the ready. This could be a setup to bump me off.

I put my hand on my gun.

"How's it hangin', Chief?"

I spun around to see Tyburn strolling up, wearing a cocky grin and a James Dean-style red jacket. Something clawed at my throat. I rubbed that smooth spot on my face. "What are you doing here?"

Tyburn hopped onto the table. "You're a sly one, Chief. And I was thinkin' you'd be out of a job by now." He took an envelope from his jacket pocket and tapped it against his palm. The packet appeared too thin to hold ten thousand dollars. "The way I see it," Tyburn went on, "this transaction makes us partners. Lawman and Joe Blow."

A flush of blood rushed into my throat and cheeks. I wanted to slug him in the teeth and forget the whole rotten thing. I would've, too, except then I really would be out of a job. "Let's get something straight. We're not partners. Never were, never will be."

"Touchy. Here." He slapped the envelope into my hand.

I opened it. Jeez! Thousand dollar bills, plus a couple hundreds.

Tyburn smirked. "Smooth move worming out those extra hundreds for yourself." He winked. "Delivery charge."

I sprang from the bench and gripped his shirt. "Listen, you smug little prick. The extra will be your neck worming inside a noose. Don't think for a minute you're going to get away with murdering your *associate*." I shoved him back. "Ain't gonna happen. You can bet your girlfriend's store on that."

Tyburn glared at me but said nothing.

♥◈♥

It was six twenty-five, and I had been waiting in the shadowy backseat of a brand new Chrysler, sweating it out, hoping this plan was going to work.

I hadn't waited long before Oswald stomped over from the bank like a guy who just got cleaned out in a poker game. He opened the driver's door and threw himself inside.

"I figured these fancy wheels must be yours," I said. "Chrysler only made 1,049 of this year's model."

Oswald's owl-shaped head spun around like he'd heard a mouse rustling in the leaves. "Jesus Christ! Get the hell out of my car."

"Is that any way to speak to a police chief?"

His eyebrows shot up to the headliner. "Look, I came to your office hoping it would remain your office. You came up empty, so go pack your things."

"Who said anything about empty?" I laid Tyburn's envelope on the backrest with a light tap. Oswald squinted at it. "What's this?"

"Pictures. Ten Grover Clevelands. Only president elected twice in non-successive terms. Consider it company reimbursement for what you just shelled out to the bank. Our little secret."

Oswald snatched the envelope and peered inside. His eyebrows took another ride up as if he'd drawn four aces. His fingers walked through the bills. "I see another president in there."

"Two Benjamins. Franklin wasn't a president, but he's worth a hundred Washingtons. He's there to whisper in your ear, *no questions*. Now I suggest you put away your new friends and trot on over to that council meeting. Inform the members that you hope the council will continue to put their faith and trust in your fine, upstanding insurance company. And while you're at it, in Defiance's new police chief." I opened the door. "Toodle-oo."

# CHAPTER 19

I drove off from having my little chat with Oswald, relieved to know I'd be holding onto my job as chief of the "pond"—as Trixie's husband would put it— and staying alive. But not so thrilled about losing my grip on Tyburn. Even if that snake was to get away with bank robbery, which he wouldn't, murder was a play that guaranteed him a seat in the chair. And I'd be there when he got the juice.

⊘⊙⊘

After finishing paperwork early the next morning, I wanted to get out into the brisk fresh air. I'd never patrolled before. Might be interesting. Might even spot more Klan posters to tear down.

I cruised east through town. The sun rose above the hills, and far-out shades of blue spread across the sky. A man limped out of Uncle Lewy's, buttoning his jacket against the chill. His shoulders drooped, and a cigarette hung from his lips. Probably a veteran who'd just fueled up for yet another day's work on a tractor or in a factory.

On a whim, I drove out onto the highway and parked behind the billboard where goat-man Boots had suggested catching speeders. Without one of those fancy new radars I'd read about, I had to guess the speed of each passing vehicle until I got on his tail.

I'd never written a ticket. Got one once back home for missing a stop sign. They didn't give tickets if you were going to church in Terrebonne Parish. But I hardly ever went to church. Besides, it was a Monday.

After listening to a dozen or more cars swish by, at what seemed legal speed, I heard a car ripping up the pavement. I lit up the Fury, but the vehicle was a state police cruiser. Dread gripped me like a second skin.

While wondering if I was still on Jerry-the-trooper's hit list, a black Ford pickup flung past like a colt breaking for an open gate. I slammed the throttle and took off after him in a spray of gravel.

Reaching a steady speed behind him, I switched on my gumballs. The driver caught the light show in his mir-ror and jerked his head. Easy to imagine the sinking feel-ing in the poor guy's gut.

I pulled in front of the vehicle and got out, ticket book in hand. I started toward the pickup and raised my arm to shield the early sun from my eyes. Well, I'll be. Ham Wentworth. He rolled down his window and placed both hands on the steering wheel.

I approached, not intending to write a ticket. Profes-sional courtesy.

Ham stared straight out his windshield with a smirk. "You're supposed to ask for my driver's license and reg-istration."

My stomach knotted up. I was the goddamn police chief and wasn't about to be treated like a recruit. "Do you know how fast you were going, sir?"

"Just doing the speed limit, Chief."

"Is that right? The speed limit's fifty. I clocked you doing sixty-four." I still didn't want to give him a ticket.

Yet, I didn't want to look wimpish, either.

"Really?" Ham said as if that was a real shocker.

"Afraid so. You may've thought you were doing the speed limit, but your mind may've been on other things. Like those llamas of yours. I can understand that."

"As a matter of fact," Ham turned to me. "I just came from Hector Manfield's place and picked up these clippers he sharpened for me." He lifted them from the seat. "I've got shearing to do this morning before heading out to Albuquerque."

I nodded. "I see. A lot on your mind."

"That's right. And I'm hoping that you—"

"Will give you a warning?"

"Yeah, a warning."

"Can't do that, sir. I don't give warnings just because drivers have thoughts floating around in their heads. Everyone does, it's natural."

Ham went back to staring out the windshield. A cheek muscle quivered like a pulse. He leaned, as if reaching for his wallet.

"No need for that. This here pickup of yours is a 1948 F-Series Ford Truck. They're known to have faulty speedometers. It wouldn't be right to ticket you because of a mechanical problem you didn't know about."

Ham turned to me, stared for a moment, then threw his head back and howled like a wolf. "Chief, you are really something. Listen, come on over to my place for a cup of coffee. There's something I want to talk about."

❧❧

I hated sitting on Ham's porch furniture. The chairs were made of gnarly tree branches that should've been sanded smooth or something. Cushions would've been nice.

Holding two steaming mugs of coffee, Ham backed out through the screen door.

"So." I wrapped my hands around a warm mug. "Today's haircut day for the llamas, and then you're off to Albuquerque."

"I'll only shear the two I'm taking there to show. And speaking of show—" He raised his mug and slurped. "I heard Oswald put on a pretty good one for the city council last night."

I blew on my coffee. He must have friends on the council. "Is that right?"

"He was in such high spirits, everyone thought he had a little something extra in his snuff."

"You never know." I sipped my coffee. Same ol' tar.

Ham chuckled. "Particularly since he'd just shelled out ten grand to a bank."

He was fishing for information. I put my coffee on the tree-stump table and leaned forward. "You've got to understand insurance people. I was in the shrimping business back in Louisiana, and one time a fella I knew lost his boat in Hurricane Flossy. Terrible winds, ninety miles an hour. Lost everything. Equipment, the works. The very next day his insurance man, just as nice as could be, wrote him a check for forty-two thousand dollars. It's hard for normal folks like you and me to understand because we only use our brains. But insurance men use premium calculations, actuarial tables, and profit and loss charts with colored up and down whatchamacallit graphs."

Ham nodded and sipped his coffee. "I see what you mean. Please the customer."

I picked up my coffee and leaned back. "Precisely."

"Now that you've made Oswald happy, I guess you've got time to crack down on speeders."

"He may be happy, but I'm not. Not until I nail Tyburn for pulling the heist and murdering Gregory." To be polite, I took another dangerous sip of coffee.

"Gregory? That's a rough patch of road. Did you forget about your trooper friends?"

"I'll do my best to avoid them."

"You're beating a dead horse."

"What horse?" I shifted in my chair, and it creaked like an old saddle.

"Tyburn. You won't get anything out of him. You told me there were two other robbers. This Gregory fella who got stabbed was one. Anything on the other guy?"

I shook my head. "I'm not exactly tripping over leads."

"In that case, focus on Gregory. What do you know about him?"

"He's from Santa Fe. No family except a sister. Robbed a bank in Wichita and stabbed a teller."

"You had someone search his house there in Santa Fe, I assume."

"No, but that's a good idea. I'll send someone."

"Make sure they know what the fuck they're doing. You can't just walk into some dead guy's house."

"I'll get a court order."

"And while you're farting around doing that, the sister or someone will sweep through the house. May already have. But in case they haven't, if you want, I'll detour up to Santa Fe on my way to Albuquerque. Save you time and red tape. I might even get a lead on that third accomplice."

"Do I need to deputize you or anything?"

"Don't worry about it. I have ways of getting around."

∽∾∽

Back at the station that afternoon, I worked at finding the third accomplice. If Abby knew Tyburn's friends, maybe I could wring some names out of her. I called the store.

"Gustafson's, this is Dexter speaking."

"Dexter, Bucky here. Put Abby on." I drummed my fingers on the desk.

"She ain't here."

"She sick or something?"

"Maybe. She's been actin' strange lately."

I switched the phone to my other ear. "Strange? How?"

"Kinda quiet. She was gone all day yesterday. Out of town somewhere. Don't tell her I told you, but she got a speeding ticket. Saw it on her desk."

Dexter always was a gossip. "Who gave it to her?"

"Amarillo police department"

"Amarillo! That's in Texas. Where is she now?"

"Couldn't say."

"Did she just walk out without a word?"

"She got in late then said she had an errand to run. Been havin' morning stomach problems."

Probably pregnant. That's all the town would need. Another little Tyburn. "All right, then. By the way, have you seen any strangers come in lately?"

"Like who?"

"Like someone you've never seen before, but who looks like a bank robber."

"You mean like Tyburn?"

"Could be."

"He called Abby just before she left. I answered the phone."

"You happen to overhear anything?"

"Mamma taught me not to eavesdrop."

"Didn't *accidently* overhear something?"

"Uh-uh."

We hung up, and I rocked in my chair, wondering how tight those two really were.

"Chief?" Mrs. Rheingold's voice came over the intercom. "Your fair maiden is on the line for you."

Fair maiden? I picked up. "This is Chief Bucky."

"Chief Bucky, it's Trixie," she sniffled.

I tightened. "What's going on?"

"You've got to come over. Only you. It's my husband. I've—I've killed him."

# CHAPTER 20

With siren screaming, I peeled rubber and sped west into the setting sun, a giant red ball heading for the fields. Near Trixie's, I switched off the siren. The last thing I wanted was nosy neighbors flocking to a murder scene.

I pulled into her driveway, jumped out, and trotted up the walk, shotgun at hand. The door stood open a crack, I crept in.

"Trixie!" No answer. I checked the living room then paced through the dining room into the kitchen. A stack of Green Stamp booklets sat on the counter. I called Trixie's name again and stepped down into the den. The pool table had a short length of chain on it. My skin felt clammy. "Trixie!"

Did she run away? Where's the body?

I checked behind the bar.

Intending to search the back of the house, I retraced my steps through the foyer to the living room, my neck damp. I placed my shotgun behind a wing chair and took out a handkerchief. Clicking footsteps from behind. I spun around.

"I'm sorry, Bucky Bucky." Trixie stood in the foyer, her cheeks stained with tears. Her hand fluttered to her throat like her voice wanted to say something and couldn't. Her mouth quivered, and her whole face went to pieces in sobs.

The front door clicked shut. Jerry!

He was not at all dead, but very much alive and in his trooper uniform. His eyes flashed, and I didn't like what I saw in them. Didn't like the gun in his hand either.

My pulse shot up along with my hands.

"Good thinking, Chief." Jerry tossed his head sideways. Vertical ridges and valleys lined his fleshy face. "Hands against the wall, feet back."

Wanting to move fast and knock his gun away, I kept my feet close to the wall.

"I said feet back!"

Now, even the slightest false move would land me on my face.

Jerry lifted my gun from its holster. "Turn around and get into the living room." My gun stuck in his waistband.

"Wait a minute!" I shouted. I wanted Jerry looking at me and not at the shotgun leaning against the back of the wing chair. "What about Trixie?" I made exaggerated arm movements for her to come. "I want her to tell me what's going on."

"Shut the fuck up and keep moving." Jerry's eyes were like coal pressed into heaps of soft tissue.

I backed into the room, keeping myself between Jerry and the shotgun before dropping into the wing chair. Trixie eased into a second wing chair a few feet beside me. Jerry sat on his snooze couch. The giant bear stood in the corner by the fireplace.

"Let's hear it, Trixie," I said. I was pretty steamed, not just faking it for Jerry's sake. "Were you dreaming about killing your husband? Or maybe this guy isn't even your husband."

She didn't say anything, just sniffled and stared at her hands, twisting a handkerchief like a braided rope.

"I'm her husband, all right," Jerry offered. "We've been happily married six years this month. Trixie always appreciates my remembering our anniversary. Isn't that right, sugarplum?"

His face didn't exactly look sugary.

She closed her eyes, and he snorted. "That's a woman for you. You know what Freud said about women?" He leaned back against the cushion and crossed his legs. "Go ahead, guess."

I continued staring at Trixie. Her face, streaked with mascara. Jerry must've forced her into this, though she sure as hell put on a convincing phone performance.

"Okay, you don't want to guess. I'll tell you. Freud said, 'Women, what *do* they want?' Even he couldn't figure them out."

"I'll remember that."

Jerry smirked. But there was something else there, too. Something tugging at the corners of his mouth—a trickster smirk of a guy enjoying a private punch line. He brushed up a sleeve to check his watch. "In about a half hour, you won't remember anything."

Trixie threw her hands to her face and, again, burst into sobs.

My bones froze. "Now wait a minute! Whatever you think happened between Trixie and me is wrong."

"A witness saw you two smooching it up in a parking lot. He'll testify to that at the inquest."

"Trixie, tell him this is bullshit."

She was crying, bent over with her head in her hands. "I'm sorry. I'm so sorry." She looked up at me, her eyes red as cayenne peppers. "I didn't know he was going to—"

"Shut up!" Jerry spat and lurched forward. He took a

breath and leaned back. "Poor dear. I'm afraid she can't help you."

This setup served one purpose. To kill me in a way that would somehow allow Trooper Jerry Hale to walk free. Trixie must've been in on the plan to get me out of town, but drew the line at actually having me killed to death.

After swearing me in, Judge Thompson said I'd have enemies. But he didn't say they'd be murdering enemies that gave thirty-minute warnings.

I had to get my shotgun from behind the chair. Trying to sound offhanded, I said, "Since we're all friends and have time on our hands, I'd like to know what brought us here together."

"You're a real smartass. Not smart, there's a difference." Jerry jabbed his finger at me. "You were put on notice about sticking your nose where it didn't belong. If you'd been smart, you'd have gotten the hell out of town."

"I thought your protocol lesson only concerned the Mayfair."

"Protocol also covers respect for the legal system."

"Like letting Tyburn get away with bank robbery?"

"You know fucking well what the jury said about that. That's what I mean by the legal system. Your harassment of Tyburn has been out of line."

I didn't mention Tyburn also being a murderer, but no point arguing about that, since Jerry seemed to be okay murdering people himself. "Fine. Now that I've been put on notice about the legal system, can I go?"

"Hear that Trixie? Smartass is also a comedian." He turned to me. "You're way past receiving notices. I tried to encourage you at the Mayfair to stay healthy by going back to the fucking Ozarks."

Jerry's geography was off, but correcting him

wouldn't be smart. Smart would be getting to my shot-gun. "I take it your make-believe snooze on the couch was supposed to scare me into leaving. Take up hog farming and marry my cousin."

"Make-believe?" Jerry's lips drooped like a bulldog. "You knew?"

"Not until now. You snored very convincingly. It take much practice? My daddy was a shrimper who snored so loud the boat rocked." I tried to calculate how many steps to the shotgun.

Jerry shook his head. "Came natural." He snapped his fingers at Trixie, who was again twisting her handker-chief. "Hey! Do I really snore?"

She made a small fretful noise that didn't really amount to speech.

"Speak up!"

"You don't snore," she said meekly.

"So," I said. "Since your health intervention didn't work, I take it we're now on Plan B." Take two steps, then dive behind the chair.

"The health intervention was, as you put it, Plan B. Plan A occurred ten minutes before that when the captain told you quite clearly on the Mayfair porch to get lost."

"So now we're on Plan C?" Grab it, pump, and fire.

Jerry peered at his watch, again. "Call it what you want."

But Jerry could get off one or two rounds by then. I scanned the room. "What exactly is Plan C?"

"It covers capital offenses." He put the gun in his lap and fished out a cigarette from a gold case on the glass coffee table.

The table also held a ceramic vase, a crystal ashtray, and a large brass lighter shaped like a shark. If only Trix-ie would do something. Bump the vase. Break it. Any-thing to help out.

I thought real hard. *Trixie, I'm sending a mental signal. Do something!*

She didn't even twitch. I sighed inwardly. There was only one way to save myself, and it would take courage because I was afraid. That's the only way to tell being brave from being stupid.

Jerry put the cigarette in his mouth and picked up the lighter. Flame erupted from the shark's mouth with the roar of a blowtorch. Bending his head toward the flame, Jerry sucked a deep drag.

I had to get to him. Charge him. "Say, mind if I have one?" I prepared to lunge.

Jerry seized his gun with amazing reflexes. "You get out of that chair, Trixie will have a lot of cleaning to do."

I leaned back. After a moment, I gripped my throat. "I'm real thirsty, do you think Trixie could get me a glass of water?"

Jerry gazed at his watch and seemed to think it over. Probably wondering if it was a trick. "Trixie!" He snapped his fingers. "You heard the man."

She got up, and I caught her eye and blinked hard. She had to do something to distract him.

On her return, she bumped into the back of my chair. She handed me the water and sat down.

Jerry took a fierce drag of his cigarette, glanced at the ashtray on the table, and flicked his ash into it. After each puff, he repeated the action.

As Jerry leaned forward to flick off another ash, I glanced at Trixie. Her eyes were on me. She squeezed them shut and lowered her chin.

A signal! Suddenly I felt miraculously alive. But what did the signal mean? Maybe she had a plan. A new thought. I'd get Jerry talking. Give her a chance to act on whatever she was signaling. "So, Jerry," I began, conversationally, "you mentioned capital offenses."

Jerry blew smoke out his nostrils like an angry bull. "Glad you reminded me." He crushed his cigarette brutally into the ashtray with the look of someone about to do something important. He strutted over to me and hovered with hunched shoulders and a pointed gun. It was easy for me to feel like the helpless prey of some deadly animal.

"Capital offenses cover such crimes as sticking your nose into such matters as Mexican paper. And I'm not talking pesos."

Uh-oh! This has nothing to do with Mayfair protocol, but with Overstreet's Mexican bearer bonds. I now understood what Ham meant about troopers being under Overstreet's control. All I could think to say was, "I don't follow."

"I'm going to ask you a question. And if I don't like the answer, I'll offer you a prompt. In the foot, then in the belly, so you can roll around a long time thinking it over. I'm sure you know how it works. A Socratic dialogue."

"Socratic?"

"I encourage you to reflect, and together—" He wagged the gun back and forth. "—we search for the truth to an important question. No philosophical training is needed, but if I think you're not trying to help us reach a consensus. Well, you remember what happened to Socrates? His fellow Athenians forced him to put a gun to his head and blow his own brains out. So, who told you?"

I stared at the gun now aimed at my foot. I laughed. Just one little hiccup. I wouldn't dare mention Dusty's name, or Dusty would have more to worry about than the Georgia police.

I frowned to buy time. Even went so far as to say, "Huh?"

Jerry pressed the gun barrel against my foot. "You'd better clean out your think pipes."

"Geesh, this is hard. You know how it is, you're talking to somebody and he says something and the next fellow says something, and before you know it, you've heard something."

Jerry cocked the gun. "Last chance."

I was imagining my life hopping along on one foot when the answer popped into my mind. "Ah, now I remember. Chief Parker told me."

Jerry's coal-like eyes darkened. "Is that so?" He backhanded his gun barrel across my face. My cheekbone caught fire. Blood splattered on Trixie, and she yelped.

"Very convenient since Parker's dead. I don't believe you."

My face hurt like a fucker. I yanked out a handkerchief. Time was running out. I had to do something. Now.

A soft thump sounded outside the front door. Jerry froze like a lethal animal with a scent. He dashed to the window.

Shit! He'll see the shotgun.

# CHAPTER 21

Jerry peered outside and shook his head. "It's only the newspaper being delivered."

He was too far away for me to do anything, and I couldn't wait for Trixie's help. When Jerry came back, I'd jump him and get him in the neck breaker hold I'd learned wrestling in school. I planted my right foot, ready to push off.

"Well, I'll be," Jerry chirped. "What's this sticking out from under your chair?"

Under my——I looked at Trixie. She flashed a weak smile, on and off. Suddenly I found myself staring up the barrel of my shotgun.

"Stashing extra firepower, are we?"

Trixie must've tried to hide it when she bumped my chair and then signaled by nodding toward the floor.

Jerry pumped the shotgun. "Smooth action. Now, about this person you talked to."

"Oh, for Christ's sake, Jerry, leave him alone." Trixie stood and reached for a cigarette on the table. She suddenly had a little more pep, though her hand trembled when she lit up. She strolled to the giant bear in the corner. An elbow rested on her wrist, her cigarette held high between two fingers. "The clerk at the Mayfair told him. I know because—"

"Shh!" Jerry raised his hand, tramped to the window, and peered out. He snapped his fingers at me. "Throw me your bracelets."

I hesitated. No way would I let Jerry handcuff me. "What for?"

"None of your fucking business." Jerry fluttered his fingers. "Come on, come on."

I tossed over the cuffs. "What's going on?"

Jerry stuffed the handcuffs into his back pocket and eyed his watch for the hundredth time. "Right on schedule. My neighbor across the street just pulled into his driveway."

Trixie strayed over to an ashtray on the mantelpiece and tapped her ash. The neighbor was probably the one who'd made a pass at her, the one who'd witnessed the kiss, the one planning to testify at the inquest. I caught Trixie's eye and blinked hard. Do something!

She looked away and sucked in a lungful from her cigarette. "He'll be coming over in a minute to play pool." She blasted smoke from the side of her mouth and plucked a piece of tobacco from her tongue. "They amuse themselves every week at this time."

"All right," her husband blurted and licked his lips. "He just got out of his car."

Jerry didn't exactly rub his hands together like a fiend, but he did a good imitation of a diabolical scientist about to destroy the planet.

"Next, he's going to get his mail and take it inside. He'll fart around a couple minutes and then come out with a six-pack of Falstaff under his arm. He'll cross the street, and about halfway up our walk he's going to hear two gunshots from inside. He'll rush to the door and ring the bell. Getting no answer, he'll pound on the door and shout. Eventually he's going to remember he has a key for when he house-sits and run home for it." Jerry studied his watch, as if seconds mattered.

Trixie jabbed her cigarette into the ashtray and moved away from the fireplace. "Jerry, please. Don't do this."

He strode over to her. On the way, he tossed the shotgun onto the couch. He put a knuckle under her chin and thumbed the streaks of mascara beneath each eye. "Don't worry, sugarplum, the chief's not going to rape you. But it'll look like he tried."

Jerry clutched a hunk of her blouse and ripped it off, bra and all. Then he cocked his arm back and let loose with a vicious left hook he must've thrown a thousand times as a boxer. She screamed and stumbled back against the bear. Blood gushed from her mouth.

I sprang to my feet. Jerry's quick reflexes had me in his pistol sights. "Don't try it, asshole. Get your ass back down."

He strode again to the window, peeped at his watch, and stared out.

This was my last chance. "What's going to happen when he opens the door?"

"Shut up. Here he comes. It'll take him thirty seconds to reach the porch."

Jerry hurried over to Trixie. She was leaning limp-kneed against the bear. Her jaw sagged to one side, as if unhinged. He swung his gun toward my head. "Here's what's going down, asshole. He'll come in and discover me handcuffed to the pool table and you two lying here on the floor, having shot each other."

He took a step back, pulled my revolver from his belt, and pointed it at Trixie's chest. "Sorry, sugarplum, but I have to answer to a higher calling."

The gun exploded with a puff of smoke and an ear-drum-bursting blast. Paralyzed by surprise and shock, I stared at Trixie. She clutched her heart. Her other hand seized the bear's arm.

They tumbled forward. Jerry tried to sidestep, but the bear caught his left shoulder. I flew from my chair and head-butted Jerry onto the glass table. It shattered. Jerry howled. I clawed over him to the sofa and grabbed my shotgun. At the same time, Jerry raised my revolver.

We both fired.

The front door opened.

# CHAPTER 22

The pounding shook the room. My eyes snapped open and I groped for the light. Normally, I wouldn't sputter to life for another hour. I trudged to the front door to find Ham holding a bulging canvas sack.

"Oh, it's you," I said woozily and stared off at a mass of black clouds. A weather system was rolling in from somewhere.

"Who'd you expect, troopers?" He tossed the sack to me like a medicine ball, sending me stumbling back. "Read about you while I was away. I take it you settled an old score." He lumbered inside and nodded at my bandaged cheek. "Must've come with a price."

"Long story." I pushed the door closed with my toe, shuffled to the kitchen table, and plunked down the sack. It made a tantalizing chinking sound. I loosened the sack's cord. "Are these what I think they are?" I scooped out a fistful of silver dollars.

"Two hundred and fifty Lady Liberties." Ham flopped into a chair and tossed his hat on the table, along with a crumpled manila folder. "Think you can brew up some coffee? Been driving all night."

"Sure." I put water on the hotplate and got dressed,

came back and picked up the coffee jar. "The story said a trooper fired at you but missed, so you blasted his head off. Fill me in with the grim details, and then I'll tell you what to do with this silver."

"It started the day I questioned Overstreet's butler at the mansion. After I left, I called back to question a woman I saw there, Trixie. When I asked to meet with her, for a few questions, she covered the mouthpiece and talked to someone—maybe to sketch out a quick plan to get me out of town."

"Love taps hadn't done the trick."

I explained my rendezvous with Trixie at the Speedy Mart, and that she had kissed me.

Ham frowned as he watched me prepare the coffee. "Sounds like a setup."

"They'd arranged for someone to witness the kiss." I poured our coffees. "First they wanted to scare me into thinking Jerry was going to kill me, hoping I'd hightail it. When that didn't work, they cooked up a final solution. No more scare tactics." I went on to relay Jerry's plan.

Ham took a slurp of coffee and made a face like he'd sucked in rat poison. He reached for the coffee jar. "Instant Nescafé?" He opened it and shook a shot's worth into his cup. "If I'm going to drink horse piss, I want it to be horse piss I can taste. How'd you manage to fuck up their plans?"

"It happened in a blur. The husband shot the wife, a stuffed bear fell on the husband, and I got lucky and shot him."

"Why'd he shoot his wife?"

"Said he had to answer to a higher calling."

"What the hell's that mean?"

I shrugged. Maybe Overstreet was Jerry's higher calling, but I didn't want to tell Ham that. Or about the Mexican bearer bonds. Might compromise Dusty. Besides, maybe by keeping my mouth shut, Overstreet might change his mind about killing me.

"Then what happened?"

"The neighbor came through the door and saw the whole mess. I called Sheriff Rakoff. He came over, checked around, said it looked like a lover's quarrel that got out of hand. The husband shot the wife, and in self-defense, I shot him. He asked if I had a problem with that. He said it in a way that told me I'd better not."

"Rakoff's tied in with that whole trooper bunch."

*Great. Now he's certain to be my enemy.* I gripped a fistful of silver dollars from the sack and let them dribble through my fingers. "Now, about these."

"I got to Gregory's place after nightfall. It was locked up tighter than a well digger's ass. Double locks on the doors, windows barred. It looked bad until I found a key in the bottom of the mailbox. I'll say this, Gregory knew how to celebrate his newfound wealth. Empty champagne bottles everywhere. The living room had a hi-fi system with speakers taller than my llamas. The whole place was crammed with new furniture, almost all of it knocked over. Someone had to have gotten there before me to tear up the house that way, and I suspected that meant they probably hadn't found the silver. So I did some searching of my own. Tapped the walls for cavities, checked for false cabinet bottoms, and finally yanked up a Mexican throw rug in the hallway. Bingo. A loose floorboard."

"But only the one sack of silver under it?"

"But room for several more." He opened the manila folder he'd brought with him. "This was there, too. Birth certificate, army discharge papers, and a photo of a burning house."

I only glanced at the documents. "The rest of the silver, whatever he didn't spend, must be with Tyburn and the other robber. So much for my brilliant theory about Tyburn double-crossing his partners and burying the loot in the desert. You said you'd tell me what to do with what's left of Gregory's share."

"You're going to use it as bait."

❧❧❧

Ham pushed off for home to get some sleep, and I went to Sally's for breakfast. The air outside was raw and the far off sky lit with jagged spears of white light. A rainstorm was coming.

I loved breakfast at Sally's. Thick bacon and moist omelets with names like lumberjack, coal miner, and cowpuncher; hotcakes such as lemon chickpea, marshmallow, barbecue pork, and a new one I hadn't tried: caterpillar. But the best aromas came from the fresh soups and spicy chilies served all day long.

I snagged a stool at the counter. A minute later, Jolene plunked down a chocolate malt. "On the house."

I glanced around. "Free malt day?"

"It's to make up for my taking so long with it the last time. Thought I was going to see a grown man cry." She tried to smile, but it only partly worked. "What'll you have with it?"

"I'm thinking the caterpillar hotcakes."

"They'd probably go well with your chocolate malt."

I hesitated while recalling the bad rattlesnake meat. What the heck, "I'll take a stack."

Boots sat two stools away, dressed in his old army uniform, but without his hat. His white hair was as fine as if it had been sifted through gauze. He stared down at a bowl of chili and stopped chewing. His mouth got sour looking, like a baby tasting something horrible.

He pushed the bowl away. When he spoke, so much

smoke came out of his mouth I thought for a moment he must've quietly lit a cigarette. "Jolene, correct me if I'm wrong, but didn't I order the *very* spicy?"

I slid my malt, water, and butt over next to him. He had the same goaty smell. "What's the good word, Boots?"

He stared, as if trying to place me. His gaze moved to my seven-point star and his lips formed a thin line like a little whip. "If this is an official interrogation, there are two sides to every story."

*This outta be interesting.* "Have you been shooting off your musket where you shouldn't have?"

"It's my neighbor, Mrs. Gustafson, isn't it? The old hag said she was going to call you."

Mrs. Gustafson was an invalid in a wheelchair cooped up in her upstairs bedroom. She was married to Gus Gustafson, whose crime put him in prison and helped make me police chief. "She hasn't called, so in case she does, why don't you tell me your version?"

Jolene exchanged Boots's bowl of chili.

"It's the damn broken fence. Not my fault my goats get into her yard. Just because her husband's not around anymore, it's not my responsibility. I told her she should have that young fella who moved in do it."

Young fella? She lived alone except for Abby, her caregiver. Maybe he meant Dexter. "You mean the kid at Gustafson's?"

The old man waved a hand dismissively. "Someone else. And it's his fault the fence fell down in the first place. Chopping hedges, opening and closing a gate that hasn't been used in years, just so he can pull his car into the back."

If it wasn't Dexter, who—"Hold on! Does he drive an old Chevy Coupe, maybe?"

Boots nodded and blew on a spoonful of chili.

"Don't know why he can't park in the driveway."

Nice and cozy. While Mrs. Gustafson's upstairs and crippled, Tyburn and Abby play house. "This guy, ever see him with friends?"

Boots swallowed the spoonful and smacked his lips with a look of satisfaction. "Friends?"

"Yeah, you know, maybe come to visit."

"Can't say I have."

"How about cars? See any unfamiliar ones around?"

Boots shook his head. "Nope. Heard a motorcycle come and go once. Damn thing woke me up. And just as I got back to sleep, it woke me up again."

My pulse skyrocketed. Gregory had a motorcycle at the Mayfair. "You say this was in the morning?" I whipped out my notepad and pen. "What time? Wait a minute. What morning?"

"Hmm, let's see." Uncertainty flickered on Boots's face. He stuck a finger in his ear, shook it, and then studied the tip. "Monday. Must've been Monday because that's when the milkman comes." He rubbed his finger on his army pants then got back to eating chili.

On Monday Tyburn was released from jail. Also, the day of the murder.

A tingle raced up my spine. *Careful,* I told myself. *You need to get this right.* "Okay, now Boots, let's review. Last Monday a motorcycle woke you up. What time was that?"

"Umm…Around seven-thirty."

"Then what happened?"

"I told you, I went back to sleep."

"Did you look out the window first?"

Boots nodded. "Wasn't sure if the motorcycle had stopped on my property or next door."

"What'd you see?"

"What do you think? The motorcycle. Now that I recall, I also saw that young fella's car parked in the drive-way. Don't know why he can't always keep it there."

"You mean the Chevy Coupe?"

"That was the first time I'd seen it."

"Then you went back to sleep?"

"Only until that damn motorcycle woke me up again. I looked at the clock, said the hell with it, and got out of bed."

"What time was that?"

"Few minutes after eight."

"How many minutes after?"

"I don't know, just a few. Six or seven, maybe."

"Did you look out the window again?"

"Yes," he snapped. "And I saw the motorcycle pull away. Now listen, if that old hag calls, you tell her she's got to fix her own fence."

After getting out of jail early Monday morning, Ty-burn must've driven to Abby's. He got there before sev-en-thirty, the time Gregory arrived, because Boots saw his car in the driveway then. Boots also saw Gregory leave at eight-oh-six or seven. Dusty said Gregory arrived at the Mayfair between eight-twenty and eight-thirty, about twenty minutes later. I'd have to check my notes to be sure. Dusty also said Overstreet's butler phoned in Gregory's reservation around eight. That would've been during the time Gregory and Tyburn were in the house together.

"Hotcakes will be up in a jiff," Jolene said and topped off my malt from the mixer. "Looks like we're in for a downpour."

I licked at a spoonful of malt and tried to think why Gregory went to see Tyburn. They both showed cuts. Gregory's between two knuckles on his left hand, and Tyburn's lip. He said it was from shaving.

If Gregory had slugged Tyburn, it wasn't because he

was double-crossed. After all, Gregory had received his share of the silver. So whatever may have provoked him had to be serious enough to cost him his life.

Jolene put down my breakfast platter and leaned against the back counter. She rested her elbow in one hand and held her cigarette high in the other. A trail of smoke corkscrewed to the ceiling.

I lifted the top hotcake with my fork in search of caterpillars. I couldn't find any, but the hotcakes appeared a pleasant green. I nibbled a bite. Hmm. Tasted familiar.

Jolene cocked her mouth and shot out a blast of smoke. "What do they taste like?"

"Like moths."

Jolene crinkled her forehead. "They're supposed to taste buttery."

"No. They have a moth taste."

"Really? We were hoping to put a description on the menu."

"What do other people say?"

"They haven't. You're the first to order them."

A thunderclap shook the room, and seconds later raindrops battered the roof like buckshot.

# CHAPTER 23

I slammed the atlas closed and swung both feet onto my desk. So, it *was* Abby and Tyburn who ransacked Gregory's house. I had been thinking of my phone conversation with Dexter, and what he said about Abby getting a speeding ticket in Amarillo—smack between Defiance and Santa Fe. Traipsed all that way and never found Gregory's silver. Serves them right.

Dexter also said Abby and Tyburn often talk on the phone. I picked up my hat and coat.

∓

"I can't help you, Chief. We're in the middle of a crisis here. Look at my damn switchboards!"

Mr. Bedford Forrest pointed to a glass door connecting his office to a small narrow room. Inside sat three straight-backed girls in straight-backed chairs. They wore headphones and were frantically plugging and unplugging phone cords in and out of a switchboard.

Forrest appeared thin as a phone jack in his tight-fitting black-and-white checked sport coat, red bow tie, and pressed white handkerchief. He had a long face and a long title. General Manager, Defiance, Oklahoma Central

Phone System. Carrying the burden of such a high position, Forrest obviously felt it his right to put me off, as if I were a Boy Scout with a wolf badge pinned to my coat.

"If you'll notice," Forrest jabbed a thin finger toward the window, "there's a storm out there."

"I might not have," I said, slapping my water-soaked hat against my thigh, "except for having to dodge lightning bolts while crossing the street."

"Then you should understand my problem." Forrest sprang out from behind his desk. "See that poster?"

He pointed to one of several on the wall. Most showed jolly faces of men and women, even children and old people, holding shiny black telephones and having the thrill of their lives.

But the poster Forrest pointed to showed the face of a horror-stricken woman holding a telephone with a fireball shooting from the speaker. The caption read *Do not use the telephone during lightning storms!*

"There you have it," the manager said crisply. "We're in emergency mode." He paced back to his chair and sat stiffly, his eyes fixed on his operators, plugging and unplugging a jumble of wires.

I nodded toward the girls. "I see *they're* busy. But why?"

"Our operators are cutting in on conversations and ordering people to hang up."

"Not to be impolite, Mr. Forrest, but what are you doing that you can't spare me a couple minutes?"

The manager pointed toward the glass door. "Supervising."

"Yes, well, I have an important police matter I need your help with. But go ahead and supervise while I explain."

"I suppose I can do that," Forrest grumbled, his gaze glued to the operators as if at any moment one might jump up and yell, *"Fire,"* requiring him to grab a hose and dash off.

"If you recall," I began, "sometime back, the FBI had phone taps on a couple unsavory citizens in town."

"I remember. Johnston and, um…"

"Overstreet."

"Correct. Overstreet. What about it?"

"I want you to record all telephone conversations conducted at Gustafson's Grocery."

Forrest's eyes remained fixed on the glass door. "What for?"

"I suspect the carrying on of illegal activities, the nature of which I can't reveal. I expect this matter to stay between you, me, and whoever you assign to the task."

"I could simply provide you with a list of all in and out calls. Names and numbers."

"Not good enough. I have to listen to the conversations."

The manager tilted his head and scratched under his chin, then leaned forward and picked up a pencil. "I believe you said Gustafson's Grocery."

I danced from the building. The trap was set, and tonight I would plant the bait.

൞

Back at my desk, I thought about Tyburn and Gregory. I realized the question should be, not what Tyburn had against Gregory, but what Gregory had against Tyburn. After all, Tyburn had the cut lip, and Gregory had the cut knuckle. Dusty had said that when Gregory checked into the hotel, he was drunk and asked what time the bank opened. Then said something about making a deposit. A Mexican bearer bond deposit, perhaps? From all appearances, Gregory had squandered most of his share of the silver and sure as hell knew of the bonds since he'd stolen them.

I snagged a paperclip and bent it back and forth, got up, and paced. Suppose Gregory got to boozing and feeling sorry for himself. That was reasonable, since he risked his life for just over three thousand dollars, while Overstreet sat on his ass and netted thirty or more times that. Maybe after getting soused and stewing awhile, Gregory decided to pay Tyburn a visit at Abby's.

Maybe he demanded to renegotiate their deal with Overstreet, but Tyburn wouldn't go for it. The three robbers had agreed to only keep the silver. They argued, and Gregory threw Tyburn a punch. Tyburn then left the room, patched his lip, and called his daddy. His daddy ordered him to tell Gregory to check into the Mayfair and get some sleep. Either then or soon after, Gregory left. Good ol' Martin told Tyburn that Gregory was a loose cannon who needed a permanent defusing.

Two hours later, Tyburn shows up at the hotel, slinks up to Gregory's room, and does the deed. He then takes off down the back stairs to his car, leaving a juicy footprint behind. But that still leaves the question: how did he slip out of the locked room?

ⱱↄⱱↄ

The rain had stopped, but luckily for me, enough of it had flooded the roads in and out of town, that those Oklahoma City big hats had to miss an evening of cavorting with the boys—and girls—at the Mayfair and instead hunker down to a blander evening at home with their wives.

I gave the hotel's front door seven sharp raps. Shave and a haircut, six bits.

Dusty poked his head out. His eyes darted like an

anxious woodchuck. Cigar smoke hovered around his stained teeth that resembled wooden fences. "What're you doing here? You fucking crazy?"

I shouldered past him and bounced inside. "Relax, you could use some company." I strolled over to the desk. "What do you do around here besides act as towel boy to horny big shots?"

"What's it to ya?"

"Forget it, I don't know why I asked. Grab a screwdriver and come along."

"What for?"

"It's a surprise."

Dusty wandered into the back muttering to himself. He returned, and we trekked up to two-thirteen, Gregory's old room. I used the key I'd been carrying with me since Dusty took it out of the lock. The room appeared exactly as it had four days earlier, except the bed was made and the blood had been almost completely scrubbed out of the rug. I locked the door. "We're not leaving until we figure out how Tyburn escaped."

I re-pocketed the key and started tapping walls like a termite inspector. A trick I'd learned from Ham.

"I already figured it out," Dusty said.

I whirled around. "You what?"

"You know as much about being a detective as I know about handling a flea circus. First, you should always eliminate the obvious. That's fundamental to detection. See for yourself. There's only one door in this room and two windows. They're both locked, and one of them's sealed shut with paint. Only a squirrel could squeeze through the chimney or the heating duct. That pea-brain officer of yours got it wrong. Not Sparks—though he's a blockhead—the other one. His suicide theory makes as much sense as flying to the moon. There's only one rational explanation for how the murderer left this room." He pointed. "Right through that door. And I don't mean the keyhole."

"If that's true, Gregory locked the door himself before he knew he was dead."

"He'd been stabbed in the heart, not the brain. Unlike in the movies, he didn't die instantly and crumble to the floor. Instead, he locked the door the moment the killer ran out for fear he'd return."

"That's so much wiser than hanging out a *do not disturb* sign. Look, I might buy your idea about him staying alive for a bit, but—"

"I'm not saying what he did was rational, but face it, the guy had just been stabbed. Who knows what anyone would do under those circumstances?"

"If it's all the same, I'd like to explore other possibilities." I returned to tapping walls. "You probably know this old place pretty well. Any secret passages?"

"You mean besides the one leading to the torture chamber?"

I didn't even grant him a smile, instead removed a picture from the wall, tapped, and put it back. "Help me with this dresser." We pulled it from the wall, and I tapped. I jabbed at the firewall inside the fireplace with a poker.

"Do you believe me now?" Dusty said smugly.

"Not so fast. See that bloodstained throw rug? There could be a trapdoor under it."

Dusty waved me off. I pulled back the rug with a flourish, and dust flew like face powder. The floorboards beneath were old and worn, exactly like others in the room.

"Hand over your screwdriver." I took it, got on my knees, and tried unsuccessfully to pry up the floorboards.

"Now open the goddamn door," Dusty grumbled. "I've got things to do."

I stood. "Like what?"

"Like turn on the oven. There's a television show coming on, and I want to heat up my TV dinner."

"What show's that?"

"Perry Mason."

"Must be new."

"See? Something else you don't know. He's a lawyer who trips guys up on the stand. Last week's episode was called *The Case of the Man Who Didn't Smoke*. It was about a car thief, who didn't smoke, but the cops found cigarettes on him. Perry Mason figured out that he used the foil from cigarette packs to hotwire cars."

"How'd the guy do it?"

"Shoved the foil under the car's dashboard and connected the ignition points." Dusty headed for the door. "I gotta go. My dinner's not going to heat itself."

Defeated, I handed over the key. Dusty unlocked the door, and we stepped into the hallway. I turned back and took one last look at the room. "Hold on," I said and went back in. I pulled up the bedspread and glanced under the bed.

Satisfied, I checked my watch. Time to go home and dress for tonight's bait planting caper.

# CHAPTER 24

Ham had suggested I use Gregory's recovered silver as bait to catch the third bank robber. But he could be in Mexico, for all I knew. Better, I reasoned, to use it to catch Tyburn.

I would sneak into Gustafson's at night and leave Gregory's bag of silver in the Defiance National Bank bag on Abby's desk. She would discover it the next morning when she opened the store. The look on her face would be a Kodak moment. She'd probably think Tyburn had pulled a prank on her.

No matter what she thought, she'd pick up the phone and call him.

"I didn't put it there," he'd say.

"Well, somebody did," she'd say back.

Tyburn could make any number of incriminating remarks. All recorded nicely by Forrest at the phone company.

I had considered asking Dexter to plant the silver or borrow his store key and do it myself. But I didn't like involving Dexter because he might screw up and get caught, or slip up and tell someone.

This would be a one-man undercover operation.

According to the newspaper, the moon would rise at

twelve-oh-six a.m., and that there would be cloud cover. At eleven-forty, I slipped into my '35 Ford Roadster. Ten minutes later, I was rolling down Central Avenue. Everything—the streets, sidewalks, shops—were dark and quiet as some Inner Sanctum Mystery episode.

Ahead sat Gustafson's, the windows black and spooky. I cruised past and got a case of the jitters, turned a corner and stopped. Was this something a police chief should be doing?

Wait. FBI guys broke into places all the time to plant bugs. So, I'd plant silver. I smiled and slipped away from the curb.

❦

I parked in a residential area in the darkest spot between streetlights. The surrounding homes had pre-war wood frames and seemed in good repair. Best of all, they were as dark as the starless sky. I got out of my car, wearing a dark coat and jeans, and slung a travel bag full of silver over my shoulder like a burglar's swag.

Nervous as a raccoon on a hot tin roof, I took off walking too fast, caught myself, and slowed to a normal pace. I lowered the front of my cowboy hat and turned right onto Citrus Avenue. Gustafson's sat a block ahead at the corner, practically invisible in the darkness. I reached the alley at the back of the store. A few cars were parked along the street. No one around. Not even a raccoon.

I picked up an empty Nehi pop case from a stack at the door and took it to the feed shed just off the street. I stepped on the case and, with a grunt, pulled myself up onto the shed's roof.

"Hey!" a voice snapped from the street.

I froze. Too scared to turn around.

"Gimme those goddamn keys. I'll drive." A scuffle.

Drunks from the beer joint around the corner.

"You're shitfaced, man."

More scuffling.

"Ah, fuck it! It's your goddamn car."

A car started and peeled rubber.

Back to breathing again and now on all fours, I made my way across the flimsy sheet metal to the main roof. Muscling myself up, I crouched along to the bathroom window, that had always been left open a crack. Unable to see, I ran my fingers down the glass to the opening. Relieved, I dragged a sleeve across my damp forehead, lifted the window, and squeezed through.

Piece of cake. Because I'd be leaving through the back door, I made a mental note to replace the Nehi case.

Inside, I couldn't see an inch from my face. It was darker than a sack of black cats and I hadn't thought to bring a flashlight. Gustafson had once lived in this upstairs area, now used for storage. It took several minutes of bumping into boxes and columns before I made it downstairs and through the hallway to Abby's office. I felt along the ledge above the door where Gustafson had always kept the key.

Dread gripped my chest like a steel band. It wasn't there.

Now what? It could be anywhere. At the register with the shed key? Impossible to get there without bumping into stuff. Since I couldn't leave the silver on her desk, I'd drop it at her door.

Relieved that I wouldn't have to navigate the upstairs minefield again, I made it easily to the back door. Knowing it would lock when I closed it on my way out, I pushed the bar, and an alarm bell clanged so loudly I felt it down to my socks. Shit! Neighbors a mile away will hear it and think there's a fire—or a burglary!

I took off running through the dark alley, tripped over something, caught my footing, and turned up the street.

When I passed under a street light halfway to the corner, someone yelled, "Bucky, is that you?"

I glimpsed a figure across the street with a dog. While I couldn't see the person's face, the voice clearly belonged to the prune-juice-lady, Mrs. McCoy.

I kept running, turned the corner, jumped into my car, and sped home.

෬෬

I'd been home barely fifteen minutes, cursing my bad luck. Abby just happened to install a burglar alarm. Mrs. McCoy just happened to—the phone rang. Blood stopped in my veins. It must be her.

I rested my hand on the phone and tried to slow my breathing. I'd act like I just woke up. Breaking and entering—some piece of cake, all right.

"Hello," I moaned in my best sleepy voice.

"Hazelwood here, Chief. Sorry to wake you, but, um…everything okay?"

What the hell did he mean? I had planned to fake a yawn, but with my heart banging against my ribcage, I could only croak, "Of course everything's okay."

Silence.

Afraid that I sounded harsh, I added, "Actually, my stomach's upset."

"Maybe you ate something that didn't agree."

"Probably the caterpillars."

"The what?"

"Nothing. Why wouldn't I be all right?"

"Oh, yeah. A woman called and said a burglar alarm went off at Gustafson's, and that she saw you running away. I told her she must be mistaken, but that I'd check with you."

I made a fake laugh. "No kidding?"

"A Mrs. McCoy. She thought burglars were trying to kill you. Pretty Funny, huh?"

"Yeah, funny all right."

"I sent a car to the store."

My stomach dropped. Had the officers gone inside and seen the silver? I said, "I'll give Mrs. McCoy a call in the morning and assure her that she must've seen someone else." I forced myself to ask, "Did our boys go inside?"

"Negative. I also called the storeowner, and she arrived first and turned off the alarm. Told our men that everything was okay. Worked out pretty nice, don't you think?"

I swallowed. "What's that?"

"The burglar alarm. Scared the guy off."

☙☙

The next morning I sat in my office bending a paperclip. Abby must've found the silver soon after going inside, that's why she wouldn't let my officers in. She would've tried to figure out how the person got inside, discover the empty Nehi case by the shed, and put it all together.

Odds are, she must've then called Tyburn. My plan hadn't worked perfectly, but it was results that counted. I dialed the phone company.

"Mr. Forrest, how are you this fine morning?"

"Shorthanded. A pole man went and got himself electrocuted this morning."

"No kidding? You guys must pull a lot of juice."

"Not at all. The fool was a careless Negro who fell

onto high voltage wires. Of course, the widow will try to suck money out of us by claiming faulty equipment. She'll hire a lawyer and file suit. Then, after mortgaging her house and spending every cent she owns, she'll throw up her hands and give up. Our lawyers handle these people more effectively than the Klan ever could." He laughed. "That's a joke, Chief. Now, what can I do for you?"

I didn't care much for Forrest's humor, but couldn't help wondering if he knew anything about the Klan's voting for a new grand dragon. The insurance man had said lawyers did things a rat wouldn't do.

"I'd like to come in and listen to that tap you set up at Gustafson's."

"There's nothing to listen to. At least as of thirty minutes ago."

"What do you mean? There has to be something."

"I beg your pardon. You've got no call to get snippy. No one's used that phone in the last twenty-four hours."

"I'm sorry. I just thought…Well, I'd appreciate it if you'd call me the minute you get something."

I slapped the receiver into its cradle. Damn! All because of that burglar alarm. Either Tyburn went with Abby to the store, or she took the silver home with her. I'd been so close to nailing that thieving murderer. To add insult to my wound, Abby and Tyburn were now two hundred and fifty dollars richer with money I was duty-bound to return to the bank. Of course the bank already got its money—in a way. But still, how could I expect to get elected mayor to help people if the people I help are crooks?

I yanked out a phone book. If it's results that count, I better make my next call count big-time.

# CHAPTER 25

Mrs. McCoy, this is Chief Bucky. I heard you had an eventful evening last night."

"Oh, Bucky, I am so embarrassed. People must think I'm nutty as a fruitcake."

"Of course they don't, Mrs. McCoy. Sergeant Hazelwood understood. People make those mistakes all the time."

My Dale Carnegie book, *How to Win Friends and Influence People*, said that it's important to let people save face.

"I tell you," she went on, "I woke up this morning, wondering if I hadn't dreamt the whole thing. But of course, I hadn't. I was mistaken because I wasn't wearing my glasses. I had just turned off the television after watching Steve Allen. He had on Elvis Presley…or was it Esther Williams? No, she was on the night before. Oh, fiddlesticks, it's not important. I had just gone outside with Hobo, you know, my little Scottie, so he could do his duty, when I heard the most insufferable burglar alarm. Moments later, I saw someone running down the street who looked just like you. Can you imagine? It happened so fast, and without my glasses—"

"That's okay, Mrs. McCoy. Lots of people look like me."

"I'll be sure to straighten things out with Miss Abby."

Straighten? I gulped. "Straighten what out?"

"I told her last night I was certain I had seen you."

☙❧

That's just great! The bees are out of the hive now. Too upset to fiddle with the intercom, I shouted, "Mrs. Rheingold!"

She burst in running, eyeballs like giant hoops. She held a tiny brush in one hand, the other hand raised, fingernails glistening red. "What's wrong?"

"Jesus, relax." My stomach felt like a knot being pulled at both ends. "I want you to get me a malt."

"A malt! You scared the daylights out of me for a malt?"

"Just do it, will you? *Please?*"

She twirled toward the door, and her dress flared up to her knees. "When I finish what I'm doing." She wiggled her freshly painted fingertips at me and left.

I ran a hand through my hair. Tyburn must know I planted the silver to somehow trick him. If the city council found out, I'd be crawling back home to Uncle Rupert, and Tyburn would no longer be badgered about stolen silver—or the more important matter of snuffing out Gregory.

Things gnawed at my insides. Not only had I helped a murdering robber get even richer and committed the crime of breaking and entering, but I had lied to Mrs. McCoy. It came so easily, so naturally. Surprising since I'd never been successful at lying before. Even as a kid, I couldn't pull off a convincing lie. I hadn't the self-confidence for it, either gave myself away or broke down and confessed. All I could do now was sit tight and hope to get lucky with Forrest's phone tap.

Mrs. Rheingold marched in zombie fashion, hand outstretched and holding a malt with a straw and plastic spoon inside. She placed it on my desk, did her fancy twirl, and started out.

"Hey, wait a minute. Where's the extra from the canister? There's always extra."

"Not with to-go orders," she said and left.

Humph! They probably put it in another container and she drank it. I pressed my intercom button. "Thank you. Please send in Officer Sparks."

I had hit on an idea of how Tyburn got out of Gregory's room but had no evidence to back it up. Ham had told me that when I lacked evidence, it was okay to trust my instincts, and that things would often fall into place.

Sparks had followed Tyburn to the Mayfair from the beer joint, and I wanted to review what happened later. My malt was nearly empty when Sparks strolled in, cupping a cigarette in his hand.

I motioned to a chair. "It's interesting," I said, "that both you and Tyburn hold your cigarettes the same way."

"An old habit from smoking at school. Hides the cigarette." He crossed his legs, sucked in a deep drag with a loud hiss, and flicked the ash into his trouser cuff. Probably another schoolboy habit.

I nudged my miniature tire ashtray toward him. "You guys palled around together, did you?"

Sparks blew a smoke ring. "You could say that."

"That's another thing you both do. Smoke rings."

Sparks grinned, as if recalling the good ol' days.

"What's so funny?"

"Jus' remembering, that's all." Sparks leaned over and flicked his ash into the tire. "Tyburn's idea of high school was to not show up. But when he did, we had fun. One time we had this gym teacher, Mr. Whipple. He smoked Chesterfields and opened his packs by tearing the whole top off. Most people just rip off a corner. Anyway, one time we got ourselves a pack of Chesterfields and inserted a horsehair into each cigarette. Then we switched packs on him." Sparks laughed.

"They make him sick or something?"

Sparks spread his arms and smoke spiraled up from his cigarette. "We never found out. But we never saw him smoke after that."

"You and Tyburn were pretty close. What's he like? That is, from your perspective."

Sparks frowned. "My perspective is from when we were stupid-ass kids. Let's just say we drifted apart." He raised a finger to his scarred cheek. Tyburn had seared it with a cigarette after Sparks taunted him in jail.

"No special reason?" I licked the spoon from my malt.

"He got mean after reform school, and I didn't like him anymore."

"But back then, what did you like about him?"

"He'd always come up with fun things to do. Usually daring ones."

"Like lacing Whipple's cigarettes?"

"More than that." Sparks took a quick tug off his cigarette. "We'd go over to Harvey's used car lot on Central and start up engines. We'd rev 'em until they screamed. Some guy would tear out of his salesman shack, and we'd run like hell. I'll say this, Tyburn was smart. Too smart for his own good. Once he read a book on safe cracking and went to work on Gustafson's safe. He got caught, and that's when they shipped him off to reform school."

"How'd he get into the store?" I sucked the last of malt through my straw.

"Through an upstairs window."

I gulped, and malt backed into my nose. Just the thought of having anything in common with Tyburn rattled my bones.

"The old man was living up there at the time and was asleep. That made the break-in even gutsier. Tyburn knew the safe was in the office, and he managed to get the key. The trouble was, he'd somehow locked himself in. Gustafson found him the next morning with a shit-ass smile on his face. He'd cracked the safe." Sparks stubbed out his cigarette in the ashtray. "Like I say, too smart for his own good."

"Smart enough to get out of Gregory's locked room." I pulled out my notepad. "I want to go over your movements prior to going into the hotel. See if there's anything we've missed."

Sparks leaned back with his hands behind his head. "Where do you want to start?"

I opened my notepad. "At the beer joint. It was there you said the beer puller told you that Tyburn had gone to the Mayfair, right?"

"Uh-uh. Another guy at the bar told me."

I flipped through pages. "That's right, a hog farmer. So you went to the Mayfair, and what happened?" I dropped my empty malt container into the trash basket.

"Where's the extra?"

"What extra?"

"The extra malt."

I shook my head. "They don't give extra with to-go's."

"Sure they do. They put it in a coffee cup."

I knew it! "Let's get back to the Mayfair."

"Yeah, I got there at around eleven and talked to that Dusty asshole."

"Before that. When you saw Tyburn's car in the back lot. Where'd you park, exactly?"

"Across the street in the alder grove. I could keep my eye on Tyburn's car and both the front and back of the hotel."

"That's where you called me from the first time, right?"

"Yeah, both times." Sparks crossed his ankles and hooked his thumbs inside his gun belt.

"Then you went in and talked to Dusty at around eleven. He said what, that Tyburn was upstairs in Gregory's room?"

"That's right. Then I went outside and tried to reach you the second time. Find out what you wanted me to do."

I looked up from my notes. "So when you couldn't contact me, what'd you do?"

"Went up to Gregory's room. Maybe catch the two of them red-handed with the silver."

I turned back to my notes taken the day of the killing and read. "You knocked. No one answered. You put your ear to the door, heard nothing, tried the door, but it was locked. You called up Dusty for his passkey, but then saw a key in the inside lock, knew the passkey wouldn't work, kicked a hole in the door, reached in, and unlocked it."

"See what I mean about Tyburn?"

"What's that?"

"He's a smart mother fucker. Has to be, to sneak out of a locked room."

"Not that smart. Was Tyburn's car still in the lot when you went up to the room?"

"Yeah, like I said. A little after eleven."

"That means the car left sometime between eleven,

and shortly before one, when we examined the car's tire tracks leading from the lot. Have you seen the TV show, *Perry Mason?*"

Sparks shook his head. "Who's he, a detective?"

"A lawyer, and in one episode, a car thief hotwires cars by jamming tinfoil under their dashboards and connecting the ignition terminals. Does that tell you anything?"

Sparks brushed ashes off his pants. "Yeah, the lawyer stole cars."

"Forget the lawyer. Think about Tyburn's car."

"You think someone stole it?"

"No. But here's what I think happened. Tyburn planned to kill Gregory but was afraid he'd be seen leaving the hotel. So he didn't leave but made it look like he did by having someone else drive off with his car."

Sparks gave an incredulous little laugh. "You're kidding."

"Tyburn was right under our noses all along. More accurately, under the bed."

"No way!"

"Did you look under it? Because I didn't. And no one else did either. Only later did I check to see if there was room enough for a man to fit."

"If he was going to do that, he'd have left the door unlocked and a window open."

"So why didn't he?"

Sparks pulled out a Lucky Strike cigarette and a lighter, lit up and leaned back. Finally, he said, "He forgot?"

"Imagine this. Tyburn goes up to Gregory's room and knocks. Gregory lets him in and locks the door. The two talk awhile, then, on orders from Overstreet—I'll get into that later—Tyburn knifes Gregory. Tyburn probably knew Gregory carried a knife, so he took it from him at gunpoint. If not, he would've had his own knife. He must've stabbed Gregory just before you knocked. Because had he done it earlier, he would've had time to unlock the door. But since he knew you had tried the door, he couldn't very well then unlock it. In his panic, he dove under the bed, forgetting to open a window."

Sparks nodded. "He probably sweated bullets, watching our feet move around inches from his nose."

"We were stupid not to have found him."

"Now that we're talking about it, I did hear something faint coming from inside the room, but it hardly registered. It could've been Tyburn crawling under the bed. But wouldn't it have been simpler for the person picking up Tyburn's car to simply have driven him to the hotel?"

"Maybe, but with the car suddenly gone, it would look like Tyburn had left the hotel."

A soft knock came at the door. It wasn't Mrs. Rheingold's thump. She must've been away from her desk, or she'd have announced the visitor.

"Come in."

A woman entered the room. "Hello, Chief Bucky Bucky."

My breath caught in my throat. This can't be—

"Trixie?"

# CHAPTER 26

Impossible! Trixie had been shot. I saw her clutch her heart and blood dribble from between her fingers. But there she was, right in front of me.

Her mouth moved, but the words sounded like a slowed down record. Sparks's fluffy smoke ring drifted lazily across my gaze.

"Did you hear me?" the woman asked in a Yankee accent. "I'm not Trixie. I'm Dixie, her sister."

I blinked. "Oh."

"I'm sorry to have shocked you, I mean. I'm here for my sister's funeral."

"Of course, of course," I said, nodding like a bobble-head doll. "I understand." I jumped to my feet, not understanding at all. She looked exactly like Trixie but sounded different. My eyes darted around the room. "I'll get you a chair."

Sparks ground out his cigarette and stood. "I was just leaving." He nodded to her politely on his way out.

I hurried from around my desk and held the back of Sparks's empty chair. "Please." She sat, and a whiff of what smelled like that same fruity perfume Trixie had used slapped my nose.

"I'm here, Chief Bucky Bucky, because—"

I raised my hand on the trip back to my chair. "My name's Bucky Ontario. Only Trixie called me Chief Bucky Bucky. It was…well, kind of a joke."

"Oh, I'm sorry, Chief Ontario."

"Actually," I said, my composure almost entirely back, "it's Chief Bucky. Just one Bucky."

She nodded with a slight smile and rose an inch from her seat to straighten her green, fluffy dress, like the ones Trixie wore.

Dixie's face turned serious. Her eyes had those same crow's feet that Trixie had worried about. "I'm hoping you can tell me why my sister was murdered," she said. "I've heard you were there. The police report was more than vague. In fact, it was suspiciously absent of details. And state troopers treated me like a child. They insist no one knows why Jerry did it, just that he went off his rocker. One of them, a captain, had the nerve to infer that Trixie must have provoked him into killing her."

Dixie lacked Trixie's southern accent, but that seemed to be their only difference. I tried to think what to tell her. There'd be no purpose in laying out the whys and wherefores of what led up to her sister's murder. Yet, on the other hand, she had a right to know *something*.

"I'm sad to say I have to share some responsibility for your sister's death."

Dixie's jaw tightened.

I waved my hand, realizing that was a crappy start. "What I mean is, it was supposed to be me. Her husband was ordered by higher-ups to kill me."

She puffed her cheeks and blew out a scornful burst of air. "What do you mean, higher-ups?"

"I was investigating a murder—not Trixie's, someone else's—and during my investigation I uncovered information that could get powerful people in trouble."

"You're talking in circles. Who were these powerful

higher-ups, and why was Trixie murdered and not you?"

"I'm not at liberty to say names. Trixie's husband was involved in a plot to murder me, but he shot Trixie first, saving me for second. As it turned out, Trixie saved my life. After she was shot, she knocked over a giant mounted bear, and that gave me time to grab my shotgun and shoot her husband."

"How fortunate for you. Is your version of why he shot Trixie the same as the captain's? Either he went off his rocker, or she provoked him?"

"I'm not saying either. But really, I don't know."

"He didn't say anything, he just shot her?"

"He said he had to answer to a higher calling."

Her eyes squinted. "What higher calling?"

Overstreet would be my guess. "Like I say, I don't know."

"Isn't it your job to find out?" Her lips set in a fine line.

She had a point. "If Jerry were alive to stand trial, yes. But the thing is, he's not, so the case is closed."

Hard blue eyes glared at me. The same hard blue eyes Trixie used when she told me to leave her house or she'd wake up Jerry and let us shoot it out.

"I see," she said. "Higher-ups wanted you dead, but because Jerry happened to feel like killing Trixie first, you're calling the case closed."

Her thighs pushed back at the chair. She came around the desk to me, pressed her knees against my chair, and stood over me. "The thing is, to use your words," she began smoothly, "this case is *not* closed until I know why my sister was murdered." She took my hand and placed my palm over her heart. "I want you to feel this. Do you feel my heart? Do you feel the truth of what I'm telling you?"

I wasn't sure that I felt much other than the swell of

her breasts and the warm silkiness of her blouse. But of her heartbeat, there was no sign. Only of the one pounding in my ears.

She pressed my hand harder against her breastbone. "Do you feel it?" she asked again. Her eyes glistened. Like her sister, she was very dramatic.

"Yes, ma'am, I feel it." I struggled to hide any sense of arousal from my voice.

She let go of my hand and seemed to relax a little. Then, calmly, she gave me an itty-bitty smile. "Whenever you're ready, you can take your hand off my bosom."

I slipped it in my pocket to save for later, like a special cigar. She sure knew how to get a guy's attention. Must run in her family. She returned to her chair and picked up her purse. "One more thing," she said, adjusting her collar, "If I discover you're involved in a cover-up—" She pointed to my hat on the desk. "—you won't have a head to wear that on."

☙❧

Holy crap! I needed to clear my mind. Those Trixie-Dixie twins had the same blood, all right. I sat back and twisted a paperclip. I had never seen a twin before, and seeing one now felt kind of eerie. Especially knowing the other was dead.

Dixie said she'd have my head if I was involved in a cover-up. Pretty laughable. As if she'd really learn why Jerry killed her sister. After a few more days of questioning troopers and getting diddlysquat, she'd pack up and go home.

Damn! Never got her last name. I should find out. She was probably staying at the Holiday Inn, the only reasonably priced place in town with clear water and no bedbugs. I looked up the number and dialed. An old woman answered. I knew she was old because she had one of those voices where her words sputtered.

"Holiday Inn, how may I help you?"

"This is Police Chief Bucky. I believe you have a guest there named Dixie. I don't have her last name. Could you please look it up for me?"

She cleared her throat. "Is this an official inquiry, or—"

"Strictly official."

"Well, I suppose. It's Dixon, Dixie Dixon. A hard name to forget. And such a sweet young lady." Her voice lowered. "Is she wanted for something? I can be discrete."

"No. I mean she's broken no laws. But since I have your confidence, I'd like you to check the register and tell me where she's from."

"So there *is* something going on."

"Nothing's going on. She came to see me about her sister's funeral, and I didn't want to bother her with too many questions."

"Ooh. You must mean that poor girl who was shot by her husband. And to think, a state trooper." I heard a page turn. "Here it is. Checked in yesterday. Miss Dixie Dixon, San Francisco, California."

"Thanks, ma'am. Appreciate the help." I hung up and leaned back in my chair. Trixie and Dixie. To think, identical twins. One of nature's fascinations. There were other kinds of twins I'd learned about in biology class. Fraternal, Siamese—that might be all.

I pictured the two women side-by-side. Same blonde hair, shoulder length, and pulled back behind one ear. Actually, behind opposite ears. And their moles were under opposite eyes. They both had nice boobs, but I couldn't actually picture them in detail, since I'd never seen them in the flesh. Were twins' fingerprints a mirror image?

Could they read each other's minds? Probably not. Otherwise, Dixie would've known why Trixie was killed. Assuming, of course, that Trixie knew.

I didn't have to read Dixie's mind to know she was mad at me for not investigating her sister's death. That's all I'd need. Start sticking my nose in the particulars and give Overstreet and his troopers another reason to kill me. Yet, if I was careful, I might uncover Jerry's motive for killing Trixie and stay alive in the process. I'd start by learning more about Dixie.

# CHAPTER 27

L ong distance. What listing, please?"
"I'd like the number for Dixie Dixon in San Francisco, California."

"One moment." The operator didn't sound old but talked through her nose. "I have two listings. A residence and a business."

"Um, I'll take both." After getting them, I asked, "Does it say what the business is?"

A long sigh. "One moment." She must've already closed the book. "It's the law offices of Dixon and Dixon. Anything else?"

Dixon and Dixon? "Oh, no thanks."

So, she's a girl lawyer maybe married to a lawyer. Odd, since she registered at the motel as a miss.

❧❦❧

"Chief," droned Mrs. Rheingold through the intercom. "Grandpa Boots is on the line."

I sighed and picked up the phone.

"What can I do for you, Boots?"

"I'm calling about Mrs. Gustafson. Thought you ought to know. The old lady just did a half gainer out her upstairs bedroom window. She's a goner. Broken neck."

☙❧

My cruiser crunched onto the gravel and stopped beside an ambulance. Boots stood leaning against a busted gate, whittling a piece of wood, and Tyburn was next door, sitting on Mrs. Gustafson's upstairs bedroom windowsill, wearing a James Dean T-shirt. The ambulance's rear door slammed.

An attendant approached as I stepped from the car. "She's dead, Chief. We'll take her to Fromm's Mortuary."

"I heard she fell out a window."

The ambulance driver pointed up to the empty window Tyburn had been sitting at. "That one. Landed on her head. The old man over there said she was yelling at him and came toppling out, including her wheelchair. I can believe it with a window that low to the floor."

"Was she alone up there?"

The man shrugged. "Some guy came out of the house and told me he was downstairs, fixing her lunch when he saw her fall past the window."

I paced over to Boots. He stood in a pile of wood chips, holding a carved piece resembling a small whale, or perhaps nothing. "Let's hear it, Boots. What happened?"

Boots waved his knife in the air. "The dang fool. She got all riled up over nothing."

"What nothing?"

"Nothing, nothing. Forget it. She just fell out the window, that's all."

"Now listen, Boots, I need to know what happened." I didn't want to play games, so I gave it to him like they did in the movies. "We can do this the easy way here, or the hard way down at the station."

Boots folded his pocketknife and jammed it into his

pocket. "Didn't do anything I hadn't been doing for years."

"Doing what?"

Boots's eyes flitted about nervously. "Let's just make this between you and me, okay?"

"Spit it out."

Boots kicked at his woodchips. "It's that jackass kid's fault. The one I told you about who parks his car in the back."

"Did he push her out the window?" Wouldn't be Tyburn's first killing.

"No one pushed her. I told you, she was all riled up. Shaking her fist at me like a nut with curlers big as woodchucks in her hair. Then, well, she just tumbled out the window, wheelchair and all. She wouldn't have been so mad if that fool kid hadn't chopped away the hedge between our properties."

"What was she irate about?"

"Well, that's just it."

"What's it?"

Boots rubbed his thumb on the carving in his hand. "She saw me standing over there." He flipped his wrist toward a tree stump a few feet away.

"Go on."

"I was stumpin'."

"You're mumbling. What?"

"Stumpin', goddammit! *Stumpin'.*"

Oh, my God! I had heard of sheepherders stumping sheep. But, no—Boots? "Were you standing on the stump doing what I think you were doing with your goats?"

"Just one. The woman had no reason to be spying on me."

I didn't need further details. "Look, I'll put in my report that you two were arguing about the hedge. But I want you to knock it off with the goats." To give Boots something to think about, I added, "The Bible says you should be put to death for what you did. Pretty sure it says the animal, too."

Boots scratched his chest with all five fingers. "Why blame the animal?"

"Listen here," I said sternly. "What you did was illegal. Any more of this, and you'll be explaining yourself to Judge Thompson in open court."

Tyburn whistled, long and piercing. He sat on the front porch, swinging on a glider loveseat, a grin all over his face. "Hey, Chief, don'tcha wanna question me?"

I padded over. At Tyburn's side sat a large striped cat, or from the looks of its yellow saber-like claws, a small Bengal tiger. Probably Tyburn's version of a body-guard. Its owner was eating a bowl of soup that smelled like minestrone.

"Go ahead," he said, "ask if I pushed her out the window."

I slid into an expensive cushioned chair that matched the loveseat. "Did you?"

"Sorry to disappoint, but I never killed no one. As for Mrs. G, I was in the kitchen. Thought I'd heard Tarzan calling and looked out the window just as she…shall we say?…passed by. In case goat-man forgot to mention to you, he saw me open the window and look out. Maybe the goat saw, too. I think she's his favorite."

"What were you doing in Mrs. Gustafson's kitchen? For that matter, why were you in her house?" Not that I didn't already know.

"Which question do you want answered first?"

"Try number one."

"I was preparing Mrs. G's soup, just like her husband used to. There's extra left over, if you'd like some. I make it every day. That also answers question two."

"Not entirely. Do you live here?"

"Yes indeedy. All proper. Got my own room downstairs. I'd be lying if I didn't admit to visiting Abby upstairs for—" He winked. "—you know, a little huggin' and squeezin'."

"How'd that come about? You moving in, I mean?"

"It was Mrs. G's idea. With me hangin' around so much, we got to likin' each other. She treated me a whole lot better than she did her husband. We even watched television together when Abby was at the store. Perry Mason was our favorite. You probably won't believe this, but I'm going to miss her."

"That's very touching." I considered asking if he'd seen *The Case of the Man Who Didn't Smoke* episode but thought better of it. However, I did wonder about the patio set. It appeared new. New furniture and leisure time seemed to accompany new wealth. It did for Gregory. "Patio furnishings look nice. Where'd you buy them?"

"Thinking of picking up a set?"

I shrugged.

"A furniture store. Me and Abby got 'em. Including the table."

"Was that here in town?"

Tyburn put his soup down on the porch deck, and the beastly cat went to work lapping up the remainder with a tongue like a tractor scoop. "Chief, you are so easy to read." Tyburn brushed his hands. "No, we didn't buy them here in town. Let's see, was it in Tulsa or The City?" He shook his head. "You'll have to check around."

I touched that smooth spot on my face. Tyburn had a knack for putting me ill at ease. Maybe because of his knife-wielding ability. "What do you mean, easy to read?"

"You wanna run out and check if I bought this furniture with silver dollars. Go ahead and waste your time, just like you're wastin' your time tryin' to prove I killed Gregory. I ain't never monkeyed with murder."

"You more than monkeyed. It's a fact, and we both know it."

"Bullshit. Ain't no fact."

"You admit, though, that you were in Gregory's room."

"I admit that. I also admit that he was alive when I left."

"Get off it, Tyburn. I already know how you pulled it off."

"Oh, really? Please enlighten me, Mr. Lawman. This outta be good."

Could telling him hurt the prosecution later? I didn't think so. The look on Tyburn's face would be another Kodak moment. "Okay. After you stabbed him, you hid under the bed."

Tyburn stared at me with a blank face. The same blank face Ham had made after being told he would not be ticketed for speeding. But Ham then burst out laughing. Tyburn wasn't laughing. His mind appeared to be running through a number of gears. After a time, he gave a smile with his mouth, but not his eyes. A chilling smile. "You've got the wrong man, Chief."

I stood. "Good try, Tyburn. Like I told you in Potter Park, you're not going to get away with rubbing out your associate. You'll be anteing up a lot more than silver." I started off.

"Hey, Chief."

I stopped and looked back.

"Say I was a murderer. Who'd you think I'd go after next?" With a cold grin, he added, "Come around anytime."

❧❦❧

Before leaving the Gustafson place, now the Abby and Tyburn place, I went up to Mrs. Gustafson's room, and everything looked normal. I had also checked with Boots that he had seen Tyburn in the kitchen within seconds of her fall.

I spent the next morning in my office wondering what the murdering crook had to gain by knocking off Mrs. Gustafson. There would likely be no inheritance for Abby, because Mr. Gustafson was still alive, though his assets, not much more than a toothbrush and shaving gear, would be useless to him. His wife's death was, no doubt, just an unfortunate accident.

Tyburn was clever to have caught on to my clumsy attempt to learn where he might've sprinkled silver dust. By now, he probably converted his silver into paper dollars, the third guy could be in Mexico, and Gregory was dead.

But I wouldn't lose hope of proving Tyburn killed Gregory. My mind turned and turned, but it turned up nothing. From my desk, I pulled out the photos of Gregory's room and checked again for anything I might've missed.

# CHAPTER 28

I had just returned from listening to Forrest's wiretaps at the phone company. Even the most on-the-ball FBI agent would've fallen off his chair, asleep, listening to Abby gab to vendors and old ladies placing long-winded delivery orders. And there was Dexter, who spent more than his lunch breaks yakking to his girlfriend about the comic books he read for free. Abby had not talked to Tyburn once. He was either on to me, or they only talked at home.

"Chief, Miss Dixon is here," announced Mrs. Rheingold.

I pressed the intercom. "Send her in."

The door opened, and I stumbled, getting out of the chair. My nervous system hadn't yet adjusted to Dixie not being Trixie.

"Let me apologize, Chief Bucky. I had no right to—"

Jesus! An exact copy. Her face, her hair. "No—no need for that, Miss Dixon. Please, come in and have a seat. Your sister was murdered, and you've every right to know why. Her death should be investigated. At least to whatever degree possible."

"I can't tell you how much I appreciate your saying that."

"When you left yesterday, I didn't get your full name, so I made inquiries. It seems you're a lawyer with an office in San Francisco."

"My sister and I have a small practice."

"Another sister?"

"Charlotte. She's a year younger."

So Dixie wasn't married. I sure had that wrong.

"We do criminal defense for those unfortunates who get worked over by the system. Usually homosexuals and minorities."

I didn't understand exactly how that went, but rather than look stupid, I asked, "What can I do for you today?"

"I'd like you to come with me to Trixie's house."

No way did I want to spend another minute in that house. Too many gruesome memories. "Why?"

"You were there. I want you to show me what happened."

"I can tell you what happened. Jerry—"

Abruptly, she leaned over, her eyes pleading. I hoped she'd take my hand and put it somewhere soft.

"Please. It's important to me."

I knew what she wanted. Unfortunately, it wasn't a heartbeat monitor. She wanted to snoop around. "What are you hoping to find?"

She straightened her back and shut her eyes tight. She looked just like Trixie did when she lied and said Jerry thought we were making out.

"Look, Chief Bucky, I've hit a brick wall. Neither the troopers nor the sheriff will talk to me anymore. I've met with several of Trixie's friends. They all say she was a devoted wife with a peachy marriage."

"You want to search the house, don't you? Find something that will explain Trixie's murder. Because if that's it, I'm sure the place has been swept clean by people who don't miss the corners."

"I know it's a long shot." She pulled out a hankie from her purse and dabbed her eyes. Again, just like Trixie in the squad car, worrying about her husband not loving her anymore. Trixie had been faking. Maybe Dixie was, too.

"This will be my last chance to learn why Trixie was killed," she went on. "My father will arrive in the morning to pack up her things, and I want to be out of town by then."

"What about the funeral? And won't your other sister, Charlotte, be coming?"

"Father canceled it. He's taking Trixie's body back to Memphis for burial. That's where we're originally from."

"Isn't that a sudden change of plans?"

"Sudden, but not surprising. Look, are you going to help me, or not?"

❧❧❧

We pulled into Trixie's driveway, stopped, and I gripped my shotgun. It had saved my life the last time I'd been there. I turned to Dixie. "Are you okay?"

She closed her eyes and nodded rapidly. She let us in with a key she had somehow gotten, and I wondered from where.

As I suspected, the place had been cleaned up. We entered the living room, and Dixie glanced around. "Okay, tell me exactly what happened."

"Are you sure?"

"Don't leave anything out."

I told her every jaw-breaking, pistol-firing, blood-splattering, bear-toppling, table-shattering, shotgun-blasting detail. Including the neighbor's reaction when he arrived. About what the sheriff said, and what I said back.

She scribbled everything down on her legal pad with the coolness of a medical examiner doing an autopsy.

Finally, long after the time I had begun hoping she'd run out of questions, she flipped to a new page. "Let's look around."

She first checked out the Venetian blinds open enough to see the street. She then roamed over to the mantelpiece and stared at a crushed cigarette with lipstick traces in an ashtray. She picked it up and rolled it slowly between her fingers. She closed her eyes and sniffed its red tip. Finally, she put it back, gently as if returning a tiny corpse to its final resting place.

She sailed through each room of the house with me at her heels like a trusty spaniel. She paused to examine a chain on the pool table and Green Stamp booklets on the kitchen counter.

After jotting notes, she tossed her pad onto the dining room table. "Now down to business."

She headed for the bedroom to poke through drawers, paw through closets, feel around in coat pockets, and lift up mattresses—to find something that would explain Trixie's murder.

Or so I thought. She did none of that. All she did was look through Trixie's clothes. And she took a long time doing it.

Then she went to Jerry's office and eyeballed everything in his desk. I leaned against a file cabinet, bored stiff, but was glad the cabinet was locked so she couldn't rummage through it for hours. She slammed the bottom desk drawer shut.

Eager to leave, I said, "Well, I guess that's it."

"Not so fast." She opened the desk's top drawer, took out a key, and held it up. "Wanna bet what this is for?"

*Oh, man.* I checked my watch. *This could take all day.*

She unlocked the cabinet and pulled open a screeching drawer, yanked out a stack of folders, and sat on the floor with them.

Leaving her to it, I stuck my head in the closet and tapped walls.

"What are you doing?" she snapped. Probably because I wasn't searching like a seasoned pro.

"Nothing, just checking. You never know." I sat in Jerry's cushy chair, made a height adjustment, and did a little rocking. My chair should be so nice. Probably dated back to Chief Cowboy Wallis. The one he got stabbed to death in.

I'd been gazing at the closet and realized something was off. The inside was only about six feet wide. Yet, the outer wall was twice that distance. I went into the closet and tapped walls. Every tap sounded the same. I pushed on the end wall, and it didn't budge. Thumbed a card from my wallet and slid it under. A hidden chamber! I felt around for a switch or lever.

Dixie slammed the file cabinet closed. "Dammit! Nothing in there's worth anything."

I'd come out of the closet and was studying a portrait of Jerry on the outer closet wall. Elbow resting on a mantelpiece, cigarette dangling from his lips. Mr. Cool.

"Why are you staring at him?" she shouted.

"Hold on." I gripped the sides of the portrait and rotated it left and right, hoping to activate a switch that would open the secret chamber.

Nothing happened.

"That bastard!" Dixie yanked the portrait down and started to throw it on the floor when a gear-like churning sound came from inside the closet.

We stared at each other.

I poked my head inside as the wall finished pivoting. "Holy shit!"

A wee bit of light spilled into the chamber from the closet. Something red caught my eye at the far end. I reached in for a light switch.

*Click.* The chamber blazed with light.

"Unbelievable!" Dixie said, peering over my shoulder. "Look at this crap. A bastard and a racist."

On the back wall hung a red Ku-Klux-Klan flag, a poster, and several robes. Some fancy with ruffled cuffs, some plain white with peepholes. Probably worn for routine house torchings and hangings.

Whoever owned all these fancy things—decorative robes, belts, pearl-handled knifes—must be someone important in the Klan.

"I've got to write this stuff down," Dixie burst and dashed off.

I stuck around gaping. The chamber had everything a good Ku Klux Klan member would want: license plate frames, lanterns, historical pictures of Klan processions and marches, a sepia print of Civil War General Nathan Bedford Forrest that said *Our Father*.

Music sheets lay on the table—"The Klansmen's Rally Song"—a copy of the Klan's Constitution, and Klan recruitment posters like the one I saw in Sally's men's room.

When Dixie returned, I read to her a creepy card from a stack found near a film can that said *The Birth of a Nation*. "You've been visited by the Ku Klux Klan. This was a social call. Please don't make the next visit a business call."

She rolled her eyes.

"Maybe you'll like this better." I threw back a Confederate flag covering a three-drawer file cabinet.

Her eyes lit with excitement. "Do you have the key?" she asked breathlessly.

# CHAPTER 29

W hy didn't you tell me about the neighbor earlier?" I said, smacking the steering wheel. "This is not good. As a matter of fact, it's very bad." Dixie and I had just pulled away from Trixie's house.

"The man started out his front door and then turned around and went back in," Dixie said. "I thought he had forgotten something. I didn't know he was the neighbor you told me about."

"He must've seen us, and he'll know just who to tell. Believe me, we're going to be visited by very unfriendly troopers. They'll want everything we took from the house."

"Is the house outside your jurisdiction?"

"It's county, handled by the sheriff." I took a long slow breath and let it out silently. "That's all right. Sorry I snapped at you. We couldn't have done anything different, anyhow. At least we put the picture back and closed the wall."

"Maybe no one will know we were in the room."

"Let's hope the guy across the street didn't see us loading the car."

"We'd better work out a plan for handling the files."

"Oh, no," I said. "I'll work out a plan. You need to stay out of this."

"I don't think so. This was my idea. I have a right to those files."

"If it wasn't for me, we'd never have found the secret chamber."

"And if it wasn't for my sister, you'd be dead."

A nervous laugh escaped me. She had me on that one. "What do you want to do?"

"Drop me at my motel, and I'll read through every box."

"Are you kidding? That's the first place they'll check for you. Here's what we're going to do…"

❡❡❡

Dixie needed protection from the troopers. She also needed a safe place to read the files. If they held names, we were both in trouble. We could use Ham's place or Judge Thompson's office, but suppose one of them was a Klansman? Best to trust no one until we read the files.

I pulled up at the Holiday Inn. Dixie checked out and told them she was leaving town.

The most secure place I could think of for both Dixie and the files was in jail, and I happened to have one with a back entrance. If troopers raided the station, and I figured they would, a jail cell would be an unlikely place to search.

I phoned the station and talked to Sergeant Hazelwood. "Larry, who we got in lockup?"

"That peeping Tom kid. A woman IDd him a couple hours ago."

"Same kid as last time?"

"The one and only." He'd been caught a month earlier peeping through bathroom windows.

"Turn him loose. I mean, remand him to his parents." I hoped I'd used the right word.

"We can't. He's eighteen now."

"Do it anyway. And listen…" I glanced at Dixie sitting beside me. "I'm bringing someone into the jail through the back for protective custody. It's on the QT, so no one's to know. That includes troopers. I'll explain later."

∽∾∿

I entered the cell, holding two shopping bags I'd brought back from Tulsa. Dixie sat on a bunk, face drawn. She'd spent hours going over the files and hadn't touched the takeout meal Sergeant Hazelwood brought from Sally's.

"Well," I said, setting my bags down by her suitcase and pulling up a chair. "What have you learned?"

"Quite a bit." She picked up her chili and began eating. "In the hands of the FBI, this information would turn the entire town upside down. You could expect more than a dozen indictments and worldwide press coverage. Sacco and Vanzetti and the Scopes trial all rolled into one." She blew out and waved a hand by her mouth. "Phew! Even cold, this is darn good chili." She sipped from a cup of water.

"You'll have to try Sally's hotcakes in the morning."

She jutted her chin at the three cardboard boxes in front of her bunk. "The information was scattered, so I organized everything logically. This box—" She pointed. "—contains the minutes of secret meetings going back to the Oklahoma City Klan of the 1920s. At some point, a faction came here to Defiance. The second box has names of every Klan member within a hundred miles, again, starting back in the Oklahoma City days." She pulled out a sheet from the box. "Here's the most recent members."

I scanned the list. "Ah, shit, Dexter. I need to talk to that guy. Here's the barber's name." I slapped the list. "Not Hector! I worked with him. A nice guy." The next name gave me a sharp chill. "Larry Sparks! One of my officers." I blew out air. "Okay. What else you got?"

She kicked the third box. "This is the jewel of jewels. The names of murderers and their victims. As a bonus, it lays out in detail the methods of execution." She ticked off a sampling on her fingers. "Lynching, shooting, stabbing, dousing with hot tar, tearing to pieces by vicious dogs, and roasting on a skewer like a pig." She opened her notebook. "I've written a list of people whose crimes rank with those of the Nazis. They would kill—*kill*—to see these files go up in smoke."

I scanned the names.

"Fifty-six men from around here," she said. "Surely some are dead, but I'll bet many are still alive. You'll notice I've added their victims, and how they were murdered."

"Here's Overstreet. Not surprising. Bedford Forrest. He runs the phone company. He has the same name as the guy who started the Klan. I see your ex-brother-in-law, Jerry Hale made the list. No shock there. Gustafson. He'd racked up an impressive number of crimes. Councilman Farnsworth, publisher of the *Prairie Duster*." Some of the other names I recognized but had never met the people personally. "Interesting stuff, but I don't see that we're any closer to knowing why your sister was murdered."

"Maybe Trixie's marriage was on the rocks, and she threatened to get Jerry in trouble for having this crap. According to this—" She pulled out a sheet of paper from a box. "—Jerry was more than simply a Klan member."

*Grand Titans of the Dominion*, Jerry Hale and Bedford Forrest.

*Grand Dragon of the Realm*, Orville Overstreet.

"Wait a minute." I took the sheet. "I've heard of this grand dragon. The Klan is having an election to appoint a new one. A little Negro girl got beat up because she overheard men talking about it. Overstreet must be the current dragon, and since he's in prison, an election makes sense. The grand dragon must be like the president, and the grand titan vice-president. I see there's two VPs. At least there were two, until Jerry dropped out. Interesting, but it doesn't help us." I handed the paper back. "Sorry, Dixie. You tried. I'll drive you to the airport in the morning."

She leaned against the concrete wall beside the bunk and sighed then nudged with her toe one of the bags I'd brought. "What's this?"

"I bought you some things in Tulsa."

She peeked inside.

"I don't know if they'll fit, but it doesn't matter. If anybody asks, they were Trixie's clothes, and you're keeping them for sentimental reasons. I took off the tags. There's also a teddy bear. Tomorrow, first thing, we'll go to the post office and you'll mail them home."

"I don't get it."

"The troopers will want to know what we removed from Trixie's house. If they search your package before it's shipped, this is all they'll find. Call it an insurance policy."

"I'm not leaving until I know what Jerry's title of *Grand Titan of the Dominion* means. It might give us a clue why he killed Trixie. I know it's grasping at straws, but it's all we've got. Do you have any friends who might know?"

No point arguing with her. I glanced at my watch. It was awfully late to be calling on Ham. Wait a minute. "I

do know someone. Does the name Dusty show up anywhere?"

Dixie ran her finger down the membership list.

"While you're at it," I added, "check for the names
Judge Thompson and Larry Hazelwood." I really hoped
Sergeant Hazelwood was clean because he already knew
Dixie was here, and I would need him to offer cover.

# CHAPTER 30

I asked Dixie to wait in my car, while I dropped by Hazelwood's desk to tell him about the files and that Dixie would be sticking around. Because folks often listened in on party lines, I didn't dare use the phone. I also told him, "There's a good chance troopers may come looking for me. Tell them you don't know where I am. Above all, don't mention Dixie or the files. Not even to our own men."

"Be careful. If anyone in those files knows you have them, you'll become a target. Same for Miss Dixon."

To play it safe, we took my own car to Dusty's, leaving the cruiser at the station. To be doubly safe, I parked on the unmarked dirt road across from the Mayfair. The moon was just rising, giving us enough light to peek inside the barn. No limos.

We padded around to the front door. At night, the building appeared spooky enough to use in a horror movie. The door was locked, so I gave it seven hard raps. Shave and a haircut, six bits.

I peered through the peephole, and a blue light came on behind the counter. Soon the front door creaked open, and Dusty poked his muzzle out.

"Tarnation! Can't you leave me alone?" Dusty stood

in the dim moonlight smelling like a cigar factory, and without a cigar. Rat-faced and wearing a white gown and floppy cap, he looked like someone from the last century. He glanced at Dixie. "Who the hell's she?"

Dixie wedged between us and took Dusty's hand. "I'm Dixie, and I'm very happy to meet you, Dusty. May we come in?" Her voice took on the sound of a charming southern belle. Just like her late sister's.

Dusty's lips wiggled, but only grunts came out, as if he was trying to cough up a fur ball.

"We'll take that as a yes," I said, and Dixie and I slipped inside.

"N—Now, now hold on a s—second," Dusty sputtered.

I found a light switch by the front desk. "Let's all sit down," I said and pointed to a stuffed chair and loveseat so threadbare they should've been burnt.

Dixie hooked her arm through Dusty's and guided him to the chair. "Dusty, I'm in a jam and need your help."

She settled beside me on the loveseat, her knees together and covered by her checkered dress. Opening her purse, she snapped out a crisp one hundred dollar bill. She extended her arm to Dusty, the bill between two lovely slim fingers.

Dusty shifted awkwardly. He stared at the bill with eyes no longer squinting from sleep.

"Please, Dusty. Take it." She gave her fingers a little flutter.

Dusty smoothed his crusty mustache with his full-sized thumb. "Depends on what kind of help you're wantin'."

"Oh, for Christ's sake," I said and grabbed the bill. "Here." I thrust it into Dusty's hand. "It's nothing that's going to get you in trouble. Look, Trooper Jerry Hale murdered Dixie's sister. I'm sure you know all about it. Dixie wants to know why."

Dusty squinted. "What makes you think I'd know?"

In her perfect southern accent, Dixie said sweetly, "Well, you must have known he was in the Klan."

"I don't talk about the Klan."

Dixie's fingers dipped back into her purse, and out came another Ben Franklin. "Whatever you tell us is strictly confidential." She rose from her chair and slipped Benji into Dusty's pajama pocket.

"What do you want to know?"

She again dug into her purse, but this time pulled out a sheet of paper from the files and handed it to him. "I'm interested in knowing about the grand dragon of the realm and grand titan of the dominion."

Dusty's red-rimmed eyes slid over the page. He nodded. "The grand dragon of the realm is him who presides over the whole state. That's Orville Overstreet." He tapped the sheet. "Like it says here."

"Not likely," I corrected, "since he's in prison."

"That means the second officer, the grand titan of the dominion, moves up."

"But there's two names," I offered. "Bedford Forrest and Jerry Hale."

"Only one of 'em's goin' to be grand dragon. My bet's on the one who ain't dead."

I frowned. "But what if Jerry Hale wasn't dead?"

"That would depend."

"On what?" I asked.

"On how the Ghouls vote. Them's the Klan members."

"I see," Dixie said and settled back against the cushion. Nobody spoke for several long seconds, and then she asked, "What generally determines the election's outcome? Popularity?"

"It gets down to what they call purity. The purest one wins. Simple as that."

"Jesus! How the hell are we supposed to know what that means?" I blurted.

"It means the candidate with an impure mark against him loses."

Dixie's forehead wrinkled. "Suppose there was something about Jerry's wife that was considered impure. Would that work against him winning the election?"

"Knock him right out of the box."

Dixie nodded slowly. Very slowly.

☙❧

I led Dixie through the station's back entrance and into her guest quarters. She'd been quiet during the ride back from Dusty's, and although I had questions, she obviously wasn't in the mood to talk.

Back home, I discovered that I'd had visitors. It wasn't hard to guess who and how they got in. The crummy door lock wouldn't keep out a rat with a toothpick. A trooper's boot to the door did the trick. A move Sparks used at the Mayfair. My mind raced as I made my way through the clutter and scanned the empty drawers. Had they found anything linking me to the files?

The phone rang, and I picked it up. "Hello."

"It's Hazelwood, Chief. Troopers were here looking for you."

"Just like I figured. They were here too."

"They claimed that Trooper Hale's residence was a crime scene, and that items had been illegally removed. They searched the storage lockers and your office. Even your cruiser. They never went into the jail, so your prisoner's still safe for now."

"What else did they say?"

"That you'd hear from the captain, and they'd be back."

"Good. And if they show up again, here's what you're to tell them…"

ↄ౨ↄ౨

The next morning Dixie looked all freshened up in a blue dress and white scarf. We stopped at the post office where I sent off her new wardrobe, and she mailed a letter to her sister in San Francisco.

From there, we drove to Sally's and sat in a back booth. Dixie stirred her coffee and asked, "Do you think the troopers know about the existence of the files?"

I slurped my coffee. "Definitely. That's what they're after. They've already searched my place and the station, and might march through that door any minute. If they do, you're going to put on that southern charm of yours. Which reminds me—why is your natural voice so different than your twin sister's was? Except of course, when you slip into your southern belle act."

"It's a long story. What am I supposed to do with my southern charm?"

"You'll say, 'Ah jus' gathered up some of my sister's clothes that had sentimental value.' When they ask where they are, you'll tell them they wouldn't fit in your suitcase, so you mailed them, and they'll hightail it to the post office. The package won't go out until late afternoon."

"And that will end it, right?"

"Hell no, it won't end it. The troopers told my sergeant that I'd be hearing from the captain. And I wouldn't be surprised if they're at Trixie's right now prying up floorboards and sledge hammering walls. They'll tear that place to the ground if they have to."

Dixie inhaled deeply. "They'll find the hidden chamber."

"And the empty file cabinet."

Worry showed on her pale face. "What do we do?"

Jolene dropped by for our orders.

Dixie picked up the menu. "How's the soup here?"

Jolene waved her hand toward the other customers. "Just about everyone eats it. Someone should write a book. Omelets are also popular. If you like spicy, I suggest the cowpuncher."

"Sold," Dixie chimed.

"Sounds dangerous," I said. "Make it two."

Jolene left, and a familiar face slid in beside me. The trooper captain I met at the Mayfair. I forgot his name, or never knew it, but his nametag said Higgins.

"Neighborly of you to join us, Captain." I tried to sound casual.

He touched the brim of his hat to Dixie. "Good morning, Miss Dixon."

"Hello, Captain," she said coolly in her normal voice.

Dixie had told me that she'd seen the captain, and that he *inferred* that Trixie must've provoked Jerry into killing her.

"I heard you two were on a scavenger hunt yesterday," he said. "Tell me about it."

I turned around. Two troopers stood outside the door.

"You mean our stop at Trixie's?" Dixie said. "It was nothing, really. I just picked up some of my sister's things. Sentimental things. I'm sure you understand."

"How nice. Such as?"

"That's none of your concern, Captain. Especially since you've been rude to me throughout my entire stay."

"Well now, Miss Dixon." He straightened. A tower of a man. "I apologize if I've seemed rude, but I've answered your questions as best I can. Now I want you to answer mine."

I wondered if she knew how to prevent feeling intimidated by staring at his ear—or his dimpled chin.

"What *exactly* did you remove from the house?"

Dixie met the captain's cold gaze and held it. "All right. If you must know, clothes."

"What else?"

"A teddy bear. I—I gave it to my sister a long time ago."

"How long ago?"

"Now look—"

He smacked the table. Coffee cups tinkled in our saucers, and customers craned their necks to look. "Answer me!"

"Hold on!" I burst.

"I don't know," Dixie said with a casual chuckle. "Several years ago, I suppose."

The captain drummed his hairy fingers on the table, then his lips curved up into a thin smile. "Then tell me this, Miss Dixon, why does the teddy bear look brand new and have a price tag sticking out its butt?"

I had trouble breathing.

"Oh, for heaven's sake," Dixie countered, her eyes suddenly wet and gleaming. "It was meant for my sister's unborn child that she later miscarried. I hope you're satisfied."

The captain narrowed his eyes.

"It's obvious," she went on, brushing a tear from her cheek, "that you have rifled through the belongings I had intended to ship home. I trust you've repacked them and allowed the postal service to send them off."

The captain glared at her. A muscle quivered on one side of his jaw. Beaten, and he knew it, he muttered something that sounded like bitch, stood, and clomped off. The screen door banged behind him.

# CHAPTER 31

C an we go someplace quiet and talk?" Dixie asked. I pulled away from Sally's and turned toward Simpson Highway. "I know just the place." I picked up my mic and called Sergeant Hazelwood. "Larry, it's me. I see the troopers must've come to the station after I talked to you this morning."

"I told them you were at Sally's, like you said."

"I expect the captain will stay off our heels for a while. I'm taking Dixie over to Alsop's place to stretch her legs. I'll check back with you later."

Dixie flexed her back. "A walk sounds good. I'm used to mattresses with more thickness than a dime."

"See that sign up ahead, Alsop Plymouth Chrysler Motors?"

"Is that where you sold cars?"

I shot her a glance. "How'd you know?"

She smiled slyly. "You're not the only one to make inquiries."

I turned into the car lot. "There's a quiet stream behind the service building. A good place to talk."

Alsop stood by the food truck, wearing a sheepskin coat and holding a doughnut and cup of coffee. Damn, I missed working with the man.

I rolled down my window. "Hey, Cal, it's me, your old work slave. I'd like you to meet Miss Dixie Dixon."

Cal bent down to the window and ran his hand across his sugarcoated upper lip. "Pleased to meet you, Miss Dixon. I probably shouldn't tell you, but I've frazzled quite a few whips on your chauffeur."

"That hasn't seemed to hinder his driving abilities."

I asked, "How's my replacement working out?"

"He's committed to the car business." He winked. "Just like another young man who strutted into my showroom not so long ago."

"Miss Dixon's only in town a short while. If you don't mind, I'd like to show her the creek out back."

"Go on down and enjoy yourselves. It's too early for dogwood bloom, but you may see a few frogs."

We passed a mechanic taking a smoke break. He nodded, and I waved.

Dixie craned her neck to look back at him. "That man has a hook for a hand!"

"That's Hector. He's a Kluxer. A good mechanic, though, and I always thought him a nice guy too." Never trust appearances, I told myself and tried to recall if my Dale Carnegie book offered advice on how to judge the honesty of friendships.

We parked, strolled down to the stream, and crossed to the other side by stepping onto stones. I reached the bank, took Dixie's hand and helped her leap ashore.

She giggled and looked around. "This is so nice." She closed her eyes. "I love the smells and the quiet." She opened her eyes. "It feels like the world went *stop*."

"When we left Dusty last night, I had the feeling you'd figured out why Trixie was killed. Something about her being impure?"

Dixie pinched off a twig from a redbud tree and smelled it. "I'll start from the beginning. My father divorced my mother when Trixie and I were a year old. That's when our sister Charlotte was born. She came into this world wearing black skin."

"Wow!" I couldn't help it. "I'm sorry. I mean—nothing. Go on."

Dixie flashed a brief smile. "We were living in Memphis at the time, and my parents agreed that mother and Charlotte would move to San Francisco. Both my mother and father wanted us, the twins, to live with them, and neither would back down. Finally, after days of bickering, father took a coin from his pocket. 'Heads,' he said, 'and Dixie goes with you and Trixie stays here. Tails, you take Trixie and I keep Dixie.' Heads came up."

I held up a dogwood branch for Dixie to duck under. "Did you see much of Trixie over the years?"

"Never. My father wouldn't allow it. He couldn't forgive my mother."

"It must've been a bummer growing up. You know, knowing you had a twin but never getting to see her."

"We didn't know about each other. At least I didn't, and I'm pretty sure Trixie didn't either."

"Gosh. When did you find out?"

"Two days after she died."

A sick feeling washed over me. "You never even got to see your own twin?"

"Believe me." She sniffled. "It breaks my heart."

"In the house, I saw you press one of her dresses against your cheek. That's what gave me the idea to buy the clothes. How'd you know she called me Bucky Bucky?"

"The captain referred to you that way."

I thought a moment. "Trixie must've said that to Jerry, and he mentioned it to the captain. They probably had a good laugh. What about your father? Did you ever meet him?"

"Not that I remember. He canceled the funeral after learning Charlotte and Mother were coming."

"Geesh. Never got to know your own father."

"Mother showed me his picture just before my coming here. A snapshot taken the day Trixie and I were brought home from the hospital. It made me wonder if it was me in my father's arms."

We reached a fallen log across the path. "Want to sit and rest a while?"

"I'm enjoying the walk." She held my shoulder, and we climbed over. A salamander wriggled out from under the log and disappeared into the faded leaves.

I said, "You were going to tell me about Trixie and the Klan."

"Everything came together when Dusty said Jerry would lose the election if he was tainted with impurities."

"What impurities did he have?"

"A sister-in-law named Charlotte." She looked at me. "You see, Trixie might've learned about her from father and made the mistake of telling Jerry."

Dixie snapped off a soapberry leaf as we ducked under a branch.

I shook my head. "But she was only his half sister-in-law."

"Doesn't matter to the Klan. By killing Trixie, Jerry severed his connection to Charlotte." Dixie tossed the leaf into the stream, stood, and watched it float away. "Like Dusty said, the candidate with impurities gets knocked out of the box. I'm sure Jerry's vote-getting strategy was one the Ghouls appreciated."

It looked like Overstreet wasn't Jerry's higher calling after all. Instead, it was being Grand Dragon of the Realm. "Pretty damn awful. Don't you worry about the troopers. You'll be safe back home."

She stopped and took my hands, looked into my eyes and said, "Tell me what she was like."

"Wha—" I pulled my hands free. "Jeez. To be honest, I hardly knew her."

"But you spent time with her."

"Not that much. Let's see." I had to think. "One, two, three…four times. And they were all really short."

"That's four times more than me. Come on, tell me." She rose up on her toes, cheeks red with excitement. "*Please*. Her girlfriends only told me platitudes. 'Oh, she was *so* sweet.'"

"Well, once she—" I wiped my forehead.

"Come on, what?"

"Nothing. She was really a nice personable person."

"That's not what you were going to say."

I threw up my hands. "Okay, I'll say it. She kissed me."

Dixie's eyes shot wide. "Kissed you! What for?"

"Well, to tell you the truth, I told her she was beautiful."

Dixie giggled. "That's why she kissed you?"

"It's not like it sounds."

"However it sounds, I want to hear everything." Her eyes darted around. "Come on, let's sit up there." She pointed to a rock that stuck out over the stream.

We sat with our feet dangling over the water.

"Start at the beginning. The first time you two met."

I told her about Trixie's giddiness from champagne, and that it had spilled on her dress, and about the butler who washed and ironed it. And about how Trixie came bouncing into Mrs. Overstreet's dining room all bubbly, and that she had told Martin his son Tyburn was a dream.

I veered off track and told Dixie how I thought Tyburn had robbed the bank and killed Gregory at the Mayfair. And how afterward Tyburn hid under the bed.

I was about to describe the next time with Trixie when I suddenly had a weird feeling. "Why are you looking at me like that?"

She wrinkled her forehead. "What do you mean?"

"The way you're staring. It—it feels weird."

"How do you mean?"

I waved my hand. "Forget it. It's just me. The second time I saw her was in my squad car." I chewed my lip a moment, then shook my head and said, "I don't think you understand. Sitting beside you feels exactly like sitting beside Trixie. I've got to tell you, it's a little on the freaky side."

She nodded, her eyes soft. "I understand. Did she kiss you in the street or in your car or where?"

"In the car, but that's not the point!" My face felt hot.

She patted my knee gently. "It's all right. You two were in the car. Go on."

"Right. I asked her about Tyburn, and she said she saw him put his car in the garage, and later said hi to him in the house. The next time I saw her—"

"Wait a minute. What about the kiss? Does it make you nervous talking about it?"

"See?" I wagged my finger at her. "That's another thing. She pulled the same little trick you just did. Except with her, it was when I took her hand off my shotgun. She told me I had gentle hands, and then asked if her saying that made me nervous. Just like you did." My voice raised a notch. "You two talk the same—except for her accent—you look the same, and do everything the same." I turned away. After a few moments, I slanted her a glance. "One thing though, you don't smoke."

She smiled. "I appreciate you telling me this. I'm sorry it upsets you."

"Oh, forget it. I'm just—shh. Do you hear that?"

"Sounds like dogs."

I got to my feet. "They're getting closer."

She stood and pointed. "Look!"

"Uh-oh." My stomach made a hard thump. "I sense trouble."

"There they are!" shouted a man in overalls and a cowboy hat. Two German shepherds tugged the leash of their stiff-kneed handler.

# CHAPTER 32

If either of you move off that rock—" Rakoff tumbled over the log and then shuffled to his feet. "—I guarantee you won't get ten yards."

I whispered through the side of my mouth, "Stay still. Dogs like those tore out Chief Parker's throat. We're not going anywhere, Sheriff," I shouted.

Rakoff staggered to a halt and yanked out his gun. He put a hand on one knee and bent over. "Chief," he hollered, huffing like he'd just conquered Mount Everest, "lay your gun down on the rock."

The handler fought to hold the dogs. Barking and flinging saliva, like they'd been promised raw meat—and knew where to get it.

I placed my gun on the rock. "What's this about?"

"You know damn well what it's about," the sheriff snarled. "Get your asses over here."

We climbed down, and I said, "Suppose you tell me anyway."

"Grand theft. Both of you."

Dixie and I glanced at each other, then I said to Rakoff, "You're out of your mind."

"Cute hiding place you two came up with. Wedged in a cell bunk."

My stomach sank to my toes. "What are you talking about?"

"The item you stole from Trooper Hale's house."

"And what item was that?"

"You know damn well what. A thousand-dollar Mexican bearer bond."

ↂↂↂ

"Come right in folks and make yourself at home. Sorry you missed supper, but here at the Garfield County hotel, breakfast is served bright and early." Sheriff Rakoff's wiry eyebrows jiggled on a face hard as carved wood.

He swung the cell door closed with a clang that made Dixie and me flinch.

The county jail was in Enid, fifteen miles northwest of Defiance. Our shared cell had everything one would expect from a penal system. That is, one from the Middle Ages. Our bunks had straw pallets about as thick as a blanket. The blanket was made practically of thin air, and the open toilet had no seat.

I gripped the bars. "What do you want, Sheriff?"

His eyebrows bunched up and he frowned. "Want? I don't want anything."

"We know damn well this is a setup. One you'll regret."

"Talk like that can get you false teeth." He showed me his in a tight grin while he placed the cell key against his palm and bashed it against my fingers.

"Aagh!"

"Or broken bones."

Dixie gripped the bars. "You bastard! Go ahead, smash my fingers too."

Rakoff drew back his hand, and Dixie squeezed her eyes shut. When she opened them, he had sauntered off chuckling.

She came to me. "Are they broken?" she asked.

My fingers looked like claws. I wiggled them a fraction. "I hope not."

She padded to the sink and turned on the tap. "Here, run them under water."

I leaned my forearms on the basin, letting cool water splash over my fingers. "We're really screwed."

"How did they know where to find the files?"

"Sergeant Hazelwood's the only one who knew. He also knew we were at the stream."

"You shouldn't have told him."

"I always tell either him or Mrs. Rheingold where I'll be. But you're right. It was a mistake. They probably put a gun to his head."

"What's this about the Mexican bearer bond we're accused of stealing?"

"They must've planted it in our cell."

"We need a lawyer with a state license." She clutched the cell door and yelled, "Hey, Sheriff! We have a right to a phone call." She turned to me. "Do you know a good lawyer?"

I shook my head. "Tyburn had one, but I don't know his number."

She looked around. The three other cells were empty. "Why'd he put us in the same cell?"

"Because he's an asshole. Plus he needs room for the drunks. You'd better check your pillow for puke."

She threw the pillow onto the floor and herself onto the bunk. "Argh, I don't believe this!"

I tossed the towel into the corner and wondered if grand theft carried a more severe penalty than, say, bank robbery.

*ↄ⌒ↄ⌒ↄ*

Early the next morning, a deputy wheeled a cart up to our cell. Its wooden wheels thumped-thumped on the cold concrete floor. He was an old-timer with more white hair than George Washington's grandmother. "Glad to see everyone up and chipper," he drawled. The cell was hot and smelly. He swatted a fly off his face, a face that looked like a crumpled cigarette-pack. He ordered us to stand back, opened the cell door, and rolled in the cart.

I didn't sleep much, because the lights had stayed on all night, and not because we were afraid of the dark.

"Where's the sheriff?" Dixie demanded. "We have a right to a phone call."

"It's only seven o'clock. He'll stroll in about nine, maybe ten. Could even be eleven."

I took a tray from the cart. It held two bowls of burnt oatmeal and spoons. The deputy wheeled the cart out, locked up, and left.

"Listen," Dixie said, as I handed her a bowl. "I've got a plan to get us out of here."

I grabbed my bowl and shoveled a glob of oatmeal into my mouth. "Tastes like burnt rubber." I heaped in another spoonful. "What plan? Rakoff and the troopers are holding all the cards."

She smiled. "We've got better cards. Aces and eights."

"Is that right?" I sat on the bunk and pointed to her bowl. "Enjoy. With those cards, this will be your last meal."

She frowned. "I thought those were good cards."

"Not for Wild Bill Hickok. He was assassinated holding aces and eights. It's called the dead man's hand."

"Oh. I guess I got it mixed up. Never mind. Remember the notes I wrote on my pad?"

"What about them?"

She sniffed her oatmeal and put it down. "I sent them to Charlotte."

I jumped to my feet. "How'd you do that?"

"I included them with the letter I airmailed to her from the post office. They named fifty-six murderers and their victims."

I tossed my empty bowl in the sink and paced in a circle. "This is fantastic. They're going to have to let us go."

"We still need a lawyer."

A door opened down a hall, and footsteps approached. Sheriff Rakoff appeared from the shadows with an oily smile. "Y'all slept well, I trust."

Dixie gripped the bars. "I demand to make a call."

Rakoff brushed his fingertips across her fingers. "You can demand all you want, lady. But you'll make a phone call when I damn well say you'll make a phone call."

She dropped her hands and scowled. "You realize you're breaking the law."

"Don't worry your pretty white face about that. And if you don't start showing me respect, you won't see your visitor."

I started to reach for the bars, but dropped my hands. "What visitor?"

Rakoff flashed his shiny false teeth. "I'll fetch him." He disappeared toward the hall door.

It opened. "You've got ten minutes," Rakoff said. "But be careful, they're dangerous."

I whispered to Dixie, "It's probably Sergeant Hazelwood. He must feel lower than snake poop."

A middle-aged man in a black fedora approached the cell jiggling coins in his pocket. He had a nice haircut, a well-fitting suit, and the look of someone seeing a ghost.

Dixie gasped.

"Hello, Dixie," the man said, gathering his wits. He removed his hand from his pocket and his hat from his head. He fingered the brim nervously.

"Hello, Father," Dixie squeaked out.

*My God! Their eyes and facial structures are identical.*

Not a muscle moved in the man's face. "I'm in town to arrange the transport of Trixie's body back home for her funeral," he said finally. "I came here to be sure you're—well, to be sure you're still alive."

Dixie's head twitched. "Of course I'm alive. Why wouldn't I be?"

"Trixie's house burnt down, and I'm—"

"*What?*" Her head swiveled to me. I shrugged.

"Anyway," her father said, "I'm glad you're okay. I have to go." He turned.

"Wait," she yelled. "Do I look okay to you?"

He stopped, paused, and then turned around. "They said you stole something from the house."

"Maybe I did. What of it?"

"You're a lawyer. I'm sure you knew what you were doing." He turned and disappeared from sight.

Dixie gripped the bars. "I'm coming to Trixie's funeral, and you can't stop me," she shouted. "I'm going to tell everyone what an *asshole you are!*"

Her anger was shocking, though she had a lot to be angry about. His footsteps stopped then started up again. A steel door opened and closed.

Dixie went to the sink. She poured a cup of water, took it to the bunk, and sank back against the wall, her chest heaving.

I sat on the concrete floor and crossed my legs. Hard to imagine. Abandoning your own daughter. "If you want to cry or anything, it's okay."

She smiled faintly. "Thanks. You're a sweet man, Chief Bucky."

We stayed quiet with our own thoughts. From what Dixie's father had said, the troopers must've burnt down Trixie's house and found the hidden chamber with the empty metal cabinet. After threatening Sergeant Hazelwood, they took out the files from under the bunk and replaced them with a Mexican bond. Then they got the dogs and sheriff to track us down.

I stretched my legs out and leaned back against the bars. *We'll be out of here once we get that lawyer.* The door down the hall opened, and I scrambled to my feet. There were two sets of footsteps. Maybe Dixie's father had decided to be fatherly and had arranged for a hearing with Judge Thompson. A surprising, but familiar voice sang out. "On your feet, boys and girls. I'm bringing in a special guest."

# CHAPTER 33

The trooper captain approached the cell then turned around. "Come on, little girl," he called. "Don't be shy."

"I'm not shy, my shoe came off," tooted a brazen voice. A big, straight-backed Negro woman appeared with curly hair parted on one side. Her gold teardrop earrings dangled just above her slim shoulders, and her clacking mile-high heels matched her red skirt.

"Charlotte!" Dixie cried and flew off the bunk. "What are you doing here?"

Before Charlotte could answer, the captain, who stood with one hand behind his back, guffawed. "I just had to see this. Don't mind me, you girls go right ahead and get all slobbery."

"Oh, Dixie, baby." The two sisters hugged through the bars. "What are they doing to you?"

"Nice and sweet," the captain purred. "All that black-and-white love."

I snarled, "Why don't you shut the crap up?"

The captain sighed. "Such language. And in front of these lovely ladies." He laid an arm across Charlotte's wide shoulder. "I know you people have a lot of catching up to do, so I'll make my departure." He started off. "Oh, how stupid of me. I almost forgot." He held up an envelope that looked like something the dog got hold of. "The postmaster asked me to deliver this. It's addressed to you, Miss Charlotte. I'm sorry, but it fell victim to some newfangled sorting machine they're using at the post office, and its contents got all shredded to bits."

I flopped onto the bunk, head in my hands. *Aces and eights.*

☙❧

Charlotte went to the courthouse and met with Judge Thompson. She pleaded for an immediate preliminary hearing.

In the courtroom, three hours later, were Sheriff Rakoff, Dixie, and myself. Charlotte, unlicensed in the state to practice law, watched from the gallery.

The judge entered the courtroom without glancing at anyone. He had a hard, no-nonsense face that had learned to control its expression long ago. He scanned his desk as if searching for something. "Why don't I see a complaint, Sheriff? What's this about?"

The sheriff coughed in his fist. "With all due respect, your honor, City Attorney Lovelace has another twenty-four hours to—"

"Stop!" The judge raised his hand. "And you planned to have—" He pointed to Dixie. "What's your name, miss?"

"Dixie Dixon, Your Honor."

"You planned to have Miss Dixon and Chief Bucky sit in jail until Lovelace gets around to business?" He nodded and narrowed his eyes at the sheriff. "I know it's considered a small detail, but shouldn't you have allowed them a phone call?"

"Well, I—we—"

"Never mind. When you and Lovelace get your act together, come back. Until then, these people are to be released. Chief, I suggest you and Miss Dixon get a lawyer. Neither of you are to leave town. Next case."

℘ↄℰↄ

The Dixon sisters and I drifted out onto the courthouse steps. The last sunlight had faded from the horizon, turning the cloudless sky a pale violet.

Dixie looked up and down the street. "I'm famished. Where's a decent place to eat around here?"

Charlotte pointed to a Chinese restaurant across the street. "Let's go there. I'd rather not eat off a crate in some redneck kitchen."

I understood Charlotte's point. Restaurants in Defiance weren't integrated like they were in California, and contrary to Charlotte's expectation, even those owned by Chinese. She'd have to enter through the rear and enjoy her chop suey by the slop bucket.

"I have another idea," I said. "I'll order takeout while you two read the gravestone near the sidewalk." I pointed to the lawn in front of the courthouse. "Then we'll check you into a motel and eat there."

Charlotte's face clouded with confusion. "Did you say gravestone?"

"Sure. Beneath it is a brand new car buried last month in celebration of the state's fiftieth birthday. They'll dig it up in fifty years." Proudly, I added, "I was the official photographer."

℘ↄℰↄ

The Holiday Inn was full due to a rodeo in nearby Enid, so I drove the girls to Ben's Beds and Breakfast, just down the street. I took the long way, checking in my mirror to be sure I wasn't being followed.

Ben placed a key on the guest register and turned the book to face Dixie. "There's only one room available," he said and brushed a greasy strand of hair off his forehead. One of those guys trying to fake a full crop with hair swept ear to ear and greased against his dome.

He pointed to Charlotte, standing off to the side, flipping through a fishing magazine. "Drop her off on East Church Street where she'll find a Negro hotel and a liquor store."

Charlotte's eyebrows arched. She placed her magazine on the rack and leisurely approached the counter. A head taller than the little man, she gave him a big broad Pepsodent smile. "Have you ever heard of the NAACP, sir?"

Ben tried to smirk, but it looked like something got stuck beneath his denture.

"I didn't think so. How about that famous court case, *Brown versus The Board of Education?* Now you've surely heard about that. It was in the news not long ago."

Ben gave a condescending shrug, like it kind of rang a bell.

"Of course you have. The Supreme Court ordered the integration of all—that is *all*—public schools. I'm a lawyer, and I'm going to teach you something few white folks around here know. Buried in among all the itty-bitty fine print of that famous case, it says motels in said contiguous and non-contiguous states must adhere to the aforementioned order. What all that mumbo jumbo means is that you have to rent a room to me or go to jail and pay a five-hundred-dollar fine. Now, I see on the wall it says all rooms ten dollars. My sister and I will pay you twenty dollars for this room." She picked up the key and wagged it before his face. "You can consider yourself five hundred-twenty dollars and one jail stay ahead." She turned to me. "Chief, would you be so kind as to bring along our bags?"

Once settled in the room, Charlotte said to Dixie, "What was in the envelope you were going to send me that got *accidently* shredded?"

"It was a list of local Ku-Klux-Klan members that we found, and I wanted you to hold it for safe keeping. Can you believe that the Klan still exists around here?"

"Lucky me," Charlotte said with a broad grin. "Maybe I'll get to meet one."

A shiver shot through me. I wished Charlotte hadn't come. With all that was going on, no telling what danger she was in. "Sorry, Charlotte, not this trip. Let's eat."

While we dug into hot Chinese food and cold beer, Dixie told Charlotte about the last few days' events, including the fun-filled visit with her father.

Charlotte dumped a packet of soy sauce into a carton of chow mein and fluffed it up with chopsticks. "The judge didn't seem keen on the sheriff. I'm sure he'll allow bail at your hearing."

"Or simply dismiss the case," Dixie added. "Charlotte neglected to mention that possibility."

"Would've if you'd waited half a second."

I kept trying to get fried rice into my mouth with chopsticks, but could only manage two or three measly grains. "How come you two are so good with chopsticks?" I reached into a paper bag for a fork.

Charlotte clicked her chopsticks together. "Chinatown. We live there."

I retrieved a handful of spoons from the bag.

Dixie scooted a carton over to me with her chopsticks. "Try the hot and sour soup."

"Then again," Charlotte said, chopsticks hovering before her full red lips and supporting a tantalizing heap of fried rice, "if your case goes to trial, you'll need a good ol' boy lawyer that can connect with the jury."

"Charlotte!" Dixie snapped, "You're awful. There's no reason in hell for this case to go to trial. We were set up only to intimidate Chief Bucky into leaving office. We'll make sure that's brought out at the hearing."

Charlotte brushed some crumbs off her red skirt. "Let me tell you something, Chief. To you, I probably don't seem very smart, but I've read more than just picture books, so I know all about southern white boys with guns and badges—" She gave me a stern up-and-down look. "—who don't cotton to anyone messing with their way of life. White or black. And if someone does, they try to make sure of two things. First, that the person pays a severe penalty, and second, that penalty serves as an example to others thinking of performing the same deed."

I slurped a spoonful of soup. My Dale Carnegie book said that the only way to get the best of an argument was to avoid it. If I had avoided Dixie's request to investigate Trixie's murder, I'd be solving the Gregory murder case, and not be in this fix.

Charlotte hadn't finished. "Chief, here's something you don't have to be a nuclear physicist, or even wide-awake, to understand." She jabbed her chopsticks into another box. "If a complaint is filed, you'll have a couple of stiff counts against you, and you can say bye-bye to your gun and badge. At least until you're cleared." She dropped a morsel from her chopsticks onto her tongue and grinned. "That is, *if* you're cleared."

I pushed away my soup and picked up a beer. "I don't find that particularly funny."

"Sure you don't. That's what makes it funny."

Dixie stood. "Playtime's over, Charlotte. We need to get to work. We've less than twenty-four hours to convince Lovelace not to file charges. I'm going to draw up a plan." She reached for her notepad.

"Failing that," Charlotte said, "we'll have to hire a lawyer with an Oklahoma license. And he better be goddamn good, or Bucky's going to lose his star, and I'm going to lose a law partner. I'll start making calls."

And while they're making plans and calls, I'd go see Overstreet. The one man who could assure that Charlotte didn't lose her law partner.

# CHAPTER 34

At five-fifteen I pulled up to the gate of the McAlester State Penitentiary and flashed the guard my identification.

"You've been expected, Chief Bucky. Please park in a visitor's slot, and someone will take you to see Warden Palmer."

Inside, I handed over my gun and was given three pages of rules to read and sign. Frankly, the place gave me the creeps. Gun towers, barbed wire, gray walls, the clanking sound of metal doors. I scrawled my name on the last page, and an officer led me down a hallway, up a staircase and to a door that said *WARDEN*. He knocked once, opened the door, and nodded for me to go in.

A man about fifty with a buzz cut and sleeveless sweater over a shirt and tie sprang from his chair and charged from around his desk with a big hand and a bigger smile. "Chief Bucky, so glad to meet you." We shook hands. "Please, have a seat."

We sat in comfortable chairs around a coffee table. The room had lots of built-in bookcases and pictures of important looking men. A knock came at the door.

"Come in," the warden said and got up. A man in a blue shirt and matching trousers brought an ice bucket into the room. "Put it on the table," the warden said and opened a desk drawer.

The trusty, I assumed that's who he was, laid the bucket down, gave me a quick on-and-off smile, and left. The warden put a bottle of whiskey and two glasses on the table. "I was pleased to receive your call," he said. "But before I bring in Mr. Overstreet, we need to talk."

I swallowed. *Bring in?* I had to talk with Overstreet, privately. "Um, okay. What about?"

He poured our drinks, raised his glass as if offering a toast, and downed a long slug. "Tell me, Chief, just between us, what's Overstreet got on the governor?"

"Huh?" I squirmed in my chair. "I don't follow."

"Come on. You're the only one not on Overstreet's payroll who knows the score."

"The score?"

"You pointed the finger at him. That's what got him in here."

"I pointed my finger at a murderer who happened to be connected with Overstreet and a bunch of other crooks. You have his records. What is it they don't tell you?"

"They don't tell me why the governor is kissing his ass."

I sipped my whiskey, still worrying about how I was going to see Overstreet alone. "How do you mean?"

"I've got five hundred sixty-six inmates, and Overstreet's the only one with a private cell—if you could call it that—his own menu, and unlimited visitation privileges. Now, I'd goddamn like to know why?" He gulped his drink.

"Excuse my saying this, but as warden, weren't those your decisions?"

"They were assuredly not! My marching orders come from the head of the department of corrections, and theirs from the governor. They arrive without explanations."

"I'm sorry, but I have no idea what Overstreet has on the governor." *Except that he happens to operate the governor's private sex resort, called the Mayfair Hotel, and he holds more secrets about the governor than J. Edgar Hoover.*

The warden glared at me down his nose. If I was to see Overstreet, I had to give him something.

"Okay, I will tell you this," I said and refilled his glass. "Can I count on your confidence one hundred percent?"

"Absolutely." He sipped his fresh drink.

"I was sent here by the governor himself."

The warden flew back against his chair. "That son of a bitch!" He sprang forward. "Why?"

"Let me ask you something: have you done anything to upset Overstreet? Taken away privileges, overcooked his steaks. Anything like that?"

"Jesus Christ! Is that what the governor thinks?"

I held my glass and stirred an ice cube with my finger. "He didn't say."

"Then what the hell did he say?"

I sucked air between my teeth. "The governor doesn't come right out and say a lot." I leaned in close. "But I think he's worried about you."

"Me!" His face turned red, and I expected fire to shoot from his eyes. "You'd better start making sense, and fast."

"Don't you see? Overstreet's got something on the governor, and the governor wants him to know he's doing everything he can to make his stay, you know, as pleasant as possible. I'm to pass along that message to your prisoner."

The warden sat back. "Humph. Why the hell'd he send you? Overstreet's got people coming and going every damn day. His wife, his lawyers. For God sake, even his butler."

"The governor didn't tell me." I tossed down the rest of my drink and stood. "Now, if someone could take me to the prisoner, I'll get out of your hair."

⌘

The same guard who escorted me to the warden led me out of the building and through an archway into another structure and up a staircase. A big red arrow on the wall, pointing right said, *Cellblock C.* The guard pointed left.

"The door at the end is Mr. Overstreet's. He prefers that you knock."

I paced to the door, halfway hoping to find a *Do Not Disturb* sign on it. *What if he grabs me by the throat, or tries to stab me with a shiv he may have made. After all, he is in prison—and I put him there.* I heard a football game coming from a radio and gave two light taps. Maybe he'd fallen asleep.

"It's unlocked, Bucky."

My God! He knew I was coming. I swallowed, took a deep breath, and opened the door. Overstreet reached across his dinner table and turned off the radio.

"A football fan, huh?" So far he hadn't gone for a weapon.

He got up and tossed his cloth napkin onto his supper plate that wasn't quite empty of something that smelled good. "One of my many diversions," he said.

I scanned the room. Wasn't much smaller than my own place. "You really should have a TV," I said, trying to sound causal, as I trekked past him to the window.

"If I wanted a TV, I'd have one."

"Nice view of the play yard."

"One you'll be spending time in, once Lovelace finishes with you."

I turned to face him. "That depends on you, doesn't it?"

"You here to try and make a deal?"

I'd continue with the casual approach. "You've read my mind."

He opened a small fridge. "Care for a beer?"

"If you're having one."

"I don't drink anymore. They're for guests." He pulled out two Cokes, opened them, and handed me one. "Have a seat on the couch." He sat in a cushioned rocker beside a large file cabinet with a checkerboard on top. "What do you propose?" he asked. "Because if it concerns bonds or bank robberies, those matters have been dealt with. Even if you were to welch on your agreement."

"Nothing like that. I want you to tell Lovelace to drop the false charges against Miss Dixon."

He chugged some Coke and burped silently. "Now why would I want to do a silly thing like that?"

"Because she plans to stir up a bee's nest, and you'll get stung. She knows those Klan files inside and out. And believe me, she'll love nothing better than to write letters and get folks riled up. Including the authorities. On the other hand, if Lovelace drops the charges, she goes home to San Francisco, and all's forgotten."

"What's in it for you?"

"She's had it hard. Her sister's been murdered, and I'd like to see her stay out of prison and keep her law license."

"Just one problem. I don't give a rat's ass about her staying out of prison, or losing her license."

"It would be very unpleasant for you."

He got to his feet and glared at me. *Uh-oh! Watch his*

*hands. There's a knife on the table.* He reached over and turned the radio back on. "Take your Coke and get out of here. And remember this, the fellas in the yard are going to enjoy having you around. I guarantee it."

# CHAPTER 35

The headline read *Police Chief Robs Home and Sets Fire!*

I gulped, and cereal milk ran from my mouth into my nose.

*The sheriff's department has charged Police Chief Bucky Ontario and out-of-towner, Miss Dixie Dixon, with arson and grand theft. After burglarizing a residence late Sunday, they returned early the following morning and burned the house to the ground. Sheriff Rakoff said the case is still under investigation. He would not speculate as to the motives of the accused, but did say that they, and their "negra" lawyer, met before Judge Thompson.*

*A search committee will begin interviewing for a new police chief—*

The phone rang, and I grabbed it. "Hello!"

"Chief, it's me, Charlotte. You didn't tell me you played with matches."

"Just found out myself. What about that lawyer?"

"Negative, so far."

"Unless Dixie dreamed up a brilliant plan that clears us of grand theft, and now arson, we need a goddamn lawyer—now!"

"Don't get your pants on fire, I'm working on it."

"This is no time to be cute, Charlotte."

"Simmer down. I've made a list of the six top criminal lawyers in the state. Three in Tulsa, and three in Oklahoma City. I called those in Tulsa, and none of them will touch the case."

"Why the hell not?"

"In so many words, it would be their last case, and they were too young to retire."

"Because all this involves the Klan?"

"You said it, not me."

"Okay, call the others in The City."

"And get the same answer? I don't think so. I'm going down there and meet with them. I've already made appointments without giving details."

But would a Negro—a Negro woman—be the most effective person in the world to do that?

"I know what you're thinking, Chief. First of all, neither you nor Dixie is allowed to leave town. Second, I'm all you've got. Deal with it."

"But—"

"Chief, it's Dixie. Charlotte's leaving now."

"You were going to work on convincing Lovelace not to file charges."

"I have been. I'm writing down as many names of murderers and victims as I can recall."

"You must have a good memory."

"I do. Charlotte can tell you stories. My idea is that we deal a new hand."

"Yours better have four aces this time."

"Only three. But they spell F—B—I."

"That's a laugh. Fat chance of *them* doing anything."

"You mean slim chance."

"Either way, the FBI doesn't admit there's a Mafia, much less the Klan."

"Things are changing. There's a Negro preacher named Dr. Martin Luther King who's a real spitfire. He just addressed a huge crowd in DC about civil rights."

"Yeah. And?"

"And people are taking notice. Even the president has spoken out. The talk in Washington is that Eisenhower will get Hoover moving on this civil rights thing."

"What's that have to do with the Klan?"

"Nothing. But hangings do. The ACLU and others are saying that killing Negros is a violation of their civil rights. That means these redneck states had better look out."

"Going to the FBI is dangerous. Our trooper friends will know you've got information in your head. They may want to relieve you of it, and I'm not talking about information."

"This is bigger than just you and me, Bucky. Think of it, a movement like this will be the greatest thing for Negros since reconstruction."

"I suppose. But what other ideas do you have?"

"None for now. Though we could play their game and simply admit to taking the Mexican bearer bond. I'd say it belonged to Trixie. They couldn't very well then accuse me of stealing it."

"They'd line up ten of Jerry's trooper pals to testify that the bond belonged to him before marriage."

"Frankly," she said, "on the face of it, their case is weak. But if it goes to trial, Lovelace will play to the jury's prejudices against outsiders. Including those from California *and* Louisiana."

"That's why we need a really good lawyer."

"Charlotte will find one. Like she said, a good ol' boy."

❧❦❧

I dumped my soggy golden Os into the garbage pail and drove to the station to face my officers and staff. I would've loved to tell them that the paper's editor, Councilman Farnsworth, was not only a certified Kluxer, but also one with notches in his rope. *I'd better have a lawyer before I go shooting off my mouth.*

"Good morning, Chief," Mrs. Rheingold said mournfully as I came through the door.

"Don't believe any of it." I breezed by her and into my office. "They're all lies."

I closed the door, dropped into my chair, and did some rocking. Was there anything I could do to save my job and keep Dixie and myself out of prison? I couldn't think of anything.

Sergeant Hazelwood opened the door with a soft knock, started to enter, then stopped.

"Come in, Larry."

He shuffled in as gravely as a man going to his own funeral. "Chief, I understand if you feel like putting me before a firing squad, and without the customary last cigarette." He leaned on his cane with downcast eyes.

I jumped from my desk and took the sergeant by the shoulders. "Hey, look at me."

Hazelwood raised his eyes.

"You did the only thing you could, anything else would've been suicide. Betty would be a widow, and I'd be out a first sergeant."

Hazelwood inhaled deeply. "Thanks, Chief."

I circled back to my desk. "For the record, you'd have gotten the cigarette. Have a seat. We need to talk about something."

Hazelwood hooked his cane on the desk and sat. "About your house torching escapade?" he said, with a lazy smile.

"Can you believe those fucking troopers? I swear

they're all Kluxers. Did you know Sparks is mixed up with that bunch?"

Hazelwood shifted in his chair. "Yeah, I knew."

"Jesus Christ, that's no good. Where I come from, cops hung Negros all the time. Graft and corruption up the yin yang. We're not like that."

"You could talk to him. But I know what he'll say."

"Deny it?"

"He's too smart for that. He'll admit it and say he was young and stupid. Happens a lot."

I thought of Dexter from Gustafson's. "Has Sparks ever done anything that made you suspicious?"

"Nothing with the Klan—but—" Hazelwood gazed at his shoeshine.

"Come on, out with it. What?"

"I suspected once that he'd planted false evidence. Well, not suspected, I knew."

Knew it, and the guy's still on the force! "Go on."

"He denied it. And if I hadn't actually seen him do it, I'd have believed him. He's a convincing liar."

Maybe from all those years hanging around Tyburn. "What did he plant?"

"This happened years ago when Sparks first got on the force. Smiley had accused Tyburn of shooting a BB gun through his barbershop window. Tyburn said he didn't own a BB gun and accused Sparks of doing it. But a witness was ready to testify that he saw Tyburn do the shooting. The witness later recanted, saying he wasn't sure. Tyburn's daddy had paid him off, and the whole matter was dropped.

"But not for Sparks, I take it."

"Told me he wanted to search Tyburn's car for the BB gun, and that I should come along. It was a Wednesday, Tyburn's bowling night. We took Sparks's squad car and parked behind Tyburn's car in the bowling alley lot.

Sparks pulled out a coat hanger to open Tyburn's car with, then asked me to make sure he was in the bowling alley, to know we had the right car. When I reached the door, I saw Tyburn through the glass and turned around to see that Sparks had already opened Tyburn's car door. He took a BB gun from his trunk and tossed it into Tyburn's backseat. When I confronted him, he denied it so convincingly that I questioned my own eyes."

"Then what happened?"

"We drove off, leaving the gun in Tyburn's car, and neither Sparks nor I spoke of it again. I heard later that Tyburn had the last laugh by screwing Sparks's girlfriend and bragging about it."

Mrs. Rheingold buzzed. "Chief, there's a call for Sergeant Hazelwood. It's his wife."

I gestured to the phone. "You wanna…"

Hazelwood nodded, and I pressed the intercom. "He'll take it here."

"Hello, dear. Yes, everything's fine, just like you said." Hazelwood winked at me. "What? When?…I'll let him know." He hung up with a pained expression. "The city council is in special session. And it's about you."

# CHAPTER 36

I hit the courthouse stairs like a bounding gazelle and flung open the door just as Councilman Farnsworth flung out the word fire. Had he said, "Set fire," or was he about to say, "Fire him?"

Farnsworth stared at me and pointed. "You! You're out of line barging in here."

I caught my breath while my gaze slid across the musty room. It was technically a jury room that the council used for their meetings. No pictures adorned the walls, as if a jury shouldn't be distracted from horrible crimes by pretty sights. Of the five councilmen, only Farnsworth, the *Prairie Duster* editor, had made the Klan list. Lamar Fromm, who'd no doubt been torn away from burial duty, would vote with Farnsworth.

In my corner were Alsop and Doc Carrington, or so I hoped. The swing vote would come from secretary and City Manager Benjamin Horning. The council hadn't yet replaced Maynard Johnston and Gus Gustafson, both off playing checkers with Overstreet back at McAlester.

Farnsworth sat stuffed in his chair, bouncing his fingertips together. His haggard cheeks emphasized thumb-sized shadows under his eyes.

With a stiff finger jab, I blasted back. "*You're* out of

line, Councilman, if you're making judgments about the false charges against me."

"Now, Chief Bucky," Horning cut in. "No point getting hot under the collar."

My neck was already hot. "I think it's important that the council know the facts. Facts contrary to what Councilman Farnsworth's newspaper published."

"You'll get a fair hearing when the time comes." Fromm offered, admiring his outstretched fingernails.

Horning nodded. "Sheriff Rakoff has filed serious charges against you. We can't very well ignore them, now can we?"

"Those charges are bull."

"We all fervently hope it's *bull*," Fromm piped up, "but we find it prudent to relieve you of your duties until this matter is settled."

"Suspended, huh?" I said, trying to hold my temper.

Farnsworth smirked. "Only until you're cleared, of course."

"Was the vote unanimous?"

"We haven't voted yet," Alsop said.

A spark of hope. If Alsop could be convinced to postpone the suspension, Doc Carrington and Horning would probably agree. The majority vote would save me—for the time being.

"City Attorney Lovelace hasn't filed a complaint yet," I said, "and I'm sure he won't after I meet with him and lay out the facts."

I had to play Dixie's hand. But at a different table. *Her list has to get to Lovelace, the complaint dropped, and then it goes to the FBI.*

Horning scratched his temple with his pen. "You keep mentioning facts."

"That's right. Miss Dixie Dixon and I took from her late sister's house a Mexican bearer bond. It belonged to her sister, and since anyone could claim ownership, she wanted to be sure it stayed safe with the estate."

Farnsworth's butt rose six inches off his chair. "That's no fact! I've been told on high authority that the bond belonged to the husband before marrying Mrs. Hale."

"Your high authority is wrong, Councilman. Dead wrong. Miss Dixon is, right now as we speak, getting proof from her father that the bond indeed belonged to her sister." Since I was making up my own facts, I'd throw in another. "As for the matter of Miss Dixon or me burning down her sister's house, I have proof of our whereabouts at the time of the fire."

Doc Carrington's eyes twinkled. "And where, pray tell, were you two during those wee hours of the morning?"

"In separate places," I shot back. I was about to defend Dixie's honor when Alsop shook his head slowly, as if counseling silence.

"I think we've heard enough, Chief Bucky," Alsop said. "Please step outside, and we'll let you know our decision shortly."

I rushed downstairs to a phone booth to call Dixie. "Do you have the list ready?"

"I recalled forty-eight of the fifty-six murderers, and thirty-two of their victims. When Charlotte returns, she'll take the list to the FBI in Oklahoma City."

"New game plan," I said. "We're taking them to Lovelace." Something cold struck me like ice down the back of my neck. "I hope Lovelace wasn't on the Kluxer list."

"He wasn't. But he could tip people off. This has to be handled by the FBI. We can't only think of ourselves. This is bigger than just us."

"The FBI can wait. If we don't get Lovelace to drop

this thing, Charlotte will need a new partner, and I'll be playing hide-and-seek on McAlister's playground."

A deputy knocked on the phone booth. "They're ready for you, Chief."

I nodded. "I've got to go," I told Dixie. "Sit tight. I'll be there in twenty minutes."

I flew up the stairs two at a time, my footsteps echoing off the tall walls. I skidded to a stop at the door. Pausing a moment to catch my breath and check my curl, I entered a room of stone silence. Farnsworth had both chins down and peered at his interlocked fingers across a gut that drooped over his belt. Doc Carrington sat pleasantly surveying ceiling tiles, and maybe humming a tune.

Alsop pointed to an empty chair thoughtfully placed about ten feet in front of the table. I ran my palms along the seams of my slacks and eased into the chair. A schoolboy about to be suspended for playing with matches.

"I'm afraid, Chief," Alsop began in a doomful tone, "that we cannot ignore the allegations leveled against you. We must set our personal feelings aside and faithfully carry out our responsibilities. You are therefore ordered to turn in your gun and badge at nine a.m. tomorrow, at which time you will start your suspension without pay. That is all."

☙❧

Ironically, a small wave of relief rolled over me as I left the council meeting. The suspension's postponement bought me time to convince Lovelace not to file charges. Even if the charges proved false, suspension would hurt my future career chances.

I knocked on Dixie's motel room door.

She opened it and smiled. "I see you're still wearing your handsome uniform."

"For a few more hours, at least." I stepped inside and my eyes searched the table. "Where's the list?"

She closed the door. "Don't worry, it's safe."

"Fine, bring it along, and let's go see Lovelace."

"What about, you know, me losing my head because of the information in it?"

"Yeah, well, since you're going to the FBI anyway, I guess it doesn't matter."

"You're right, it doesn't. But I'm not leaving. I've got things to do here."

I scanned the room. "What things?"

# CHAPTER 37

Dixie pointed to a stack of letters on her desk. "Community organizing. San Francisco's the perfect city to get behind Dr. King's civil protest. I've got more letters to write and—"

I threw my hat on the floor. "Don't you understand?" I tapped my watch. "We need to get the list to Lovelace before he files the complaint." I took her hand and picked up my hat. "Come on."

Dixie yanked free and folded her arms tightly across her chest. "I told you I'm not going. And I'm not giving you the list."

"You know something?" I said through clenched teeth. "Trixie could be on the irrational side now and then, and I see that same trait in you."

"I'm being very rational, and Trixie probably was too. If we give the list to Lovelace, there's no way he'll investigate. He'll ask our favorite trooper captain if he knows anything about this *Klan thing*. Or maybe he'll kick it around with the sheriff. That's sure to get results."

"It doesn't matter. The list will prove to Lovelace we're being framed. After that, go ahead and give it to the FBI, the KGB, anyone you want."

"That'll be too late. Those on the list, at least those

still alive, will have circled the wagons and covered their tracks. The feds have to be the ones to investigate, and they'll fail if Lovelace poisons the well."

"So you're willing to go to trial and trust Charlotte's lawyer—if she's gotten one—to get us off?"

"Like I said, this civil rights movement is bigger than all of us. If being a part of it means taking risks, so be it."

"Even if you lose your law license?"

She nodded.

∽∾∽

I pulled up and parked smack in front of the three-story city hall. Fifty years ago, it was a single-story structure, but as the town grew, so did the building. I trotted inside and spotted a white-haired Negro janitor kneeling beside a mop bucket outside the men's room. He appeared old enough to predate the original tile floor he was scrubbing.

"Say, where's the city attorney's office?" I asked.

The man glanced up. Lots of turkey skin under his chin. "Well, I'll be," he said with a nice easy smile and stumbled to his feet. He took my hand and shook it like he was pumping for water. "I'm proud to make your acquaintance, Chief Bucky. You're a good man."

I blinked. "Do we know each other?"

"I know you. Our new police chief with enough gumption to stand up against the Klan. I'll tell ya somethin'." His eyes checked around. "It was a blessed day for us folks when we read about you burning down that Kluxer's house." He took my elbow and leaned in. "I can give you a few more addresses if y'all want 'em." The old guy slapped his worn-out knee with a laugh that came easy and probably often.

I had to chuckle. "I'm afraid to disappoint you, Mister…"

"Folks call me Cleve. Real name's Cleveland. Don't use the last name much."

"Like I was going to say, Cleve, I didn't burn down the house, but you should keep your eye on this Dr. King fella. He's the man you want to get behind. Now if you could be so kind as to direct me—"

"Top of the stairs, to the right." He again leaned in close. "He's is a strange bird, you know."

"Oh?" I slanted a glance both ways. "How do you mean?"

"He don't allow no smokin' in his office. You want to do that, you go visit the mayor up there in the corner office. Cross ventilation."

I mounted the stairs, wishing I had time to pop in and say hello to the mayor. Take a peek at my future office with cross ventilation. That was, my maybe future office. What was Lovelace's first name? I forgot. Might be good to use it. Sound friendly. Reason with him, man to man. Maybe he'd have a nameplate on his desk.

Lovelace's secretary welcomed me into her outer office. "Good afternoon, Chief Bucky."

It felt weird being recognized all over the place by people I'd never met. She had pale skin and a dusting of freckles. Her shiny blonde hair waved down to her bony shoulders.

"You're Miss…"

She grinned, raised her ring finger and gave a wiggle. With some squinting, I recognized a wedding band with a diamond stuck to it. I'd seen better diamonds on playing cards. Her husband probably picked it up from Smiley, who operated a small pawnshop out of his two-chair barbershop. Somebody probably pawned the ring for a haircut.

"It's Mrs., as in Mrs. Roger Montgomery." She giggled and pressed both fists to her chest. "Isn't that a perfect name?"

"It sounds…um…sophisticated." I pointed to an open door. "The boss in?"

"I'm afraid not. Do you have an appointment?"

"Not exactly. When do you expect him?"

"Any minute. He had to run over to the courthouse. You can wait if you like."

I nodded. Was I too late? My heartbeat forced its way up into my temples. "Do you happen to know the nature of his courthouse visit?"

"He doesn't tell me those things."

The door opened and in strode Lovelace. Confident and with the good looks that would cause a jury to fall all over themselves. He wore a gray suit and polished brown shoes with little holes on top. Big deal. I recognized him from his picture in the paper. He had bowled a perfect three hundred.

"Mr. Lovelace." I stretched out a hand and tried not to show how mad I was. "Nice to meet you." And to soften him a little, I added, "Congratulations on your bowling a perfect score."

Lovelace's hand was limp and cold as a toad's belly. He told Mrs. Montgomery we were not to be disturbed, escorted me into his office, and closed the door. "Grab a seat on the couch."

I stayed standing. No nameplate on the desk, but screw it, there was nothing to be first name friendly about. I could see by his abrupt nature that he'd filed the complaint. "You did it, didn't you?"

"No choice." Lovelace tromped to his desk and pulled out an ashtray from a drawer. He took it to an armchair, flicked a hand toward the couch, and we sat. Lovelace fired up a menthol cigarette from a pack in his breast pocket and sucked in a lungful, as if inhaling a reefer down to his toes.

Cleve must have meant Lovelace doesn't allow *casual* smoking.

"Don't worry," Lovelace said, chin down, and holding his breath, "you'll be okay."

"You call losing my job okay?"

"Beats going to jail," he said, still holding his breath.

"That depends on why."

"Too late to worry about why," he said, and smoke blasted from his mouth toward me in a swirling cloud. "Want my advice? Move to California with your lady friends."

He crushed out the cigarette in his ashtray, paced back to his desk and dumped the butt into a Kleenex, then wiped the ashtray and put it back in the drawer. I waited as he continued his ritual of carefully folding the tissue and stuffing it into his coat pocket.

"So if I leave town, you'll drop the complaint?"

Lovelace returned to his chair. "No reason not to."

"What's your stake in this?"

"Like everyone, I answer to a higher authority."

"You mean sell out to a higher authority."

Lovelace scowled. "I'm being nice just talking to you. Face it, Chief, you're out. How you go is up to you."

"Why'd you take so long filing the complaint? Conscience eat at you?"

Lovelace lifted his chin and loosened the knot on his tie. "I had no interest in getting mixed up with this Klan thing. Believe it or not, you and I are on the same side."

"I believe not, but go on."

"I told Rakoff I wanted no part of it. That was fine with him. Wasn't his battle."

"But someone convinced him otherwise."

Lovelace was quiet a minute, stood, and headed back to his desk.

I figured here comes the ashtray again. Instead, what arrived was a picture of a younger Lovelace being presented with a bowling trophy big enough to melt into a hundred doorstops.

Inscribed on it: *First place. Men's Tulsa Annual Bowling Tournament. 1940.*

"Nice award," I said. "Must've taken a forklift to get it home."

Lovelace tapped the man in the picture presenting it. "Look familiar?"

Overstreet. "How touching. Was that the beginning of a beautiful friendship?"

"I was a poor kid just out of college. Mr. Overstreet owned the bowling alley. You might say he took a shine to me. Sent me to law school and got me my first job."

"You make him sound like a nice guy."

Lovelace shrugged. "It's no secret that I hold this job because of him."

If Lovelace was fishing for understanding, I wasn't biting. "So Rakoff was ordered to pull your strings."

Lovelace's jaw tightened. "You don't have to be crude. Overstreet's a powerful man. You should know."

"I know he's a murderer. So do you. Those Klan documents prove it."

"You mean the ones that no longer exist?"

"Easy enough to have made copies, don't you think?"

Lovelace glanced nervously at the door.

"I don't have to remind you," I continued, "that convicted murderers don't get to sit behind bars—at least for long—giving orders to their butlers. They sit behind a window clouded with gas. And you can bet your perforated shoes that Overstreet will be seated sooner than you think." I leaned forward. "Listen, Lovelace, this is your chance to break free before it's too late. This new civil rights movement has Washington sharpening its claws. Before you know it, the feds will swoop down on the Klan like hawks. Do the right thing and stand up to Overstreet."

Lovelace wheezed and got up, lumbered to the window, stuck a hand in his pocket and jingled coins like Dixie's father did during his heartwarming jail visit.

Lovelace turned and shook his head. "Can't do it." He sat down stiffly at his desk. "You should worry more about yourself. You either resign now, and I drop the complaint, or at eight o'clock tomorrow you appear before the judge. He'll set a court date, and an hour later you'll be walking around with a pinhole in your shirt."

I stood and pointed at him. "Your case stinks, and you know it."

"You don't want to face me in court. And we *will* go to court. When we do, I promise, you'll leave having a lot of free time on your hands. As for your lady friend, Miss Dixon, she'll learn that juries down here don't take well to uppity California girls. Especially lawyer types."

I stormed the stairs with a galloping fear that if Charlotte didn't get a good lawyer, I'd have more to worry about than too much free time. Before I reached the door, Cleve sidled up to me and whispered from the side of his mouth, "We gotta talk."

# CHAPTER 38

I'd been in the broom closet only a minute when Cleve slipped in and closed the door. "We thought you'd like to know, some white men are plannin' to do somethin' bad to that colored lady lawyer."

My throat squeezed so tight it hurt. "What do you mean, bad?"

"Don't know. Somethin' that won't be good."

"How do you know this?"

"Suzie, my granddaughter, works at the phone company. She tol' the wife. Said they don't like no Yankee negra woman comin' down here causin' trouble."

"Who are these people?"

"Suzy only said one name. Mr. Forrest. Bedford Forrest."

I hustled over to the motel. If Charlotte wasn't back from The City, or hadn't called, I'd send Sergeant Hazelwood there to find her and bring her back.

As for Lovelace, the battle lines were drawn, and he would come out swinging. How did he sleep, fighting a case he knew was bogus? I couldn't. Not even in his skin.

Tomorrow, Judge Thompson would set a trial date. As if that wasn't enough to squirm over, there was Charlotte's safety to worry about.

I jumped from my cruiser as Dixie opened the door. "Heard from Charlotte?" I said, angling past her into the room and glancing around.

Dixie shut the door. "She hasn't called, and I'm worried sick."

I debated whether to send Sergeant Hazelwood to find her. I'd wait before telling Dixie about Cleve. She worried enough. I checked my watch. "Have you been here the whole time?"

"I stepped out only for a sandwich."

"Charlotte may've had to wait around a lot."

"What happened with Lovelace?"

"He made a date for us with the judge at eight tomorrow."

"He might throw out the case."

"Don't count on it."

"Lovelace seems that confident?"

"Enough to believe we'll be eating off tin plates if I don't leave town."

The phone rang. Dixie dashed to it. "Hello." She smiled and nodded to me. "That's wonderful, Charlotte." She reached for her pad and pen and wrote something. "I'll go to the office and reserve him a room— What?...Oh, for goodness' sake. Our place isn't good enough?" She wrote some more. "All right."

I signaled for the phone.

"Hold on, here's Chief Bucky."

"I hope this lawyer of yours is good, because I just met with Lovelace, and he'll be coming at us bare-fisted. Now listen, I don't want to scare you, but I got a tip— well, maybe it's just a rumor—from a guy at the city hall. He said that...well, that some people in town are upset about you being here, so be careful and come straight to the motel." I hung up.

Dixie's face was cold as winter concrete. "What did

you mean, people are upset? I don't like this. Not even a little. We're in redneck country. People don't get upset with Negros, they murder them. Remember?"

"What'd you expect me to tell her, fly back home?"

"Hell yes!" Her eyes got teary. "And you should've told me about this the minute you walked in. I'm *furious* with you, Chief Bucky." She stormed into the bathroom and slammed the door.

"I'm *sorry!* Won't do it again." I peered at what she had written on the pad. *Granville Judge Drummond, Encore Hotel.* I picked up the phone and called the station.

Hazelwood told me right off that a summons for me had arrived.

"I already know about it. Anything else?"

"Um, well, yeah. It's kind of embarrassing, but I was asked to fill in as chief. You know, temporarily."

"Don't worry about it. But before Mrs. Rheingold moves you into my office, I want you to check out someone named Granville Judge Drummond. He's a lawyer down in The City. Get right on it and call me back. Ben's Beds and Breakfast, room one-oh-eight."

ↂↄↂↄ

The sun had just set, and I sat by the window, watching a full moon rise over the trees, while waiting for Charlotte and Mr. Drummond to arrive.

Finally they rolled in and parked in front of the room. Eager to get a fix on our lawyer, I opened the door. His hands clutched the doorframe as he got out of the car, as if to keep from tumbling out.

"Get a load of this guy," I said to Dixie, whose breath warmed the back of my neck. "He's either old or drunk."

"Maybe both," Dixie added sourly.

I hurried out and took his arm before he fell on his face.

"Let him be, Chief," Charlotte cried out, loping around from the driver's side. "Judge doesn't want people helping him."

I let him go, and he seemed okay. I supposed he went by his middle name.

"Just an old war wound to the knee," Judge said, while brushing off peanut shells from his chipmunk brown suit and threadbare tie that looked like it had spent the past four months crinkled in a tight ball. "I was blown to hell by a Whizbang rocket and buried alive for a while."

After steadying himself, he gave my hand a powerful shake, as if inducting me into a secret society. I had wisely shoved my hand in deep, saving myself from yelping and hopping up and down with mangled fingers. Our new lawyer didn't have the graceful moves of Fred Astaire, but he did have the spellbinding baritone voice of Edward R. Murrow. And with his silver hair, that looked combed by a Mixmaster, and bushy eyebrows that made sharp angles against his forehead, he could double for Spencer Tracy on a bad day. Maybe he'd do fine.

"Come on in and meet your new clients," Charlotte said to Judge. "Later, the chief will drive you to your hotel."

Though not consulted by Miss Bossy, I liked the idea of being alone with the man. He might talk more honestly than he would with the girls around. Although, if anyone could handle straight talk, they sure could. They're experts at it.

Charlotte made the introductions, and Judge and Dixie sat in the two chairs at the table, Charlotte and I on a bed.

"Charlotte," Judge said, "do you suppose you could

run next door and pick up some medicine? I'm all out, and—" He chuckled. "—well, my doctor would spank me pink if I missed a dose."

"Charlotte, let the chief do it," Dixie said.

I jumped up. "I'd be happy to." I wanted to keep Charlotte safe inside.

"Sit down, Chief," Charlotte insisted. "I'll get it." She went for her purse.

Judge opened his mouth to speak.

"I know what kind," Charlotte said, as if she'd run the errand a thousand times.

"I was going to suggest," Judge said, "get the big one this time."

Charlotte left, and Judge's eyes scanned the room. "I should've also suggested she get more peanuts. Happen to have any around?"

Judge's deep voice had a commanding quality that made me want to apologize for my thoughtlessness. I even patted my shirt pockets as if I'd been asked for a cigarette. "Gosh, I'm sorry, we don't."

Judge waved a hand. "The hotel lounge will have plenty." He smiled and shook a lazy finger at Dixie. "I want to tell you something, pretty lady. I'm mighty impressed with that sister of yours."

Words streamed from his lips like a singer's. He reminded me of Jefferson Davis, the shyster lawyer who got Tyburn off.

"Yessiree," Judge continued, "pretty as a belle and, my oh my, Harvard Law School. I suppose she's about the smartest woman I've ever had the pleasure of meeting."

"And if she had testicles," Dixie put in, "she'd be the smartest man." She reached for her notepad on the table. "Let's get down to business."

The telephone rang. "Excuse me," she said. "Hello.

He's right here." She handed me the phone. "It's Sergeant Hazelwood."

I stretched the cord into the bathroom and closed the door. "What've you got?"

"Chief, you're not thinking of hiring this guy?"

My stomach did a quick tumble. "Bad idea?"

"I'll put it this way, if you sue him, you won't be his first client to do so—or his second. He, um…" Hazelwood cleared his throat. "This might be a touchy subject, but he once had his license suspended. And before that, he was a judge."

I lowered the toilet cover and sat. So that's why he's called Judge. "Just tell me."

"He was a Mississippi circuit court judge who refused to sentence a Negro man to death for slapping a white woman who had before that slapped the man's child. Rather than be censured, Drummond quit. Moved to Oklahoma and became a defense lawyer and a drunk."

"Why did he have his license suspended?"

"It involved a guardianship case. Mother and father each wanted child custody. The father hired Drummond. Drummond goes into court, tanked to the gills, and for ten minutes he screws up and makes a rock-solid case—for the wife! That's not all. The husband is sitting there dying, trying to get Drummond's attention. Finally, Drummond sees him, goes over and leans in. 'Hey, you dumb fuck,' the husband spits in his ear, 'you're supposed to be *my* lawyer, arguing for me!' Drummond then turns and says to the jury, 'Now that's what Mrs. so and so's attorney will tell you.' And for the next half hour, Drummond makes an even more convincing case for the husband. And here's the kicker. The husband won."

"Well, at least he's a quick-thinking lawyer."

I got off the line and went back into the room. I stood by the window biting a hangnail while considering what to do about Judge. Charlotte had returned and was sitting on the bed listening to him.

"I agree," he was saying, "that the bearer bond charge will never stick. Now, Chief, Dixie and I believe the arson charge is the most serious. The one we need to prepare to fight. I'm asking both of you to write down for me your exact whereabouts the night of the fire. Don't leave anything out. We'll discuss it more later."

He stood and picked up a paper bag from the table. Charlotte must've brought it in. It was twisted tightly at the top, indicating its contents to be a bottle. "I'd be most grateful, Chief, if you could be so kind as to deliver me to my hotel."

"Sure, no problem." I opened the door and sighed. Too late to find another lawyer.

We pulled out from the lot, and I didn't waste time laying down the law. "I've done some checking on you, Judge, and I have serious worries about your drinking."

"Of course you do. I respect a man who lays his cards on the table." Judge took off his glasses and cleaned the tinted lenses with the end of his woolen tie. He seemed to be holding back a smile.

"So let's cut the medicinal crap," I said firmly. "I need you to promise you'll be stone sober at eight o'clock tomorrow morning when we go to court."

Judge's thick lips curled up. "Sir, you have my word. I shall fight thine enemy with every sober faculty of my being."

"Mortal combat won't be necessary, but getting the case dismissed is. What do you figure the chances are?"

"Let's see what happens tomorrow, shall we? Ah, here we are. Thank you for the lift." He winked and clucked his tongue twice. "The courthouse, eight o'clock."

He waddled off, and I wondered how one goes about suing their lawyer.

# CHAPTER 39

Well, *Charlotte*," I said in my most unfriendly tone. "Congratulations. You did a swell job checking out this lawyer of yours. Let's see, you learned he prefers getting out of cars unassisted, and you found out his favorite medicine and that it comes in size large, also his preference. You've picked the cream of the crop, all right."

I'd arrived back at the motel room to find a box of pizza on the table next to Dixie, and Charlotte on her bed watching TV and nibbling her fingernails. I fell into a chair and grabbed a slice of pizza.

"That's enough, Chief Bucky," Dixie droned, her head down and scribbling away on her pad. Probably planning a march across the Golden Gate Bridge, arm in arm with Dr. King.

"I don't think it is enough," I said, flicking a crumb of pizza crust from my knee, sending it flying. "I wonder if your sister also learned that he's been sued by two clients. That he's had his license suspended, and that he argued before a jury for the wrong side."

Charlotte pushed up from the bed and slapped off the TV. "Are you ready to get off your high horse and listen to facts?"

"Oh, yes. Please fill me in with *facts*." I grabbed my

pizza from the box and pressed back against my chair.

"Fact number one: he's been sued by three clients. Number two: up until six hours ago, he was in jail for contempt. And fact number—"

"Wait a minute. Contempt for what?"

"Throwing an eraser at a judge."

I slumped and bit off a piece of pizza. "Wonderful," I mumbled.

"Finally, he's the only lawyer I could find willing to take the case. Before you start, he promised to keep his drinking under control. *And* he agreed that Dixie will be quasi lead chair. That means she calls the shots."

"What's he costing us?"

"Twenty-five a day plus expenses. Fifty if we go to court."

"Okay, fine," I said, resigned. "It's not safe for you around here. Tomorrow we're going to get you on a plane for home."

"Dixie's already made a morning reservation," Charlotte said, removing her earrings and dropping them on the bureau.

"I'll have Sergeant Hazelwood drive you. By the way, what were you and Judge doing all afternoon? Getting acquainted over bottles of hooch?"

"I tested him. Wanted to learn his cognitive ability after drinking copious amounts of alcohol."

"And?"

"After two pints of J and B he could still say Peter Piper picked a peck of pickled peppers."

෧෨෧

I insisted on sleeping on the girls' floor that night in case Cleve was right about the Klan planning to hurt Charlotte.

"Chief, it's eleven o'clock," Charlotte said. "You need to go check on Judge."

I placed my finger on the line I was reading from the Bible in the drawer. "Why would I do that?"

Charlotte blew on her nails that she had just finished polishing. That is, what was left of them. The poor girl had to be pretty frightened. "To make sure," she said, "that he's in his room and not drinking at the bar. You'll need him sober tomorrow."

"I'm not leaving you two alone. Besides, doesn't he have that *medicine* you got for him?"

"Believe me, that's long gone. You need to be sure he's not closing the bar."

"Charlotte's right," Dixie said. She clicked her pen and set it down. "We can't risk him blowing our case. I'll go."

"Hold up, sister," Charlotte said. "You can't go into a bar alone at this hour. And suppose he's there. What will you do? Drag him up to his room by his ear? The chief will go. If anyone comes knocking, we won't answer."

I shook my head. "I don't like it."

Charlotte swung her legs off the bed, got up, and handed me my hat. "We'll be fine. Dixie can take that bath she's been wanting."

I looked at my watch. I could be there and back in less than thirty minutes. "Okay, but only answer the door to the knock of shave and a haircut, six bits."

❦

I reached the Encore in seven minutes. The hotel offered the fanciest rooms in town, and, as everyone said, the finest dining. A very snooty establishment.

I padded through the lounge, its thick fibrous carpet

surrounding my shoes. No sign of Judge.

"Excuse me," I said. The bartender was dressed like a White House waiter. "I'm looking for an elderly gentleman, Mr. Drummond. He checked in—"

"I know the gentleman to whom you refer. Is there a problem, officer?"

"Just checking to be sure he's comfortable."

"I'm sure he's quite comfortable. After he checked in, he sat at the bar, had two drinks and ate peanuts. Then he dined in the rose room. I believe he then retired to his suite."

Suite? I saw dollar signs leaping from my wallet. "Do you happen to know the number?"

"It's two-ten. I know because he said he didn't trust elevators. I assured him that they're serviced regularly."

I thanked the man then flew up the stairs to the second floor. There was no light coming from under Judge's door. I double-checked the number, then put my ear to the door, hoping to hear him snoring. No luck. *How can I be sure he's in there without waking him up?* Hated to do that. But suppose he'd slipped out to some bar? I tapped lightly. Then not so lightly. Then pretty damn hard.

"Judge, are you in there?" I pounded with my fist. "Drummond!" Shit!

I ran back down the stairs to the front desk. "Quick, grab a pass key," I told the clerk. "This is an emergency. One of your guests is not answering his door."

The young man's eyes bulged. "Yes sir—er, officer." He grabbed a key from a drawer, and we ran up to suite two-ten.

"Hurry up," I said. "Open it."

The clerk looked at me, puzzled. "This suite's empty. Are you looking for Mr. Drummond?"

"That's right."

"He's moved to a first floor suite."

Back down I flew and was relieved to see a light under Judge's door. I tapped lightly.

"Who's there?" came his deep melodious voice.

"It's Chief Bucky, Judge. Just checking to see if you need anything."

"Everything's fine, Chief. See you in the morning."

Although a bit out of breath, I had hoped to be invited in to check his condition. Then I remembered Charlotte's test. "Judge," I said.

"Yes."

"Do me a favor, repeat Peter Piper picked a peck of pickled peppers."

A brief silence, and then, "Forward or backward?"

"Fo—no, wait. Backward."

"Peppers-pickled-of-peck-a-picked-Piper-Peter."

I smiled. "Good night, sir."

☙❧

I turned north onto Simpson Highway. A half-mile up, a neon sign glowed with red letters. *Ben's Beds and Breakfast*. I glanced at my watch. I'd been gone twenty-one minutes. I stopped at a signal just short of the motel, and my blood froze. A dark pickup bounced out of the motel's lot and took off north.

I was about to run the light when three teenage boys sailed in front of me on a bicycle. One on the handlebars, one on the seat, one on the crossbar, trailed by a shaggy mongrel. They passed, and I hammered the gas, blasting through the red light.

Screeching to a stop outside the girls' room, I jumped from the car and noticed the door next to theirs wide open.

I banged their door. "Dixie, Charlotte, open up!" I shook the doorknob. "Dixie!" I heard a moan.

I ran into the adjoining room to find the connecting door open, its jam shattered. Dixie was tied face down on a bed, mouth taped. I ripped it off.

Dixie gasped and yelled, "They took her. They fucking took her."

# CHAPTER 40

I untied Dixie from the bed and freed her hands. "Undo your feet, I'll be right back."

I sprinted across the parking lot to the office. Ben had to have told the bastards the girl's room number and rented them the adjoining room.

The lights were off, and the door locked. I drove my boot into the door. Chips flew like shrapnel, and the door flung open with a crash. A light came from under the door behind the counter.

I vaulted the counter and didn't waste time stopping to try the door. Flying at it, boot raised, it burst open.

"Don't hurt me!" Ben cried, arms raised. He was possibly in need of new shorts. I shoved him against a wall by his throat, pulled out my gun, and pressed the barrel against his temple.

"You have a choice," I spat through clenched teeth. "Tell me where they took her, or check out."

"I—"

I cocked the hammer. "The next word had better be a place."

Ben swallowed. "G—Gustafson's."

That didn't make sense. "You mean the store?"

"No, no. His old catfish pond."

Dixie came running in.

I growled to Ben, "You call anyone, you'll have more than a five-hundred-dollar fine to worry about." I holstered my gun and took Dixie's hand. "Let's go."

We jumped into my cruiser and screamed north.

My adrenals pumped like fire hoses. "Who were they? How many? Did you see their faces?"

"There were three of them, at least that's all I could make out. Where are they taking her?" she cried.

"To a catfish pond about twelve miles up. They only have a ten-minute head start. What happened?"

"I was in the bathroom getting dressed when I heard a frightening crash. I thought a car had slammed through the front. Charlotte screamed, and I heard harsh voices. I ran out. The lights were off, except for the bathroom. They wore those hideous white hoods."

"What were they doing?"

"Putting a blanket over Charlotte. She yelled and fought like a cat until—" Dixie threw her hands to her face. "—until she stopped yelling and dropped to the floor." Dixie turned to me, her eyes flooded with tears. "Oh, Bucky, they might have killed her."

She covered her mouth.

"No, no, they wouldn't have taken her," I said, trying to give her hope. "We'll bring her back safe." I patted Dixie's leg. "I promise. Let's go."

# CHAPTER 41

It was near midnight, and a full moon hung straight overhead, illuminating the landscape like a huge flashlight with weak batteries.

I turned off the dirt road into the brush about a quarter-mile short of the catfish pond. "We'll stay clear of the road, circle around the pond, and come from behind." Grabbing my shotgun, I climbed out and we walked.

"But won't it take a long time to get there?"

"It's a small pond."

We trotted through the tall brush, hearing nothing but our own footsteps trampling on twigs and leaves. At the pond, we stopped and took stock. The moon reflected on the water, and the air was damp and smelled of wet vegetation.

Dixie tugged my sleeve and whispered. "Where are they?"

"Shh. Let's keep moving."

We had almost circled the pond when Dixie gripped my arm. "Look! By the shed. A pickup under that big tree."

I recognized the dark pickup that had sped from the motel.

"Stop right there, and don't turn around," a man barked behind us.

Dixie gasped. My blood chilled. Now I had to save Charlotte and protect Dixie.

"Chief, I want you to ease the shotgun onto the ground. *Nice and slow.*"

My veins felt cracked like frozen water pipes. I laid the gun down."

"That's it. Now both of you raise your hands."

My Colt was lifted from its holster.

"Now put your hands behind your back. José, tie their hands with the knot I showed you."

*Suure*, José. A phony Klan name, if I ever heard one.

"Now that you two have arrived, we can get on with the rope dance. It'll be a humdinger. One you'll want to share with the folks back home." The guy whistled a shrill, piercing blast. Three men in white hoods appeared from behind the shed. That meant at least five of them. They'd probably arrived in two cars.

"Oh, no!" Dixie cried.

One of the men dropped the pickup's tailgate with a clang, climbed aboard, and threw a rope over a tree branch. Seconds later, he looped a second rope across the branch.

"What the—" whistle-man mumbled. "They don't need two ropes. José, take this. I'll be back."

Whistle-man tramped off around the pond toward the pickup.

José had obviously been given the gun. And since he hadn't known how to tie hands, I suspected he was inexperienced in Klan pageants. Deciding to risk it, I spun around to look at him.

Startled, José jumped back awkwardly. Like the others, he was dressed in a white gown and hood. He regained his balance, crouched, and lurched forward, jabbing his rifle like a bayonet. All that fancy footwork kicked up a cloud of dust. I peered down and recognized a distinct pair of high top sneakers and red shoelaces. "Dexter!" I hissed. "Put that gun down before you hurt yourself."

"Uh—"

"Go ahead, drop it."

"I'm—I can't do that. I'm a guard."

I had to think of something. Reason with him. "Look Dexter, do you remember when you got caught hiding in the girl's locker room?"

He giggled and shuffled his feet. "Uh-huh."

"Do you remember your punishment?"

"Um—uh-huh. Had to stand at assembly and apologize to all the girls in the school."

"That didn't feel good, did it?"

"Uh-uh."

"Do you see this badge I'm wearing?"

Dexter moved his head a bit sideways.

"It's a police badge, which means I outrank you." I glanced back toward the pickup and saw someone yank off the second rope from the tree.

"We're jus' scaring the nigger girl, is all," Dexter said.

"Oh, these people!" Dixie spat.

We're running out of time. "Dexter, is the girl conscious?"

"She's *real* conscious. When they pulled her out of the car, she screeched like a riled hen."

"My God!" Dixie burst. "Look what they're doing."

Two Klansmen lifted Charlotte onto the pickup, her hands behind her back and her mouth taped.

"Listen, Dexter, I'm ordering you to untie me right now."

Dexter didn't move.

"Dexter, they're not just scaring the girl, they're about to hang her. Goddammit, untie me!"

He didn't budge.

I stomped my foot. "Now!"

Dexter flinched, dropped his rifle, and untied knots.

Afterward, I freed Dixie. She gasped. "Oh, my God!"

The man tightened the noose around Charlotte's neck.

"Listen to me," I said. "We're going to walk over there with our hands behind our backs like we're tied up. Dexter, you bring my shotgun and keep your rifle at our backs. Don't say anything. I'll do the talking. And for crap's sake, keep your finger off the trigger."

Fear flickered in Dixie's eyes as we got close to the truck. Men jumped from the pickup, leaving Charlotte alone. She let out a chilling low-pitched moan.

I whispered, "Dexter, when I leave here, you tell them we untied ourselves and then walked off. You didn't know what to do."

Whistle-man spotted us. "Hey, what the hell you doin'?"

We were about ten yards behind the pickup. All four hooded men stood off to the side. No one was armed. Exactly what I'd hoped for.

"The view's better here," I said, glancing at the rope straining against the tree branch.

Someone hopped in the pickup and started the engine. Charlotte's eyes were huge disks. She made a cry like a slaughtered cow.

I spun and grabbed my shotgun from Dexter.

The driver released the brake. The pickup pitched, and Charlotte stumbled back.

"Turn off that engine!" I shouted.

The transmission ground into gear.

I pumped my shotgun and pointed it at the driver. No good. Charlotte would catch spraying pellets. Tires spun, and gravel peppered my shins. Charlotte's body lurched forward. I swung the gun toward the rope and jerked the trigger. Charlotte's weight snapped the badly frayed rope as the pickup bolted ahead. She fell to the ground, rolling onto her side.

The pickup stopped, and the driver leaped out. I pumped the shotgun and pointed it at him. "Get over with the others," I barked. He didn't move, and I fired my second round over his head before realizing my mistake. He ran to the others.

Dixie had already helped Charlotte to her feet. She was untying her hands when whistle-man yelled, "Grab him, he's out of buckshot."

"Jump in the back, you two," I hollered. The driver charged at me, arms outstretched. I swung my shotgun, smashing the barrel with bone-crushing force against his hooded skull. I scrambled into the pickup, threw it in gear, and spun away spitting gravel.

# CHAPTER 42

How do your clients plead, Mr. Drummond?"
Four of us stood before Judge Thompson. Dixie
in a dark green dress with a tight black belt, and
me in a freshly starched uniform. Beside us, very much
the dapper gentleman, stood Judge in an elegant blue suit.
His lapel held a white carnation that matched his combed
hair and trimmed eyebrows. To our right, our adversary,
the well-groomed City Attorney Lovelace wore a gray
pinstripe suit, snakeskin boots, and a smug expression.

"Not guilty!" Judge boomed in a voice likely to rattle
Chinese teacups at the restaurant across the street. He
dropped his tone down a notch or two and added, "These
charges are patently outrageous, Your Honor. The defendants are solid citizens. Our own police chief, and an
esteemed attorney. Hardly whom you'd call thieves and
arsonists. We move for an immediate dismissal."

"Denied," Judge Thompson said flatly and flipped
pages of his calendar.

Judge cleared his throat. "In that case, your honor,
due to the unfortunate fact that Chief Bucky will be dis-
charged from his duties as police chief, we beg the court
for the earliest trial date."

The judge turned back pages and picked up his pencil. "All right. One week from today. The twenty-second, ten o'clock. Defendants are to remain free on their own recognizance and are not to leave town." He stood. "Miss Dixon, please see me in my chambers."

Dixie reached for her purse.

"Not you." The judge shook his head. "The other one." He pointed to Charlotte sitting in the gallery, wearing a high-collared green dress and pearl necklace. Her eyes widened.

I accompanied Dixie and Judge out onto the front steps.

"I'd say that went pretty well for a day's work." Judge puffed out his chest, his Masonic clasp glistening in the sun. He put a fatherly hand on my shoulder. "I know you were hoping for a dismissal, son, but I've seen enough of these cases to not expect miracles. Cheer up. Before you know it, this will all be behind you, and you'll be back maintaining law and order."

Judge scanned the street, probably looking for a bar or liquor store. "While I'm in town, I have friends I'd like to check in on. Why don't you two join me for dinner at my hotel? We'll begin work on your defense. Shall we say seven?"

"Yeah, sure," I said. What better place to blow an entire paycheck?

Judge waddled off.

"While we're waiting for Charlotte, tell me your plans for dealing with last night's party throwers," Dixie said.

"Well, Charlotte won't be around to testify. And even if she is, what could she say? 'I was kidnapped by people dressed in white, who tried to hang me?' Whistleman was probably from out-of-town and so was the pickup. That leaves Dexter. You know damn well, if he talks, he's good as dead."

She rolled her eyes. "So that means you'll do nothing."

"Now hold on," I snapped. "In case you forgot, I'll be out of a job in about fifteen minutes."

"You heard Judge. You'll soon have it back. Then do something."

Charlotte came bouncing up, glowing with delight. "I found out why Judge Thompson didn't dismiss the case."

"This ought to be interesting," Dixie said.

"He sees this case as an opportunity to put the Klan on trial. And get this, he loves Judge. Thinks he's the perfect guy to turn your defense into an attack. The press will eat him up. He also thinks you should talk to the ACLU. Get some big guns behind you."

A squad car pulled up to the curb.

"Here's Charlotte's ride to the airport," I said.

Charlotte turned to Dixie. "Why don't you go keep the officer company for a minute?"

When Dixie left, Charlotte took my hand in hers. "Chief, I want you to know I appreciate everything you've done for Dixie and for saving my big black ass. I wasn't all that sure about you in the beginning. After all," she added with a grin, "you are a southern white boy with a gun and a badge."

"Like Judge, I guess I passed your test, huh?"

She threw her head back and widened her eyes in mock indignation. "Who said anything about passing?" She let out a whooping laugh. "Give me a big hug, and let me get out of here." I wrapped my arms around her broad shoulders and looked straight at Lovelace on the courthouse steps, talking to a man I had never seen before. Lovelace caught my eye and elbowed the man. He glanced at me, and then they smiled at each other.

I returned to the jury room to turn in my gun and badge to the city council. This promised to be a nerve-racking week if there ever was one. Spend it all with Judge and Dixie going over our defense. That's if Dixie could pull herself away from her civil rights work.

I reached the top of the stairs just as Judge Thompson and three councilmen got into the elevator. Entering the jury room, I was surprised to find only Alsop. He was sitting at the table and talking on the phone.

"You're welcome, Sergeant Hazelwood." Alsop hung up.

I felt a deep, hard thud in my stomach. I really was about to lose my job. "Where'd everybody go?"

"Have a seat," Alsop said and put a cigar between his lips. He patted himself down, found a lighter in his coat pocket, and flicked a flame to the cigar. He sucked noisily until it glowed like a torch, then rolled the cigar between his fingers.

I held my breath.

He looked up at me and said matter-of-factly, "The council has decided to hold off on your suspension."

My mouth snapped open to take in much needed oxygen.

"Since your trial is only a week away, we thought it'd be less disruptive to let things ride and hope for a quick acquittal. I just notified Sergeant Hazelwood. Now then—" He drew sharply on his cigar, twisted his mouth to the side, and blew out a stream of smoke. "—I heard you've snagged a crackerjack lawyer from The City. That's good. Everything else okay?"

I could hardly believe my good fortune. However, the trial would still put a black mark on my record. As for Alsop's question, it might be best not to mention my problems with the troopers and the previous night's Klanfest. Judge may want to keep the lid on everything until the trial.

"I'm investigating a murder at the Mayfair. Kind of low key. I've been told that the hotel is strictly state trooper turf."

"Been that way forever. Any suspects?"

"As a matter of fact, Tyburn Newgate."

Alsop's eyebrows crept up. "Oh?" He leaned back in his chair and puffed. "Have proof, do you?"

I shook my head. "Uh-uh. That's the problem. The proof's right in front of me, I know it. But—" I raised my palms and sighed.

Alsop's eyes took on a faraway look. He drew a long puff from his cigar and released a plume of smoke that disappeared like fog. "When you're bound on a long bus trip, and you mislaid your ticket," he said, after a moment, "it's natural to go through your pockets, knowing full well that it's not in any of them. After all, you just checked. Then you find it in one of the pockets where you knew it couldn't be."

I heard the door open and kids voices. "Excuse us gentlemen," a woman said, "We're touring the courthouse. Would it be okay if..."

❧❧

I was back in my office only a short while when Mrs. Rheingold strolled in. "I'm glad you're staying on, Chief. The colors here wouldn't go well with Sergeant Hazelwood. He's more suited to a brighter, cheerful room."

I looked around. "I hadn't thought about it, but the walls are awfully drab."

"I suppose. By the way, Sergeant Hazelwood wants to see you."

"Tell him to come in. Also, go ahead and pick up a color chart. The place could use brightening up."

A sly smile crossed her lips. "If it means that much to you. Sure."

She left, leaving me bamboozled. Naturally, she'd want her office done, too.

Hazelwood came in and congratulated me on keeping my job, adding, "Something interesting has been going on over at Gustafson's. I thought you'd want to know about it."

"Have a seat."

Hazelwood hung his cane on the desk's edge and sat down. "My wife told me Abby has been depositing an unusually large number of silver dollars at the bank. Evidently, low-wage workers, like those at the dog food factory, are paid daily with them, so it's common to see them in merchant's deposits. But like I say, Abby's numbers have spiked."

I slapped the desk with my palms. "So *that's* how they're doing it. Funneling the silver back to the very bank Tyburn stole it from."

"That's the way it looks. I've got to get back on the desk."

I rocked in my chair, trying to think of how to nail Tyburn and Abby. Was there a way to uncover their laundering scheme? Probably not. Silver coins didn't exactly have serial numbers. I got up and paced. Might be just as well. Thanks to Mrs. McCoy telling Abby about me running away from the store, Tyburn must know I planted the bag of silver. He would think that made us partners. Like when he handed me the envelope stuffed with two extra hundred-dollar bills.

I flopped back in my chair and stared at the manila folder Ham had found hidden in Gregory's house with the bag of silver. I thought of what Alsop had said about finding proof. "You'll find it in one of the pockets where you knew it couldn't be."

I opened the folder and examined Gregory's birth certificate. Studied it, but nothing stood out. Then I skimmed his army discharge papers and found nothing. Discouraged, I picked up the last item. A Polaroid of a burning house with a close-up of two grinning teenagers in the foreground. The boy had taken the picture himself by holding the camera at arm's length. The girl had her arms around his neck, cheek-to-cheek.

Suddenly my heart stopped, and I couldn't breathe. The girl looked a lot like Abby. A hell of a lot like Abby! And the boy…I peered closer. He must be Gregory.

I played with that idea. Then grabbed my notepad and searched for what the Santa Fe police had told Hazelwood about Gregory. *As teen, set fire to house. Parents died. Sister saved.*

No wonder Abby turned pale when I told her Gregory had been murdered. He was her brother. Geesh. That changed everything. She never would've allowed Tyburn to murder her own brother. Maybe Tyburn hadn't killed Gregory. But if not him, who? Questions flooded my thoughts.

Then it hit me so hard it burned. Like tobacco juice in the eye.

# CHAPTER 43

I climbed into my squad car, thinking how smart I hadn't been. I was so convinced Tyburn had murdered Gregory that I hadn't considered other suspects. I decided from then on, when it came to murder, I'd keep an open mind.

I should've known who turned out Gregory's lights. But the original scenario still fit. Gregory showed up at Abby's house drunk and slugged Tyburn. Probably because Tyburn didn't go along with his plan to renegotiate the bank profits. Then at some point, Tyburn called his daddy. But his daddy didn't order him to murder Gregory. That job he assigned to a lowlife, Dusty. "Give him a room and an early checkout," he'd told him.

After doing the deed, Dusty put Gregory's key in the inside door lock and then cleverly managed to lock the door with his passkey from the outside.

I had no proof, but even if I did, it might not do any good. Dusty had immunity. Trooper immunity.

I hit the bell on the hotel's front desk, then turned and leaned my back against the counter. A painting above the front door showed a swamp with trees draped in Spanish moss. It reminded me of canoeing through the swamps back home. I could almost smell the vegetation.

Like a trained seal, Dusty emerged from the back, his feet slapping the floor. I pointed to the painting. "Is that a watercolor?"

"Yeah," Dusty said, voice scratchy as ever. "Painted it myself."

I turned to face him. "You don't say? If I looked close, would I see an alligator with a partial thumb in its mouth?"

"This ain't no art gallery. What do you want?"

"Just a friendly call. Your artwork reminds me of what you said about an alligator nipping your thumb. You had just killed your mamma with your .22. In the eye, as I recall."

"You should also recall that my pa was beating on her and that I had meant to kill him."

"Ah, yes, such a shame. Your pa lived, but your poor mamma died. All because of bad aim."

Dusty squinted his pea-sized eyes. "What are you gettin' at?"

"Your aim was a whole lot better with a knife, wasn't it? I know you killed Gregory, and I know how you escaped from the room."

Dusty yanked his cigar stub from between his wet lips and dropped it in the ashtray on the counter. "I'll tell you what I know. I know you've lost your fucking marbles. I can't believe you're a police chief. You'd screw up writing a jaywalking ticket."

"Nice bluff, Dusty. But I don't give a shit anymore. I've learned my lesson about this place. If the troopers and the sheriff and even the goddamn governor want to let you get away with murder, fine. I'm done caring."

"Then leave, and care enough not to come back."

"Just between you and me and that painting of yours, I'd like to know if I'm right about how you got out of the room."

"You just said you knew."

"Yeah, but it's a theoretical kind of knowing."

For the first time ever, I saw Dusty laugh. He scratched an armpit and bared his grimy teeth. "Okay," he said. "How'd I do it?"

"Magnetism."

"Magnetism?" There was that scowl again.

"After stabbing Gregory to death, you put his room key in the door's inside lock, went out and closed the door. Then you inserted your magnetized passkey in the lock and pushed the inside key back enough to turn the lock. When you withdrew your magnetized key, the inside key was drawn back into its original position." I grinned. "Pretty good detective work, huh?"

Dusty raised his hands in defeat. "Well, ya got me. Congratulations. Now, if you'll excuse me." He turned to leave.

"Come on. Is that really how you did it?"

"I know this is gonna break your heart, Sherlock, but I didn't kill Gregory. And if you had half a brain, it would've dawned on you that there were three other people in the building that morning besides me. And I can tell you, there were *only* three other people."

"That would be Tyburn, Officer Sparks, and—oh, yeah, Gregory."

"You have half a brain, after all."

"Would you swear on your poor mother's grave that you didn't kill Gregory?"

"If it meant getting rid of you once and for all, yes. Goodbye."

"Really? You're not just saying it?"

Dusty disappeared into the back.

ೲ

I returned to my office with the worrying feeling that

Dusty was telling the truth. Besides Dusty, only Tyburn and Sparks were alive in the hotel around the time of the killing.

Sparks, the killer? He couldn't have planned the murder in advance. He only went to the hotel because a hog farmer had told him Tyburn was going there.

"Bucky." It was Mrs. Rheingold on the intercom. "Miss Dixon is here to see you."

"Great. Send her in."

Dixie came in and handed me an envelope. "These are points we should discuss with Judge tonight over dinner."

"Fine. I'll review them later. I'd like to run something by you that's unrelated to our case."

She glanced at her watch.

"That is, if you have a minute."

"Okay, but quickly. I have to mail off some letters before the post office closes."

"Have a seat, and I'll try to make it fast."

She sat before the desk. "What is it?"

"Remember I told you about the murder case I was working on?"

"At the Mayfair hotel."

"Right. I'm considering the possibility of the killer being one of my men."

It took several minutes to explain Sparks's version of his movements from the time he left the barbershop to when Gregory's body was discovered.

"I'm sorry, Dixie. This is taking too long. You should probably go."

"No. This is important to you. I want to help."

Good. I needed to talk this through with someone smart. "Okay. Let's look at means, motive, and opportunity."

"Did Sparks have a knife?"

"He probably used Gregory's. Officer Murphy found an empty scabbard on his calf."

"What about motive?"

"Officer's don't make much money, so there's the silver to consider. Sparks could've knocked on Gregory's door and threatened him. You know, 'The silver or your life.'"

"Then took both and left by the back stairs."

I clicked a thumbnail against my tooth. "But there might be other reasons too."

Dixie cocked her head. "Such as?"

"Getting back at Tyburn. He tried to frame Sparks once. Said he shot a BB through a barbershop window and later humiliated him by screwing his girlfriend and bragging about it."

"You think that's motive enough for Sparks to have killed someone?"

"Sparks had other reasons for revenge. Tyburn had seared his face with a cigarette, and Sparks threatened to kill him for it. Also, let's not forget that Sparks is a Kluxer with a heart for violence."

Dixie pursed her lips. "Do you think he had time to pull it off?"

"Sparks said that after he arrived at the hotel, he saw Tyburn's car parked in the back and tried to reach me, but I was off shooting tin cans. He went inside, and Dusty told him Gregory's room number, then he went back to his car."

"He didn't go to the room?"

"Not until after failing to reach me again. Then he went up, knocked, and getting no answer, he tried the door. It was locked, so he called for Dusty, whose passkey wouldn't work because a key was lodged in the other side of the lock. Sparks then kicked a hole in the door, reached in and unlocked it."

"When would he have done the killing?"

I got up and paced behind my desk. "Suppose it happened this way." I scurried back to my chair. "While Sparks sat in his cruiser across the street with a good view of the hotel, he saw Tyburn come around from the rear of the building, get into his car and drive off. Then Sparks had a beautiful thought."

Dixie's eyes brightened. "Get even with the son of a bitch."

"Think of it—disfigurement, betrayal, humiliation. So Sparks slips up the same back staircase Tyburn had used. Knocks on Gregory's door, enters, and gives Gregory the business. Afterward, he hightails it back down the rear stairs, around the building, and in through the front door."

"A plausible theory, but how are you going to prove it?"

"Don't know. I also have to figure out how Sparks got out of the locked room." I checked my watch. "Listen, you can still make it to the post office before it closes."

She stood. "I don't know how helpful I was."

"You were great. I really appreciate it."

Dixie left, and I moved to the window to think. The sky hung low to the ground like a tarp. I thought of the photos I had taken of the crime scene.

I went back to my desk and pulled them out. I studied them carefully, as if going through my pockets again. The body, the knife, the window latches, the air vent, the chimney, the door—its hinges, the jagged hole, the keyhole—all of them. I picked up the keyhole picture and leaned back. Something struck me about the empty lock. There was a key in there that Dusty had taken out.

I flashed on the image of Sheriff Rakoff's hand palming the cell door key and smashing it against my fingers, and all at once, I got it. I pictured exactly how Sparks got out of the room.

Murphy came into the office, asking if he should pick up Gregory's abandoned motorcycle behind the Mayfair. "It's been there almost two weeks," he said.

I stood up. "Come on, I'll drive you there."

# CHAPTER 44

I had asked Sparks at the time of the murder if, when he listened at Gregory's door, he had heard noises inside. Sparks said no, that he had even stuck his ear to the door.

Later, when I explained my original theory of Tyburn hiding under the bed, he changed his tune and suddenly remembered. "Oh, yeah. Now that we're talking about it, I did hear something coming from inside."

Murphy and I marched into the hotel. *Bing, bing, bing.* "Dusty," I shouted. "Get your ass out here."

Dusty appeared from the back, chewing a dead cigar stub. "Don't you have a home?"

"Good news. I know who killed Gregory and how he escaped."

Dusty turned to Murphy. "You?"

Murphy gulped.

"Not Murphy. But you'll know who after you answer a couple questions. Sparks hollered to you from the landing to bring up the passkey to Gregory's room, right?"

"Yeah."

"But when you got there with the key, Sparks said he had just looked through the keyhole and saw a key in the lock from the inside."

"He said the passkey wouldn't work and then kicked the hole in the door."

"I'll bet—wait. You tried the door before he kicked it, right?"

"Yeah, it was locked."

"That's when you left your fingerprint on the doorknob. Okay, so we know that. We also know that Sparks said there was a key in the lock."

"Yeah. We just went over that."

"Only partly, because although Sparks peeked through the keyhole, I'll bet a dollar to a dry cigar that *you* didn't look through the keyhole."

Dusty stroked one side then the other of his grubby mustache. "I guess I didn't."

"I know you didn't. Because if you had, you'd have known there was no key in the lock."

Murphy and Dusty exchanged puzzled looks.

"Before Sparks came in the front door the second time, he had gone up the back way and knocked on Gregory's door. Gregory let him in, and Sparks slipped him the blade. Then Sparks left the room, locked the door, and with the key in his pocket, retraced his steps out the rear and returned through the front entrance."

Murphy raised a finger. "That's when he went up and kicked a hole in the door."

Dusty waved his hand. "Hold on a minute. How can you say that the key wasn't in the lock? It had to have been."

I grinned. "It was, but not until Sparks put it there after putting his boot through the door. He then reached in, inserted the key, and opened the door."

Dusty shook his head. "I'll be damned." His face scrunched. "But why'd he go to all that trouble when he could've left the door unlocked?"

"An insurance policy, in case someone saw him entering or leaving through the back entrance. With the door locked, he could safely fudge his story. Say that he forgot to tell me that before going to the room through the front, he'd gone up the back stairs and found the door locked."

Murphy's lower lip almost fell to the floor. "So Gregory didn't commit suicide."

єёєё

The sky was a deep navy blue, edging closer to black. Murphy rode Gregory's motorcycle back to the station, but I had a plan to arrest Sparks.

# CHAPTER 45

"Y"ou wanted to see me, Chief?" Sparks breezed into my office as if he hadn't a care in the world. And judging from the spring in his step, he might have even expected a promotion.

"Have a seat, Larry," I said, friendly like, as if I might just offer that promotion.

He sat slouched in a chair across the desk from me.

I raised my chin and scratched the underside. "I've got a new angle on the Gregory killing."

His left eyelid twitched. "No kidding."

"I'd like to get your thoughts on it. But first I want to double-check something. According to my notes, you went up to Gregory's room through the front entrance. That right?"

"Yeah. It's in my report."

I smiled. "That's good. And you went to the room only once, right?"

He cleared his throat. Probably wondering if he was being set up. "Uh-huh. So what's this new angle?"

He just canceled his insurance policy that said he had gone up to the room twice. First by way of the back entrance.

He slipped out a crinkled pack of Camels from his

shirt pocket, shook out the last smoke, and crumpled the empty pack.

"I'll run it by you," I said.

He looked around, as if for a wastebasket. I watched him work it out. He stuffed the wadded pack back into his shirt pocket, lit his cigarette, and sucked in a sharp drag.

I nudged an ashtray across the desk toward him. "Before getting into the new angle, I'll tell you this, Tyburn didn't murder Gregory."

He gazed at his glowing cigarette and rolled it around in his fingers. "You sure about that?" he asked evenly.

I sighed, taking my time on the exhale. "Afraid so. Doesn't add up. Gregory was the brother of Tyburn's girlfriend. She wouldn't have wanted him killed. Besides, there's no proof. All we have is Dusty's say-so that Tyburn walked into the Mayfair, asked for Gregory's room number, and went upstairs."

"Then what are you saying? That Dusty's the guy who killed him?"

I shook my head. "Dusty's been cleared."

"Well, then," Sparks waved his cigarette, and it made a dissolving smoke ring in the air, "it had to be Tyburn wanting all that silver for himself."

"But there was no silver at the hotel. Dusty would've seen if Gregory had brought it in with him."

"Okay," he squirmed in his chair, "so the silver was hidden somewhere, just like you said."

I winced at the reminder of how wrong I'd been on that score. He went on, his voice rushed. "Maybe Gregory and Tyburn argued about it. Who the fuck knows? The fact is, Tyburn was the last person to be with Gregory alive." Sparks shoved the cigarette in his mouth and sucked as if he were inhaling a malt.

I shook my head slowly. "That's not a fact. Tyburn

was the *next to last* person to be with Gregory."

Sparks stared at me while smoke jetted from his nostrils. He laughed, just one little hiccup. The only sign that anything was going on inside was a slight red flush on his face and another eyelid twitch. "Is that so?"

He hooked a thumb in his gun belt. I hoped he wasn't going to pull a quick draw. He gazed fixedly at his cigarette's wilting ash. I expected it to tumble to the floor. After more heavy silence, he leaned over and tapped his ash into my ashtray, then sat back and looked at me squarely. "All right," he said, as if he'd steeled himself for bad news. "Who *was* the last person to be with him?"

I rocked in my chair, and it squeaked like a trapped mouse, then I folded my hands and smiled patiently. "Take a guess."

He snorted another hiccup. "This is your new angle. You tell me."

I planted my forearms on the desk. "The last person to be with him was you."

He swallowed hard, sending his Adam's apple riding up and down. "You're crazy." He shifted in his chair and made a phony high-pitched laugh. "Didn't know you had such a wild sense of humor."

"I don't, when it comes to murder. I'd like to hear how you came up with the clever idea of palming Gregory's room key and slipping it into the inside lock."

He stubbed his cigarette out in the ashtray, then settled back with his hands behind his head. "Interesting theory," he said and offered a smile that crinkled the scar tissue on his cheek. "But just like with Tyburn, you've got no proof."

I stared into his eyes. "But I do have proof."

Redness drained from his face.

I slid open a drawer and pulled out three eight-by-ten

photos. "The day of the murder, Murphy made impressions of footprints behind the Mayfair's back staircase." I spread the photos on the desk before him, then stretched across and pointed to his shoes. "I'm betting one of these photos matches those clodhoppers of yours."

He lurched forward and swept the pictures off the desk. It was as though whatever connected him to reality was gone. Panic filled his now bright-red face like fire. There was anger there, too, but fear behind the fire.

"Those don't mean a fucking thing!" he yelled. "You and Murphy and I walked back there the day of the killing. Murphy will back me up."

"No he won't. Only Murphy and I went back there. You'd already left for the station to write up your report."

Sparks clutched his thighs, his eyes frantic. "Come on, Chief." He gave another high-pitched laugh. "We both know damn well Tyburn's trying to frame me. He's a scumbag. Let's work this out."

"We'll do that." I pressed the intercom. "Mrs. Rheingold." I shot a glance at Sparks, who was gnawing his lower lip. "Send them in."

The door swung open, and Hazelwood and Murphy stepped inside, guns drawn.

"On your feet, Sparks. Hands behind your head."

# CHAPTER 46

Sparks was allowed two phone calls. One local, another long distance with reverse charges.

By ten the next morning, black clouds had built up over the foothills, the air thick and heavy. Hard rain was expected by nightfall. Tyburn continued to be in my thoughts, and my thoughts told me to tell the thieving bastard that he would stay on my radar. I cruised over to the old Gustafson place, now homesteaded by Tyburn and Abby. She would be at work.

I pulled up in front, and there sat Tyburn on the porch, stretched out on his new patio furniture, sipping beer and gabbing with his daddy. Martin was all gussied up butler-like with his plastered down yellow hair and black suit. I got out of my cruiser just as Tyburn and his daddy were saying their goodbyes.

Martin and I approached each other halfway along the walk. His back straight as an ironing board, he slowed and said, "I told you my son was not a murderer." Raising his chin, he continued past.

"But he *is* a bank robber," I muttered to myself.

"Come on up, Chief," Tyburn said cheerfully. "Got a warm chair for ya. How 'bout a cold one?"

"I don't think so. Only be a minute."

Tyburn's feline bodyguard bathed itself on the table.

"At least sit down and tell me how you figured out it was Sparks who done it, the bastard. And don't worry, I ain't lookin' for no apology."

I wouldn't be much of a man if I didn't admit I was wrong. But what I said was, "It's all in the papers."

"No hard feelings, Chief. My whole life, people been accusing me of bein' a rascal."

"Oh, you're more than a rascal. Just not a murderer. At least as far as I know."

The screen door opened, and out came Abby. "Hello, Chief."

I stood. "Hello, Abby. I thought you'd be at the store." I wanted to add, *exchanging stolen silver for bank receipts.*

"Stay seated," she said. "I only came out to say hi."

She put a hand to the stomach portion of a bulky blue sweater.

I asked if something was wrong.

"Mornings are hard lately. I'll be going into the store soon."

"She's been throwin' up," Tyburn said, as if genuinely concerned.

"You might want to see Doc Carrington," I told her, figuring she had morning sickness as a result of their *huggin' and squeezin'* that Tyburn had once mentioned.

"Maybe I'll do that." She eyed Tyburn with a mischievous smile. "Does he know?"

Tyburn took a swig of beer, his fist wrapped around the neck of the bottle. "Nah, he don't know."

"Does it matter?"

Tyburn pulled her onto his lap and the two giggled. "Not one tiny bit."

"Go ahead and tell him," she said. "I want to see his face."

Tyburn wrapped his arms around her waist, all snuggly. "It's like this, Chief. You've heard of Bonnie and Clyde?" A sly smile played at the corners of his lips.

Confused, all I could do was rub that smooth spot on my cheek. Then blood rushed to my face.

"Look at him," Abby burst gleefully. "He got it."

"That's us," Tyburn said. "At least it used to be. We're retired now. Bonnie and Clyde and brother Greg. May he rest in peace."

Abby hopped off Tyburn's lap. "I've got to get ready for work. Be seeing you, Chief." She disappeared inside.

I stood. "You know something, Tyburn? Your kind never retires. You'll do something stupid, and when you do, I'll pounce on you like a ton of your stolen silver dollars."

Tyburn smiled his crafty smile. "I don't see that happenin', Chief. I see you and me gettin' along just fine. Lawman and Joe Blow."

ഗ്രരൂ

I was home cleaning my camera, trying to forget about Tyburn and think about dinner when the phone rang.

"Hello Chief. This is Mrs. Rheingold. Enjoying your new fame?"

"Actually, I'm thinking of what to do for dinner."

"Well, then, how would you like to join me? I've got a pot roast in the oven. Bring a bottle of wine, and we'll toast to your magnificent detective work. Then I'll show you my color charts so we can choose something for our offices."

*Our* offices. I knew it. "Sounds great. I haven't had pot roast since my grandmother made it."

"I'd also suggest you invite your friend, Miss Dixon,

but she's leaving town. That's why I'm calling. She wants you to drop by her motel."

"What do you mean leaving? She can't leave."

☙❧

A fine rain like the spray from a sprinkler kept my windshield wipers working on the ride over to Dixie's motel. How could she possibly ignore the judge's—the real judge's—order not to leave town? This didn't make sense.

She greeted me at the door. "Come in and sit down while I finish packing."

"Wait a minute, where are you going?"

"Home. I guess you haven't heard. Lovelace has dropped the charges against us."

"*No!*" I collapsed into a chair. "That's fantastic."

"He called me personally. Don't ask why. I have no idea. He really laid on the southern charm. Said what a nice person I was, and that after questioning Rakoff some more, things didn't seem quite right." She waved a dismissive hand. "He started to go on, so I told him fine and hung up."

"I can tell you what happened. Judge Thompson didn't know that Farnsworth was a gold-star member of the Klan when he informed the council that he would allow the defense leeway. When word reached Overstreet, Lovelace's chain got yanked, and he pulled the plug."

"I would've loved exposing every one of those scumbags in court. Especially those who tried to hang Charlotte. I would, too, except for the time involved and the fact that I wouldn't risk bringing Charlotte back to testify. I'll see that the FBI gets my list." She glanced around the room one more time and closed her suitcase.

"Now you'll have lots of time to organize for Dr. King."

A horn beeped, and Dixie peered out the window. "That's my ride."

"Well, I guess that's it," I said, getting to my feet.

She looked at me with her whole face smiling. "I'm so glad you understand. Negro civil rights are something we should all support." She took my cold hands with her soft, warm ones. "I want to thank you from the bottom of my heart for all your help."

The taxi driver came in and took her suitcase.

She hugged me and kissed my cheek. "Goodbye, Chief Bucky Bucky."

It was sad watching Dixie drive off. She really understood me. Like that time on the rock when I got upset with her reminding me so much of Trixie.

I'd also miss Charlotte and her playful ribbing. I used to feel the same sadness when Uncle Rupert left after spending the holidays with the family. Of course, he always spread pressure as well. He'd urge me to aim for Mount Everest, so I'd at least make it up the next mound. When he left, real life set in again, and the mound grew larger until I started the climb. The gloominess always went away, but still…

# CHAPTER 47

Thunderclaps crashed, and rain poured down in sheets as I headed out to Mrs. Rheingold's for pot roast. She lived a few miles past the Mayfair Hotel. I hadn't felt this good since I sold five cars in one day to the police department I now ran. I had solved Gregory's murder and didn't need to worry about keeping my job. Dixie was of course disappointed being denied a day in court with the Klan, but she could still pursue justice with the FBI. I'll give her Willow and Bart's number. The agents who had earlier put away the town's corrupt officials. With all the publicity, the Kluxers would probably do as Hazelwood said: Go back under a rock until something new ruffled their feathers.

I neared the Mayfair Hotel. Through the beating windshield wipers, I saw a car approaching from the opposite direction. It skidded to a stop on the water-drenched road, backed up, and turned into the Mayfair's parking lot.

I slowed down. Several men hopped from the sedan. Curious, I made a U-turn and pulled in behind the car. Two men, hunched against the chilling rain were leading a grim-faced Dusty out of the hotel in handcuffs. Another guy stood by the car. His jacket said Georgia State Police.

I jumped from my cruiser, hurried over, and shouted through the deafening downpour, "Say, what's going on?"

"We got a call from an Officer Sparks that a fugitive was here. A Bobby Joe Jenkins, aka Dusty Miller."

"What?"

"That's right. He murdered his parents forty-one years ago."

I shook my head vigorously. "No, no. He killed just one parent, his mother."

"Negative. Both mother and father. Blew their heads off with a shotgun."

THE END

## About the Author

Bill A. Brier grew up in California and went to Holly-wood High School. After serving in the air force as a combat cameraman, he hired on at Disney Studios, as a film loader, and advanced from there.

He earned a master's degree in psychology—a big help when working with *Trumpish* Hollywood producers—"You're fired!" During his more than twenty-five years in the movie business as a cameraman, film editor, and general manager, Brier worked on everything from the hilarious, *The Love Bug*, to the creepy, *The Exorcist*, to the far out, *Star Trek* and *Battlestar Galactica*.

Eight years ago, Brier switched from reading scripts to writing mysteries and driving race cars. After completing three award-winning novels, he signed with Black Opal Books. His first novel, *The Devil Orders Takeout*, published in April 2017, is a standalone mystery/thriller about a devoted father and husband who makes a deal with a real-life devil to protect his golf-prodigy son—

after his wife and older son are killed in a mysterious accident—and pays hell for it.

Brier lives in Southern California with his wife, dogs, and chickens. He writes every day and golfs infrequently (that damn right knee!). His five children and eight grandchildren keep him busy going to birthday parties, and he never misses one!

*The Brier Patch*, Brier's humorous and engaging blog about his wild and woolly early days in Hollywood, is on his website, BillBrier.com, along with contests, which will award the grand prizewinners $1,000.

www.ingramcontent.com/pod-product-compliance
Lightning Source LLC
Chambersburg PA
CBHW060951120726
47910CB00002B/588